River of Death

by

Earl Underwood

Book 3

A Detective Jack Storm Mystery

Shoppe Foreman Publishing
Guthrie, Oklahoma USA

Published by
Shoppe Foreman Publishing
Oklahoma City, Oklahoma
www.ShoppeForeman.com

Cover image by Dm Cherry ©

Printed in the United States of America
Printing/manufacturing information
can be found on the last page.

ISBN-13: 978-1727548853
ISBN-10: 172754885X

River of Death

by

Earl Underwood

Dedication

To my parents, Mary Alice and Jesse Underwood, who brought me into this world and taught me that life is about living it.

My brother Carl and my sister Mary, whom I miss every day. They were taken much too soon.

My late wife, Susan, who gave me so much encouragement to write.

My children, Michael, Scott, Shaunie and Dejah. Thank you for always keeping in touch with me, especially through the tough times.

My grandchildren, Victoria, Erica, Zachary and Mika. I love you beyond words.

Acknowledgements

A SPECIAL THANKS TO LINDA WARD. Yes, folks, she is a real person, not just a character in my books. She is a big fan of my writing and a very special person to me. She is a retired CSI Supervisor from the Lake County Sheriff's Department in Florida. We worked together for many years, and based on her knowledge of crime scenes and forensics, I value her opinion highly.

To my brother-in-law, Bill Plant, enjoy your brief role as a Judge.

A new character in this novel is Brenda Skipper, Special Agent with the FBI. She is also a real person. I worked with her daughter, Shelia, in law enforcement for many years. Shelia always had a smile for everyone. I have a place in my heart for special people, and she is one of those.

Another new character is Nickie Young, an exceptional young lady. Nickie has been my housekeeper for almost a year now, and I truly value her. Nickie, I hope that you like your character and the part she played.

Larry Foreman is not only my publisher and editor, but a good friend. I thank you Larry, from the bottom of my heart, for all you do to help me. Hang in there, I only have about another hundred stories to write.

Forward

WHEN I BEGAN MY WRITING QUEST, I didn't know where to start. After three years of retirement I needed to do something to help fill my time. I told my wife that I wanted to write a book, and she suggested I write about what I knew, to get the feel of writing before attempting a novel. She advised me to "get my feet wet" by writing my autobiography/family history. Being from North Carolina, my kids and grandchildren had no knowledge of my relatives or where I came from. So, my first book was exactly that, an autobiography written for them. Once it was in print, I was hooked.

After I began writing in earnest, I soon completed my first novel, a science fiction thriller. I was quite pleased with it. From then on it was a book a year, from writing, to editing, to publication. I was fortunate to find Larry Foreman, who took on my projects and made me look good. For that I'm extremely grateful.

This novel is the third novel in the Detective Jack Storm Mystery Series, and will be the seventh book I've had published. When I began writing this third "Jack Storm" book, I attempted something I hadn't tried before. I wrote the book with two different stories running parallel to each other and coming together only at the end. It was a challenge, and a lot of hard work and long nights. I'm pleased at how it came out, and I personally think it is the best one in the Detective Jack Storm Mystery Series – so far. I think that most of my readers will agree with me.

My next novel, *Blind Justice*, is in the planning stages at this moment. I have a lot of projects in mind for the future, and there *will* be more Jack Storm coming, but not for a while. I hope to finish *Blind Justice* in 2019, and hopefully, Jack will be back in 2020.

To family, friends and all others who read my books, I thank you from the bottom of my heart for your loyalty and for your feedback.

Earl Underwood, 2018

Chapter 1

KYLE THOMAS, and his best friend Jose Mercado, sat on the bank of the Miami River, their cane fishing poles tightly wedged in the muddy bank. They were laughing and skipping stones across the dark waters of the river, each trying to be the first to skim one all the way across the water to the opposite bank. This particular section of the river was not as trash-laden or murky as it was further inland. Maybe because it was so close to the downtown section of Miami and the Chamber needed to keep it clean-looking for the tourists, and possibly in a small part, for the nearby residents, but it was still nowhere near pristine.

Both of the boys were in their early teens and having a blast. For the past hour they had been considering jumping into the water to cool off, each waiting for the other to make the first move. It wasn't that they were afraid, even though there was possibly a *gator* or two in the area. They hadn't seen any evidence of one in the almost three hours they had been there, so their trepidation was beginning to wane. The five-gallon plastic bucket they had brought to put their catch in was almost empty because the few fish they did manage to catch were simply too small to keep, nowhere near large enough for eating. They even tried using a couple of the small ones for bait, with visions of catching a whopper, one they could take home to show off their fishing prowess. So far those efforts were in vain; the big ones deftly eluding their hooks.

"Okay, Kyle, I'm going in. It's just too dang hot out here," Jose said, rising and stripping off his tee-shirt.

"Wait for me, I'm coming too," a suddenly emboldened Kyle said, quickly taking off his shirt, also.

Both boys took a running jump, landing in the murky river about five feet out from the bank, the splashes causing large ripples to spread out in ever-widening circles, until they tapered off and barely made splashes upon hitting the bank's edge. The coolness of the water suddenly contacting their sun-baked skin was refreshing, although it took their breath away for a split second. Steam vapors rose from their partially submerged bodies, a testament to how hot it was in the South Florida sun in mid-July.

They began using lazy strokes, swimming across the river, and once reaching the other side, climbing out onto the bank. Laughing and turning around they both took a running start and once again dove into the river, the chill of the water not affecting them nearly as much now. While they splashed each other playfully they unknowingly drifted down the river for approximately half a city block. When they realized what was happening they attempted to swim back to their poles, but the current was working hard against them.

"We'll have to swim to the bank and climb out, or we'll drift further away," Kyle said to Jose.

"Okay, but we're going to have to climb through those

thick cattails, and who knows what lies in wait for us," Jose said, grinning malevolently at Kyle.

"Not funny, man. There could be a gator hiding in there."

"Oh, come on, bro. There ain't any gators in here – too much noise and boat traffic," Jose said, quickly striking out for the bank where the thick strand of cattails ranged from five to well over eight feet in height.

Both of the boys reached the bank at nearly the same time, but about ten feet apart, laughing and clowning as they climbed up the muddy slope. They carefully pushed through the thick cluster of cattails as they slowly made their way to the top.

Suddenly Jose screamed out, "Kyle, there's a dead woman in here!"

"Quit joking around, Jose. We need to get back to our poles. It's almost time to head home."

"Hey, bro, I'm not kidding. I almost stepped on her. Come over here, dude," Jose said, the tremor in his voice convincing Kyle to quickly head his way.

"You had better not be joking around, Jose," Kyle said as he made his way through the cattails.

The two boys stood amid the thick strand of cattails in dark, knee-deep water, staring at the blonde-haired woman lying face up in the shallow water. Her cloudy, sightless eyes were wide open and staring directly into the sun, a look of pure terror frozen on her face. Her severely sun-burned skin was beginning to peel away. Patches of her skin were already eaten away, probably from the crabs prevalent in the river. The woman's semi-nude body was wedged between some of the cattails at the edge of the steep bank; it was obvious she had been there for a while. The area she was in was not readily visible from the top of the bank and the road.

The boys quickly scrambled up the slick muddy bank in a panic and ran to the highway. They quickly flagged down a passing motorist and convinced the skeptical driver of the car to call the police on his cell phone. They stood in a group at the top of the bank, all three deliberately trying to avoid looking down at the area where the body was floating, even though they couldn't see it from where they stood. Within a few minutes several Miami police units were on the scene and began blocking one lane of traffic.

Once the visibly shaken boys pointed out where the body was located, one of the officers began to carefully make his way down the slick steep bank. His shoes slipped on the damp grass and only by planting his feet against a large clump of brush was he able to prevent himself from sliding out of control. At the bottom of the bank he cautiously parted the thick strand of cattails, and then keyed his radio, advising the other units there was indeed a body.

The two shaken boys were going to be a little late getting home on this day, but what a story they had to tell their friends.

Chapter 2

"WE THE JURY, find the defendant guilty, as to the charge of first degree murder." The Foreman read from a slip of paper to the packed courtroom.

"The defendant shall be transported to the Dade County jail to await sentencing three days from now," Judge Bill Plant said, ordering the officers to take the defendant, Juan Castro, AKA *El Scorpion*, to a jail cell. "I would like to thank the jurors for their civic duty, and at this time they are free to go."

As *El Scorpion* stood between the two officers, he cast a look back at Jack Storm who was seated in the courtroom. He gave a slight smile, nodded his head, and turned to leave the room with the officers.

"What was that about?" Dakota asked.

"What, the smile and nod?" Stormy replied.

"Yeah, what the hell did he have to smile about? You know he has to figure he's getting the chair."

"I don't know, and I really don't care. He's getting what he deserves and that means case closed!" Stormy said with conviction.

"Luckily Pablo's resources came through and found

out where *El Scorpion* had fled, for you that is," Dakota said, as they arose and joined the throng of people leaving the courtroom.

"Also, I'm glad the local authorities over there were so co-operative with the extradition. Otherwise we would be twiddling our thumbs as he lived a life of luxury while in the process of getting away with murder," Stormy replied as he and Dakota exited the building.

As they walked to the car, Stormy's cell phone began vibrating, reminding him he had set it on the quiet mode during the court proceedings. He looked at the number and recognized the caller, Leo Sharp.

"Hey, Leo, I guess you heard the verdict," Stormy said as he answered the call, continuing on to the parking lot with Dakota.

"Yep, I just now received the news. Was there really any doubt as to the outcome?" Leo replied.

"Well, you know how things go these days. Juries are usually pretty good, but once in a while you get one that will surprise you with their idiocy," Stormy said with a chuckle.

They reached the car and once inside the call switched over to the Bluetooth, now coming through the dashboard speaker. Stormy started the car and turned the air to high, trying to kill the stifling heat inside quickly.

"I know you didn't call just to congratulate me," Stormy said, keeping the car parked as he talked.

"Nope, I just wanted to let you know we pulled another floater from the Miami River a couple of hours ago," Leo said.

"Why do I have a feeling this is not just a Miami P.D.

case you're calling about?" Stormy said.

"Because you're that famous detective who caught the elusive *El Scorpion* and also you're so darn astute," Leo said laughing heartily.

"Cut me some slack, Leo. I just got lucky that my informant came through," Stormy said with a laugh. "Now why would a floater, out of my jurisdiction, be of any interest to me? It's in your jurisdiction isn't it?"

"Oh yeah…*we're* definitely working it. I just wanted to give you a heads up. The victim is from Hialeah."

"What's his name? Do I know him?" Stormy asked, slightly puzzled.

"Not *his* name…*her* name. Her prints came back to a Stefanie Taylor living on West Sixty-fifth Street in your city. Does that name ring a bell?" Leo asked.

"Not really. Am I supposed to know her?" Stormy asked.

"Oh my God, are you sure Leo?" Dakota yelled at the dash speaker.

"What's wrong, Dakota? Do you know who it is?" Stormy asked suddenly startled at Dakota's outburst.

"You wouldn't know her, but that's Linda Ward's sister," she responded, tears welling up in her eyes.

"Are you sure? How do you know that?" Leo asked.

"A little while back I had lunch with her and Linda. I ran into them while shopping, and we decided to grab a bite together. She was so nice. Her husband will be devastated. They were just married recently, her second one," Dakota responded, shaking her head in disbelief.

"Have you notified her husband or family yet, Leo?" Stormy asked.

"No, we checked with DMV and found she had a driver's license, which was suspended by the way. We sent a detective to the address listed on it, but she didn't reside there any longer…not for quite a while it seems. The current resident had never even heard of her. I had no way of knowing it was Linda's sister. Oh my God, she'll be so devastated," Leo replied, the somber tone coming through in his voice.

"You want us to take her down to identify the body?" Stormy asked.

"I would certainly appreciate that, Stormy. Maybe she can take the news coming from you a little better than a phone call from me or Doc Davis. I know you and Linda have a great working relationship," Leo responded.

"We'll head back to the station now and I'll break the news to her," Stormy said.

"Do you know how she died, Leo?" Dakota asked.

"Not yet. She was in shallow water near the bank, so it's possible she drowned. The detective on the scene figures she may have been dead for at least a couple of days, maybe longer, due to the condition of the body. We'll have to determine if it was foul play or an accident. I'm leaning towards foul play, mainly due to the state of undress she was in. Of course that will be up to Doc Davis to decide, so I'll keep you in the loop as I find out more," Leo said.

"If she's been missing for several days, maybe her husband has filed a missing persons report. We'll also check that out when we get back to Hialeah," Dakota responded.

"Thanks, Leo. I'll get back to you after we take Linda down to the morgue to identify the body," Stormy said, disconnecting the call and hurriedly backing out of the parking space.

The drive back to HPD was mostly in silence, although it was obvious that Dakota was distressed. Stormy concentrated on his driving while trying to comfort Dakota at the same time. He knew that Linda was going to be devastated, but she was a strong woman. He knew that losing a loved one was hard; he would do everything he could to comfort her in her time of need. His relationship with her was borne out of working together for so long. She was almost like a sister to him, as well as a great friend, and he was dreading his task of breaking the news to her.

Stormy pulled out his cell phone and called the office, asking Adria to patch him through to the Captain. His friend and former boss, John Paradis, had retired and now there was a newly assigned captain taking his place. Roscoe Carter had been selected and transferred to the Detective Bureau to take the reins. Stormy didn't really know much about him other than he had been in Vice for years as a lieutenant and was promoted to captain for his new assignment.

"Captain Carter speaking."

"Captain, Detective Storm here. I just got off the phone with Leo Sharp at Miami P.D. and the news is not good. They just pulled a body out of the Miami River, and it appears to be the sister of our CSI supervisor, Linda Ward. I need you to have her report to your office as soon as possible. I know her very well and would like to be the one to break the news to her. Dakota and I will be there within twenty minutes," Stormy said.

"Oh my God! I know Linda, but not that well. So yes,

you're right. You should be the one to tell her. I'll make the call as soon as we hang up," Captain Carter said. "Are you sure it's her sister?"

"Based on the prints, Miami pulled and ran, and, Dakota recognized the name, yes, it's her. I plan to take Linda to the Morgue for positive identification later," Stormy replied.

****

Captain Carter stared at the phone for a minute before replacing it to the cradle. He didn't know Linda that well, other than the few instances where he had to go over evidence with her for narcotic cases his men worked. He had risen through the ranks to sergeant and had been placed in Vice, at his request, three years ago. He had been promoted to lieutenant shortly afterwards and was allowed to stay while the resident lieutenant was granted his own request to go to Patrol. When Captain Paradis had retired, Captain Carter was tapped to be his replacement in the Detective Bureau. He now commanded over forty detectives, four sergeants and two lieutenants. The Bureau was comprised of a Crimes Persons Unit, Crimes Property Unit and Auto Theft Division. He only hoped he could do half the job that John Paradis had performed during his tenure. Now, he had to gain the trust of the detectives who would be working for him and show them that he not only had their back, but could be approachable. Picking up the phone once again he dialed CSI. When Linda answered, he asked her if she could come to his office as soon as possible. To her credit she didn't ask why, just said she was on her way.

****

Stormy hung up his phone and turned to Dakota, who was staring out the window, her tear-streaked face highlighted in the reflection of the glass. Stormy reached over and clasped her hand, giving it a gentle squeeze. She attempted a smile without turning to him, appreciating the gesture.

"I know that I didn't know her that well but my heart is breaking for Linda," she finally said, her words catching in her throat.

"I know. I feel the same and I'm not looking forward to breaking the news to her," Stormy said.

Chapter 3

MARC BUTLER SAT on the covered deck of his houseboat, out of the blazing July sun, sipping one of the ice cold beers he had pulled from the ice chest by his lounge chair. The houseboat wasn't much to look at but it was paid for in full and he would begin performing the multitude of cosmetic repairs soon, but not today. It was just too damn hot to do anything but stay in the shade and drink cold beers.

About a year ago he had bought the boat from a sixty-year-old lady in a distress sale. Her husband had passed away, and she wanted to go to California to live with or be near her children. She had no family left in Miami, and her friends understood her wanting to be near them. The houseboat needed painting, caulking in some areas and in general, minor repairs. The price she gave to Marc was more than reasonable, and he paid her with cash, in full. Luckily, a few months earlier, he had inherited the estate of an aunt he hardly knew. It seems he was the only next of kin she had. It wasn't a fortune but enough to allow him to live for a while without having to worry about working. To help stretch the money he had taken on the job of being an Uber driver. It gave him the freedom from punching a time clock, allowing him the option of turning down fares if he so felt. Today was one of those days he had turned his cell off, not in the mood to drive noisy and sometimes smelly people around town.

The boat was presently anchored on the north side of the Miami River, just east of where the Dolphin Expressway crossed over. The noise from the traffic was loud, but bearable, for now. Marc had plans to move the boat further west on the river to a quieter area, maybe near Hialeah. Quieter area! What a joke. With the exploding population all over Dade County there weren't many quiet areas left.

Normally he would be content just doing nothing, but today he had a lot on his mind. For the past hour he had been thinking of how his career in law enforcement had been cut short about a year ago. It still galled him to think about it. He could have probably applied somewhere else, but at the time of his termination he never considered it. He drank himself into a stupor for several months, wallowing in self-pity, refusing to believe he had done anything wrong to justify firing him.

Several months earlier he had, with some clarity, sobered up and become determined to make the person responsible for his firing pay the price...the ultimate price. Linda Ward would soon find out that he wasn't a person you wanted to screw with.

With a long-range plan in mind, he set out to begin the process of drawing out Linda, getting her in his clutches, and exacting his revenge.

****

The bar was dark, noisy and smelly. Marc didn't smoke cigarettes, so the smoke-filled room was stifling to him at first, causing him to consider leaving and going to another bar. But he suffered through it as he needed a small out of the way place where he wouldn't be remembered. Soon he saw his target. A young Cuban girl who couldn't be more than twenty years old sat alone at the bar. Marc knew immediately that she was probably a hooker, looking for some fast cash in exchange for a quick lay. She was not an overly pretty girl, probably explaining why she sat alone. She was not fat but a little overweight, a mild case of acne on her face and a tattoo of a butterfly on her neck. She would be the perfect victim – someone no one would miss for a while.

"Hi, can I buy you a drink, pretty lady," Marc said as he took a seat beside her at the bar.

The girl slowly turned and looked at Marc, not believing her luck tonight.

"Hey, handsome. Sure you can. I'll take a Canadian Mist and Coke," she replied with a smile.

Marc motioned to the barkeep and ordered another beer for himself and the Mist for the girl.

"So, what's your name, honey?" Marc asked.

"You first, big guy," she replied, still smiling.

"I'm Steven," Marc said without hesitation, having been prepared to use a phony name before arriving. "Now, what's yours?"

"My name is Lilly, Lilly Sanchez, Steven. Pleased to meet you."

The drinks arrived, and they made small talk for a while. After several more drinks, Lilly asked Marc, "You want to go somewhere and have a little fun?

"Sure. How much is it gonna cost me?" Marc asked.

"Since you're so handsome, how does fifty sound?"

"I can handle that," Marc said, pulling out two twenties and a ten from his wallet and handing it over to Lilly.

"Okay, hon, let's get out of this dump."

Marc paid the tab and they left the bar. Once they were in the car, Marc drove to an abandoned warehouse about a mile from the bar. The warehouse sat on the Miami river and had apparently been empty for quite some time.

"Hey, we can't go to your place, Steven?" Lilly asked, a little alarm creeping into her voice.

"My sister is down visiting and with her and the kid there it would be a little awkward" Marc replied with an apologetic smile. "Besides, what I want we can do in the car. Unless you want me to take you back to the bar."

"No, this will be fine. What do you want to do?" She asked.

"Take off you top and bra," Marc replied, feigning excitement.

"My, you waste no time, do you," she said as she began pulling her top up over her head.

"No, I really don't."

When Lilly had her arms stretched over her head with the top almost off, Marc quickly reached out and put both of his hands on her throat, part of her top covering his fingers. As he started to squeeze Lilly panicked and tried to grab his arms. With her arms still ensconced in her top and above her head, she couldn't grab him. She began screaming and kicking the dash of the car. As Marc squeezed harder her resistance became feeble and finally, she stopped breathing.

Marc sat there for several minutes, contemplating what he had just done. Guilt washed over him immediately and his heart began palpitating wildly. Quickly he snapped out of it and got out of the car. It didn't stop him from throwing up, the act he had committed filling him with revulsion. He walked around the car and opened the passenger door. He lifted Lilly's lifeless body from the seat and dragged her to the top of the river bank, where he then rolled her down the embankment. He watched as her body stopped – the top half in the water and the other half on the bank.

When he returned to the car he almost stepped in the vomit he had spewed on the ground. Reverting back to his police training, he wondered if DNA could be obtained from vomit. Taking no chances, he espied a shovel leaning against the warehouse wall. Quickly fetching it, he walked to the side of the warehouse and dug a foot deep hole in the soft dirt. He went back and carefully scooped up the vomit and carried it to the hole where he covered it. There was an old tire leaning against the wall so he laid it down on the ground covering the freshly dug earth. It was the best he could do for now. It would be a real streak of luck if an investigating team found the spot.

As Marc drove back to his houseboat he thought of what he had done. It was the first time he had killed anyone, and it left him sick to his stomach. That was his first; he hoped that the second, which was necessary for his plan, would be a lot easier to handle.

Chapter 4

STORMY AND DAKOTA managed to arrive at the Detective Bureau before Linda Ward. They entered the room and spotted Captain Carter standing by the coffee pot chatting with another detective. He glanced up and, seeing Stormy, excused himself to the detective and motioned Stormy and Dakota to come to his office.

Once they were inside he asked, "Either of you want a cup of coffee before Linda arrives?" They both declined and took seats at Captain Carter's bequest.

"Are you sure that it is Linda's sister?" Captain Carter asked as he sipped his coffee.

"I can only tell you what Leo told me. He said the prints were hers and even pulled up a driver's license with her picture on it. I assume that the investigating detectives compared her to the picture when they went to the Medical Examiner's Office," Stormy replied.

"Are you okay, Dakota. You seem to be taking this hard," the Captain said, looking over at Dakota with concern.

"She was familiar with Linda's sister. In fact they just had lunch together with Linda not that long ago," Stormy answered quietly.

"I'm so sorry, Dakota. Do you want to be here when Linda arrives?"

"Yes, sir. She will need the support and we *are* good friends. Maybe I'll be able to help her cope with this loss in some way," Dakota replied, wiping a slowly forming tear from the corner of her eye.

About that time the Captain's phone buzzed. He picked it up and was told by his secretary that Linda had arrived.

After hanging up the phone, Captain Carter turned to Stormy and said. "Linda is here. I'll give you and Dakota privacy to break the news to her. I will be just outside if you need me. She may take it better from you guys since I haven't had many dealings with her."

"Thanks, Captain, and if you could, have someone bring in some water and tissues. I think we'll need them," Stormy said, glancing over at Dakota.

Captain Carter left the room and Stormy stood by the door, as a perplexed Linda walked in the room.

"What's going on, Stormy?" She asked as she took a seat.

"I...uh...well Linda, I have some bad news," Stormy said.

"What kind of bad news. Someone screw up another crime scene," Linda said with a short laugh. You could tell by the look on her face she knew it was something more serious than a "messed up crime scene."

"Stormy, go get a cup of coffee, and bring me one," Dakota said, giving Stormy a meaningful look.

Stormy arose and left the room, grateful for Dakota's foresight. Evidently she could see that Stormy was going to have a hard time breaking the news to Linda and decided to spare him that task.

As Stormy stood by the coffee pot, he suddenly heard a wail of anguish through the closed door. Dakota had closed the blinds to the large window so the other detectives couldn't see inside. Tears suddenly welled up in Stormy's eyes, his heart breaking for Linda. He espied Adria walking towards him carrying a box of tissues and a glass of water, not realizing that the Captain had already taken care of that. He silently took them from her anyhow and foregoing the coffee, returned to Captain Carter's office.

When he entered he saw that Dakota had moved her chair next to Linda's and had her arms around her. Without saying anything Dakota held out her hand for the tissues. Stormy handed her the box and took the seat behind the Captain's desk.

Linda sobbed for several more minutes, her head buried in Dakota's shoulder. They both were using the tissues to wipe their eyes. Finally, Linda gave a final shudder and straightened up, blowing her nose and wiping her eyes again. She looked at the glass of water on the desk where Stormy had placed it. She took it and swallowed several sips before looking at Stormy.

"Stormy, you find the bastard that did this. You hear me...find him," Linda said with her eyes watering up again.

"Linda, it's a Miami P.D. homicide case. The crime happened in their jurisdiction," Stormy replied.

"I don't care where it happened. I want *you* to find him."

"I'll check with the Captain and see if I can approach

Leo about helping with the investigation," Stormy said.

"And Stormy, I want to know when you find him, and who he is," Linda said, almost spitting out the words.

Stormy just looked at her. He knew that if the perp was here in this room now, Linda would have no problem putting a bullet in his head...but he wasn't going to let her ruin her career and possibly go to prison for a rash act.

"I'll do that, Linda. But only after you've had some time to think about it," Stormy said, knowing he had no intentions of giving her the name before an arrest.

"I don't need time to think about it, Jack Storm. Whoever it is needs to pay and pay dearly," Linda said, determination and grief written all over here face.

"And they will. The courts will make sure of that. But first we have to find out who did it," Stormy said.

"Now, I would like to go see my sister," Linda said as she stood.

****

"Is she going to be alright?" Doc Davis asked Stormy.

"She'll handle it Doc. She just needs time," Stormy replied.

They had arrived at the Medical Examiner's Office fifteen minutes earlier. After giving Linda his condolences, Doc Davis led the way into the holding room. There were banks of cold, stainless steel doors on the walls, most of them containing deceased remains.

Doc pulled open a door and slid out the tray from the wall. There was a body bag, zipped up and laying on the cold slab. The autopsy hadn't been conducted as of yet, but would be this very day. Doc Davis reached over to unzip the bag but was surprised when Linda gripped his wrist.

"Could I please have a minute, Doc? I'll open it myself, but I'd like to be alone for a minute."

Doc Davis glanced over at Stormy, who gave a slight nod. They turned and began walking out of the room.

"Take all the time you need, Linda," Doc said over his shoulder. "We'll be just outside the door."

Linda stood over the bag containing the body of her sister for nearly a minute before she slowly began to unzip it. She pulled the zipper down only exposing the head. She immediately recognized her sister and dropped to her knees. She stayed in that position for a minute before standing back up. She used the back of her hand and stroked her sister's face, silently saying a prayer. The tears were still coming, but she took deep breaths and fought to control her emotions. Finally, she zipped the bag closed and spoke to her sister.

"I will find out who did this to you, Stefanie...I promise. And who ever it was, they are going to pay," Linda whispered, as she dried her eyes.

Linda walked out of the cold sterile room and gave Doc a hug.

"It's her...that's my sister Stefanie," Linda said.

"I'm ready to go home," she said to Stormy.

****

The drive back was mostly in silence. Dakota asked if she needed to stop for a drink or anything before they got back to the office. Linda declined and lapsed into silence once again.

When they arrived back at the office, the Captain was waiting and told Linda to take the day off, or as long as she needed. Linda told him she needed to go back to work, but the Captain told her she was to at least take the rest of the day off, and that was an order.

Linda gave Dakota a long hug and then gave Stormy one. She reached up and whispered in his ear, "I mean it, Stormy. When you find out who it was I want to know."

"Would you like for me to come with you for a while, Linda?" Dakota asked.

"No, I'll be fine. I just need to be alone, and I do have some calls to make and a funeral to make preparations for."

Then she turned and walked out of the building.

Chapter 5

CONSUELO ALVAREZ SAT in her hotel suite at the Loews, on Miami Beach, lost in thought. She had checked in using an alias, Roberta Estes. She never checked into a hotel using her real name; too many people wanted to either see her dead, or in jail.

She had received a call with a business proposition...a very lucrative one. She needed to break someone out of the Dade County Jail and in return she would receive one million dollars. She had made a lot of money since she had been released from prison in Cuba and sent to the United States during the *Mariel boatlift*. Castro had promised to allow thousands of Cubans to immigrate to the United States under the Carter Administration in 1980. Mixed in with the thousands of desperate Cubans were many more thousands of released prisoners, most violent murderers. It was a way for Castro to deplete the prison population and cut his costs immensely. Needless to say, the crime rate for South Florida spiked dramatically, and quickly.

Consuelo's first reaction was to say "no, hell no!" Especially when she was given the name of the person she was to spring. She had recognized the name immediately, as it had been all over the news for months. Some guy who used the moniker, *El Scorpion*. But a million dollars was nothing to sneeze at, so she had flown to Miami from Colombia to look into it.

****

Juan Castro, aka The Scorpion, sat in his dank, smelly and small holding cell at the Dade County jail. He sat on his bunk with his back against the cold concrete block wall. He had just hung up from placing a call to someone that could possibly get him out of this cell, and out of the country. Juan had gone by many names in his profession, that of a highly paid assassin, but his birth name was Juan Castro. He hadn't been vain enough to give himself the name of *El Scorpion*, which had been bestowed upon him early in his career by his peers. The word was that when Juan was in town, "someone was going to feel the sting of the scorpion." The name *Scorpion* was thus born and bestowed upon Juan ever since that utterance.

The call he had just placed was to another colleague, one he had never met but had heard the name in the circles he ran in, Consuelo Alvarez, and he had memorized her number for future reference. Her record of kills and the methods she used were legendary, and he couldn't think of anyone else to call. He had obtained a cell phone from one of the inmates. Contrary to the public's belief, you could get most anything you wanted in jail or prison. Most of the inmates knew his name and reputation, and the respect they showed was evident when they were granted an hour outside the cell for exercise. That was where he had arranged to obtain the phone. The promise of a good payday was enough to convince the inmate to make the arrangements. That and the thought of the possible consequences of saying no to *El Scorpion*. Now he had to wait and hope that the cells weren't shaken down and the phone found before he could make the call.

****

Consuelo was a professional assassin, not some common criminal who knew how to break someone out of jail. But, the more she thought of it, the more it intrigued her. And a million dollars wasn't something to dismiss lightly.

She had told the caller to give her a day to think on it and to call back. She put her thinking cap on and decided to give it some serious deliberation. After spending most of the day going through various scenarios, she suddenly hit upon an idea. But, first she needed to contact an old friend from the past. Pablo Gondar!

A little over a year earlier she had done a favor for Pablo, a big one, and he owed her. She had gone to New Orleans and executed an ex-cop who had almost killed Pablo. It had been a piece of cake for her. She had preyed upon the sexual greed some men had, and it had cost Rolando Fuentes his life. Now, she needed a favor from Pablo. It was time to collect the debt, so she dug out her small black phone book and found his number. She placed the call, but it went directly to voice mail. She left her first name and simply said, "Consuelo. Call me. We need to meet."

Consuelo sat by the window, staring out over the Atlantic Ocean, lost in her thoughts. She had an idea but would need resources from Pablo. She had no sooner thought of his name when the phone rang. She picked up her cell and answered.

"Hola, mi amiga," Pablo answered.

"Hello, Pablo. How have you been, *mi amigo*?"

"Good. What can I do for you, Consuelo? You didn't just call out of the blue to chat, now did you?" Pablo asked with a short laugh.

"No, but I do need to meet with you. It could mean a lot of money to you. Give me a place and time. Better yet, how about on Miami Beach?" Consuelo said.

"Miami Beach? I can do that. Where do you want to meet?"

"Are you familiar with the Klima Restaurant and Bar?" Consuelo asked.

"I've actually been there before...great food, authentic Spanish cuisine. What time?"

"How about seven...I'll treat you to dinner."

"See you there at seven, Consuelo," Pablo replied as he broke the connection.

Consuelo looked at her watch and saw that she had plenty of time to go to the spa before dressing for dinner. Hopefully it would be a productive meeting with Pablo.

Before going down to the spa she went to her closet and selected a dress and shoes for dinner. It was an upscale restaurant, but she didn't want to overdress and stand out too much.

Chapter 6

STORMY AND DAKOTA dropped Linda off in the Detective Bureau parking lot, by her department-issued vehicle. She gave each of them a hug, told them she would be okay and that she would call later. She gave a long and searching look at Stormy, silently relaying the same message to him she had whispered in his ear earlier.

When they entered the Bureau, Captain Carter motioned them to his office. Stormy stopped by the coffee pot but saw that it contained barely enough for a cup. He poured it anyhow and, loading it with cream, walked into the Captain's office. Dakota was already sitting in front of his desk.

"You can't live without coffee, can you Stormy?" Dakota said with a slight smile.

"Makes the world go 'round, Dakota, makes the world go 'round," he replied laughing.

"Where is Linda?" Captain Carter asked.

"She followed your orders, Captain – she went home. Said she had to make calls to family and friends, preparations for a funeral. She seemed to be okay."

"Good! Make sure you and Dakota keep a check on her.

Did she identify her sister's body?"

"Yes, sir, and I need to call Leo Sharp and advise him she did so, although I'm sure Doc Davis has already made the call," Stormy said as he took a swig of the coffee, made a face and placed the cup on the desk.

"What's wrong? Coffee too strong for you," Dakota said, noticing the face he made.

"My God! Has that pot been sitting there all day? That's some strong stuff," Stormy said.

"Make sure you take that cup of *mud* with you when you leave," Captain Carter said, laughing.

"Captain, would you mind if I ask Leo if I can assist him in the investigation in Stefanie's death?" Stormy asked.

"It's a Miami P.D. homicide case, Stormy. What makes you think they will allow you to help and what possible benefit would you be to them?"

"Well, the victim *is* from Hialeah. Maybe I could do some legwork for them in our city...free their detectives up to concentrate the Miami end. Since the victim affects part of our family here at the Hialeah P.D. I feel like I have to make some kind of effort to help. I'm just asking as a favor," Stormy said.

"Do you have anything heavy pending. I don't want you to drop your cases for this," Carter replied.

"I have nothing going on that can't wait for a few days. Dakota can be here in case Linda needs her," Stormy said.

"Very well, if Leo agrees I don't have a problem loaning you out for a few days. Just make sure you keep me apprised of any developments."

"I will, and thanks, Captain. I'll go touch bases with

Leo now," Stormy said.

When they had left the Captain's office, Dakota said with a little sarcasm, "Hey, partner, thanks for inviting me to go with you."

"Sorry, Dakota. I wasn't slighting you at all. I really want you...no, I need you here to keep an eye on Linda. She will need a shoulder to lean on for a few days, and you both are such good friends. Could you please do this for me?" Stormy asked.

"No problem, Stormy. I was just pulling your chain a little. I will be glad to be there for her – that is if she will let me," Dakota said, smiling.

Stormy sat down at his desk and pulled Leo's number up on his cell. It was picked up on the second ring.

"Leo, Stormy here."

"Yeah, your name popped up in the screen. Anyone else and they would have had to wait for a callback. I'm up to my elbows in paperwork right now. What can I do for you, pal?" Leo said.

"I assume Doc Davis called and told you that Linda had made a positive I.D. on her sister, right?"

"Yep, he called right after she was there. He's conducting the autopsy as we speak," Leo replied.

"And I have another question...rather a request, for you," Stormy said.

"Let me guess. You want to be in on the investigation, right?" Leo said laughing.

"Damn, Leo. I knew you were a great detective, but a mind reader also?" Stormy replied, also laughing.

"Flattery will get you everywhere, pal. I just know how you think, and I would have asked you if the tables were reversed. Of course you can assist in the investigation, if your boss agrees," Leo said.

"It's a done deal. I asked him just before calling you, and he gave his blessing, for a few days at least. Thanks, buddy. I'll be over this afternoon, and you can fill me in on the case," Stormy said as he broke the connection.

Chapter 7

One month earlier

IT WAS A THURSDAY NIGHT, and Marc Butler was sitting in a bar just on the outskirts of downtown Miami. He had picked this location because it was, first, not near where he lived, and, second, it wasn't too crowded and no one seemed to pay him any attention. He didn't want to be remembered in case any investigators came around asking questions. He had disguised himself a little without making it too obvious. He had for the last two weeks been growing a beard. He wore jeans and a ball cap. He fit in with the locals who were everyday workers just grabbing a drink before heading home.

As he nursed his beer, he thought back to his first kill, ashamed that he couldn't even remember the name she had given him. He had been so guilt-ridden for several days afterwards that he wasn't sure he could follow through with another killing. But he had to in order to get the person he wanted.

He had watched the news for several days and when the girl he had murdered and dumped into the Miami River had been found, it just seemed to be another of the daily homicides in Dade County. After two days there was no other mention of her in the news...although he knew that undoubtedly the case was being worked.

Now, here he was, waiting for the right girl to come in. He had to be careful where he dumped the body, so that was the reason he had come downtown.

Marc ordered his third beer and was planning to leave after he finished it since no prospects had come into the bar. It had to be a young girl, not strong looking, and alone. There had been several, but they were either with someone or not an easy, vulnerable mark.

As he raised his beer to his mouth, he heard the door open. He glanced over and saw that a twenty-something girl wearing a waitress uniform had entered. She must have just gotten off work and was having a drink before going home. She took a seat at the bar, two seats down from Marc. He glanced over at the same time she looked at him. He gave a tentative smile, raised his bottle and nodded at her. She gave a slight smile and nodded back. The bartender asked her what she wanted to drink, and she asked for a beer also.

"Must have been busy night for you," Marc said, turning his stool slightly facing her.

"You have no idea. My feet are totally killing me. I had to do a double shift today and on top of that I didn't get much sleep last night. So, yep, I'm beat," she said as the barkeep set her beer in front of her.

As she dug in her purse for money, Marc smiled and said, "I got it. You can consider it your last tip of the night before you go home and get some sleep."

"Tip? You sure you're not coming on to me," she said with a smile.

"Nope, you look like a hard worker, and I just wanted to do something nice for you...that is okay, right?" Marc said

"Sorry, I didn't mean to come off flippant. Sure, I appreciate it, Mr..."

"Oh, sorry, Fred, Fred Stone," Marc replied.

"I'm Jan," she replied, not giving a last name.

"Well, Jan. Enjoy the beer."

Jan got up and moved to the seat next to Marc, sliding her beer down the bar as she moved. They sat there without saying anything for a minute. Then Marc laughed.

"What's so funny?" Jan asked.

"I was just thinking. You spent all day waiting on others, so you must be hungry. You want to go and grab a bite somewhere before you turn in for the night?" Marc asked.

Jan swirled her beer and seemed to be in thought before answering.

"Nah, I appreciate it, Fred, but one, I don't go off with someone I don't know. And two, how do you know I didn't eat at work. We do get breaks, you know," she said with a chuckle.

"No problem, just offering. I need to leave myself, early day at work tomorrow," Marc said, turning up his beer bottle and finishing the last of it.

"Maybe I'll see you here again, and we can go have that meal you offered," Jan said.

"Sure, I come in mostly on Thursdays, so I'll look for you. Have a good night, Jan," Marc said as he stood and walked to the door.

When Marc went outside he looked around and observed that there were only three cars in the parking lot. One was probably the bartender's, one was his, so the remaining one must be hers, he thought. He saw that she had parked at the end of the building away from the outside light, her car mostly in darkness. Careless girl, he thought. He walked over to the back of the building and was almost completely invisible as he stood near her car, leaning against the bar. He only had to wait about fifteen minutes before he heard the door to the bar opening. He took a sneak peek around the corner and, sure enough, it was Jan walking to her car.

Marc waited, holding his breath as if he thought she could hear it. When she reached the driver's door, she turned slightly, facing the light to find the keys in her purse. She never heard Marc walk up behind her. She must have sensed his presence because she began to turn around. Marc had taken Judo classes years ago and knew where to strike a person on the side of their neck to render them unconscious. Before she could make the turn, he struck her as hard as he could. Jan collapsed to the ground, out like a light.

Marc waited a minute and watched for anyone that would be a witness, but saw no one. He opened his front passenger door and walked back to where Jan lay on the ground. He quickly picked her up and put her in the passenger's seat of his car. Reaching in the back seat, he retrieved a roll of duct tape he had brought just in case. He tore off a strip and placed it on her mouth. Tearing off another long strip he wrapped her wrists and ankles tightly and then fastened her seat belt. He got into the driver's seat, quickly started the car, and backed out of the parking lot, heading back towards Okeechobee Road. Earlier in the day he had scouted the area and found a deserted area, out of view of the road, on a canal that fed off the Miami River.

Jan was still unconscious when he pulled onto the over-grown dirt path leading to the canal. He parked the car, killed the headlights and scanned the area. There were a lot of homeless people in Miami, and he wanted to make sure there were none in this area. There were no buildings, but that didn't seem to stop the vagrants from camping out in the open. After a few minutes he determined that the area was deserted. He exited the car and walked around to the passenger's side. When he opened the door he could hear Jan moaning slightly. She would be coming around soon so he had to hurry. He unfastened her seat belt and lifted her out of the car. He carried her down to the bank of the canal and deposited her on the ground. Her mouth was al-ready taped, so he pinched her nostrils together. She began gasping and her chest labored, trying to suck in precious air. Suddenly her eyes flew open, wide and in panic. She stared at Marc, her eyes pleading for him to stop. He couldn't bear to watch, so he turned his head. She began bucking and thrashing wildly, so he sat on her chest and arms. Soon, she stopped moving, and her body relaxed in the throes of death.

Marc stood and looked down at her, seeing that her eyes were wide open and staring lifelessly up at him. He took the tape off her wrists and mouth, aware that prints could be lifted from the sticky residue, and the smooth side of the tape. He rolled the tape up into a ball and stuffed it into his pants pocket.

To give the needed appearance of a sexual assault, which he had no intentions of committing, he ripped her dress and pulled it down to her waist. He then jerked on her bra until it ripped loose, leaving it hanging below her ample breasts. For a minute he thought he was going to throw up again, but he took a couple of deep breaths and shook it off. He lifted her body and walked to the top of the bank. Laying her on the ground he rolled her down the embankment and watched as she slid into the murky water. He hoped she would stay in place, but he could see that she was beginning to slowly float away from the bank. So be it, he had to leave before someone wandered by, even if it was a desolate area. He jogged back to his car and left the scene, heading home to clean up.

Part two of his plan was in play now. In a week or two he would find one more victim, the one he needed to draw Linda out.

This time the heinous act was a little easier, but still he didn't like the feeling. It made him feel like a monster... and maybe he was...but he still didn't like it.

Chapter 8

PABLO ARRIVED at the Klima Restaurant and Bar promptly at seven. He parked his car about a block away, the only available space he could find. South Beach is a busy place at night, and the sidewalks were flooded with locals and tourists. As he walked to the restaurant he could hear the music flooding from clubs and bars along the way. He loved South Beach and came over every chance he got. The establishments were a little pricey for him but he managed. He had eaten at the Klima once before, as a guest of one of his friends, one who made a lot more money than he did.

Although swanky and expensive, the Klima had an open seating arrangement and tended to be quite noisy when crowded. It had been voted one of the ten most romantic restaurants on Miami Beach. The food was authentic Spanish cuisine, and live music made conversations a little difficult. He enjoyed the food but to be honest, he enjoyed the food on Southwest Eighth Street in Hialeah. In fact, he enjoyed food anywhere.

He walked into the restaurant, noting that it wasn't as busy as the last time he had been here. The night was still young, and he was sure it would be packed with partying people before he left. He looked around and spotted Consuelo sitting at one of the few two-top tables. She hadn't seen him yet, so as he walked to her he observed how beautiful she was. He hadn't seen her for a while now, and the last time he had spoken with her was to arrange for Rolando's untimely demise in New Orleans. He owed her for that, and more than likely she was here to collect, in some way.

"Consuelo, *Te ves hermosa*, you look beautiful," he said as he stopped at the table.

"Pablo, you look good as well. Please, *amigo*, have a seat," Consuelo replied.

Pablo took a seat at the table and smiled at her. She smiled back and asked, "How have you been, my friend?"

"I've been good. Still have some pain from the gunshot Rolando rendered me. But, other than that, good!" Pablo answered.

"Well, I hope you're hungry. I hear the food is good here and was highly recommended to me by a friend," Consuelo said.

"I've eaten here once before. The food is good, but to be honest, I've had better," Pablo said.

"Oh, you've eaten here *before*?" Consuelo replied, raising her eyebrows.

"Yes, but it was a business meeting of sorts. Normally I go for the low-brow places," Pablo said, laughing.

"Well, order anything you like...dinner is on me tonight, my friend."

"I'm sure that I will pay in one way or another," Pablo

said with a chuckle.

Before they could say anything else, the waiter appeared and began filling their glasses with iced water. He handed them the leather-bound menus and said he would return in a few minutes to take their order.

"I suppose we should look at the menu and be ready to order when he returns," Consuelo said as she opened the menu.

Once they had decided what they were going to order, Pablo said, "Now, I know you didn't invite me to dinner just to catch up on old times, Consuelo. What am I really here for?"

"Why Pablo, can't I just visit with an old friend," Consuelo said, with a phony pout.

"Sure you can, but I know there is something more you want," Pablo said, grinning.

"Once we order I'll tell you, okay?"

As if on cue the waiter appeared to take their order. Consuelo ordered a fresh Ceviche, citric vinaigrette with avocado and cilantro for an appetizer and fresh Mediterranean monk fish for the entree. Pablo ordered an appetizer of croquetas Jotas Iberian ham and opted to try the monk fish also. Pablo asked for a beer and Consuelo ordered a gin and tonic.

"Gin! T hats like drinking kerosene," Pablo said with a turned-up nose.

"I like it. I guess it's an acquired taste, but I do like it," she said.

"Okay...what's going on, Consuelo?" Pablo asked.

Looking around the room as she took another sip of her drink, Consuelo leaned over and speaking softly said, "I have been approached about a job...one which I will need some help with. You are local and have contacts and resources that I don't. I need your help."

"What sort of job?" Pablo asked.

"I need to break someone out of jail. And, arrange for him to leave the country," Consuelo said, still speaking softly, even though there were few patrons near them.

"Which jail...and who is it that you need to spring?" Pablo asked, slightly interested.

"Well, he's in the Dade County jail presently, but in a few days he will be transported to a holding facility in South Miami, the Metropolitan Correctional Center I believe it's called."

"That's the one Manuel Noriega, the Panamanian dictator, was held in until he died this year. I thought they weren't using that facility any longer," Pablo said.

"I only know what I was told...maybe it's being used selectively or something," Consuelo said, pausing as the waiter arrived with their appetizers.

As Pablo picked up one of the ham croquettes he asked, "And who is this prisoner that wants you to break him out?"

"He is Juan Castro...or maybe you know him better as *El Scorpion*," Consuelo replied, as she watched for a reaction from Pablo.

Pablo had just put the croquette in his mouth and began to chew when Consuelo revealed the name. He began choking and had to grab his glass of water, quickly gulping a swallow.

"Are you totally *loco*?" He practically yelled, causing several diners to look his way.

"Lower your voice, Pablo. No, I'm not loco, and if you

don't want to make a quick 100k, then finish your meal and I'll find someone else," Consuelo said, tightly.

"Oh, I'm interested, it's just that this man will have more guards than Noriega did. What did you have in mind for me to do?" Pablo asked.

Pablo was in conflict now. He had been responsible for finding where The Scorpion had fled to and had subsequently told Stormy. He couldn't tell that to Consuelo since he didn't know how she would react to learning that he was a confidential informant for Jack Storm. He only had one way out and that was to pass the job on to someone else. Stormy would never forgive him for freeing the man...and Stormy *would* find out, of that he had no doubt. Nope, he would have to pass this one even though it was a helluva lot of money to pass up on.

"Let's finish our meal and take a walk down to the beach, away from prying ears. I have a plan and need your input to refine it," Consuelo said as she put a piece of avocado into her mouth.

They made small talk until the main course arrived. The monk fish was out of this world and Pablo had to admit, the food was much better than the previous time he had eaten here. Consuelo paid the check, left a sizable tip and they left the restaurant.

Once they had walked the two blocks to the beach, they found a bench near the sand and sat down. There were no other people within thirty yards of them, so Consuelo felt free to talk. Pablo had been in deep thought as they walked to the beach, and he had reached a decision.

"First, I want to tell you, Consuelo, that I appreciate

you considering me for this job. But, it's out of my expertise. It would take more than 100k just to hire the necessary number of men to pull this off, even if I could find them. On the other hand, I can put you in touch with someone who will possibly do it, but, be prepared to pay more," Pablo said.

"I understand, Pablo. If you have someone, please have them contact me as soon as possible. Here is my cell number," she said as she handed him a card containing only a phone number. She had once entertained the thought of making business cards that said, *Have gun...will travel*, after watching an old television series from the sixties. She quickly discarded the idea – one, because it was cliché, and two, because it was too blatant of an advertisement for her profession. She settled for just a phone number on a metallic card. It had class and carried a semblance of mystique.

"If he is *interested,* he'll be calling you within the next couple of hours. I'll contact him once I leave here," Pablo said.

As Pablo walked back to his car he decided that he wouldn't say anything to Stormy about what Consuelo was planning. He valued his life too much, and he knew what she was capable of if she ever found out. He only hoped that Stormy never found out; he valued their friendship too much.

Pablo sat in his car and dialed the number for one of his contacts. He hardly ever did business with Pepe Lopez. He considered him a little unbalanced and too demanding. Usually Pepe would want the lion's share of any deal presented to him. If he tried that with Consuelo he would fail...she was not stupid by any stretch of the imagination and would quickly tell him to get lost. He sure could have used a good payday but not at the expense of losing his relationship, and friendship, with Stormy. It was better this way. Then Pepe answered the phone.

Pablo spent about ten minutes explaining as much as he knew about what Consuelo wanted. Finally, Pepe said his goodbyes and that he would make the call to Consuelo.

****

Consuelo had just arrived at her room at the hotel when the call came in. She quickly kicked off her shoes and sat in one of the plush easy chairs by the expansive window. She answered the phone.

"Hello," she said, avoiding giving her name at this time.

"Is this the lady that needs some expert help with a problem?"

"Yes, and you are?" Consuelo asked.

"Just call me Pepe, for now. Fill me in on what you need, and I'll give you my price. And yes, I won't mention the name but I know who you are referring to...and I have no problem with him. So that won't play a part in determining if I can do it. Actually, and I'm surprised I am saying this, I am in awe of the man," Pepe said.

Consuelo explained to Pepe what she needed, also without mentioning The Scorpion's name. She stressed that it would have to go down in about three days. That is when The Scorpion was to be transported to the Metropolitan facility in Kendall. She explained that she needed a passport with his picture, which she would provide, and a change of clothes. Also, there would have to be a car furnished for a lengthy trip. When she had finished, Pepe told her he would call back, and then let her know if he could provide what she needed within the three days, and how much it would cost her. He promised to call back within the hour.

Consuelo decided to take a shower, but she took her phone into the bathroom just in case. She needed to go to a quick print shop after Pepe called back...if he was interested.

Chapter 9

"STORMY, GOOD TO SEE YOU AGAIN," Leo said as Stormy walked off the elevator and over to Leo's desk.

"Great to see you again, Leo," Jack Storm replied, as he shook hands with his friend.

"How is Shaunie doing? When is she going to have that baby?" Leo asked.

"She's doing great, other than being uncomfortable lying in bed. The baby will be here any day now...just waiting," Stormy said with a big grin. It was obvious that he was a happy man who was about to become a father for the first time.

"So, do you know what it's going to be, or how many," Leo asked, laughing.

"There's going to be only one, as far as we know, and no, we don't know what it's going to be yet, nor do we want to. We're going to be happy whatever it is."

"Well, give her my best and be sure to let me know when the big event happens," Leo said.

"So, where are you on the case? Have there been any

more bodies found?" Stormy asked, getting down to business.

"No, so far only the three. And how far as we have gotten...not far. We have Identified all of them now. We have been trying to see if they knew each other...had anything in common that connected them. So far, we're hitting a wall. At this point it doesn't seen they knew each other at all," Leo said.

"Well, if solving homicides was easy, they wouldn't need us, would they?" Stormy replied.

For the next couple of hours Leo and Stormy went over the reports, looking for that one particular thing that would give them a lead. The autopsies had revealed that although the women's clothes were either removed or torn, there had been no sexual assault. That was a glaring point that they struggled with. It seemed that either the women fought their attacker and the clothes were ripped in the fight, or the attacker began by ripping their clothes before they were killed. But, why go to all that trouble and then not rape them? According to the autopsy report they all died by strangulation. No prints were found on the necks of the victims nor anywhere else. The submersion in the water and elapsed time had probably dissolved any prints that would have been present, or, gloves were worn.

It seemed they had their work cut out for them, and Stormy suggested that he would return to Hialeah and begin following up on the last days that Linda Ward's sister, Stefanie Taylor, was alive. Where she worked, who she saw last and other bits of information would be a start. Stormy told Leo he was heading back to Hialeah and would keep in touch with him, especially if he came up with anything.

****

Stormy arrived in Hialeah and drove to Stefanie's last known address. He parked in front of the apartment building on West Sixty-fifth Street, the address he had been given by Leo. When he reached the apartment number, he knocked on the door.

A man opened the door and asked, "Can I help you?"

"I'm Detective Storm of the Hialeah Police Department, Stormy said as he produced his I.D. case, displaying his badge. Are you Mr. Taylor?"

"No, sir I'm Robert Johnson. What can I do for you?" The man replied.

"I'm trying to locate a couple by the last name of Taylor who used to live here. Did you know them?" Stormy asked.

"No, I've only lived here for about three months. The rental office is just down at the end of the building. Maybe they can help you," the man replied.

Stormy thanked him and walked down to the office. He spoke with the manager and found out that Stefanie had moved out about four months earlier. Stormy asked if by chance he had an address where she had moved to. Surprisingly, the manager did! He said she had left in good graces and had left the address she was moving to in case some packages she had ordered online came here instead of her new address. The manager wrote down the address and gave it to Stormy.

Stormy called the office, and Dakota answered the

phone.

"Hey, Stormy. Where are you?" Dakota asked.

"Out and about. Checking out addresses to see if anyone knew Stefanie and maybe saw anything unusual the night she vanished. How is Linda doing?"

"She's hanging in there...chomping at the bit to come back to work. The Captain told her not for a few days yet," Dakota replied.

"Well, keep an eye on her...she's conflicted right now. If you need me, call."

"Will do. Keep me up to date, okay?" Dakota said.

"I will. I'll try to stop by the office before heading home," Stormy said, hanging up the phone.

The address the apartment manager had given Stormy was at a new apartment complex in Miami Lakes. In fact, it was only about five blocks from his old address. He started his car and headed up Sixteenth Avenue, and within minutes he was at the address. He parked his car in front of the management office and looked around. It was a fairly new three-story building and the area was neat and well maintained. He walked to the office and entered.

"May I help you?" The young lady at a desk asked.

"I'm Detective Storm and trying to locate a family by the last name of Taylor. I understand they may have moved here in the last few months."

"Yes sir, the Taylors do live here. Are they in some type of trouble?" She asked.

"No, I just need to speak with Mr. Taylor. If you will direct me to their apartment, I would appreciate it," Stormy said, with his most disarming smile.

"They are on the ground floor at the far end of the

building, apartment 114."

"Thank you, I won't be long. Have a nice day," Stormy said as he turned to leave the office.

"I don't think anyone is home. I've received several calls from Mr. Taylor asking about his wife. Stefanie I think her name is. He said he has called for two days now, and she is not answering her phone," the girl said.

"Where was Mr. Taylor calling from?"

"Somewhere out of state...he's a truck driver and is gone days at a time."

"I'll need a pass key to the apartment," Stormy said.

"I don't know if I am allowed to do that, Detective," she replied, obviously confused.

"Miss, this is a homicide investigation. I need to get inside and determine what happened. A key works better than my foot...if you get my drift," Stormy said.

"Yes, sir. But I'll be calling my supervisor to let him know what's happening. Is Mr. Taylor the victim? His wife?" She asked as she produced a master key.

"Mrs. Taylor was found deceased today. If Mr. Taylor calls, please, don't say anything about her death. Here is my card and number. If he calls back, have him call me at once," Stormy said.

Stormy walked to the end of the building and stopped in front of apartment 114. He knocked on the door several times, and when no one answered, he inserted the master key and opened the door, not sure what to expect.

The apartment was spotless, clean and tidy. Stefanie was a good housekeeper from what he observed in the living and dining room. He walked back to the bedroom and slowly pushed the door open. The bedroom was also immaculate, the bed still made, no signs of anyone having slept there recently. A blinking light caught his eye, and he saw the phone and answering machine on the nightstand. He walked over and pushed the play button. He listened to several messages, all from her husband, the worry showing through in his voice from one message to the next.

Stormy left the apartment, not yet calling CSI. since there was no visible crime scene there to be processed. He would have them come by later anyhow, just to be safe.

As he left the apartment a woman was leaving her apartment next door at the same time. Stormy approached her and asked if she knew Stefanie Taylor and her husband.

"Not very well. They haven't been living here very long and usually kept to themselves. I believe her husband travels a bit, out of town a lot. I've spoken to her in passing, but we never had a real conversation," the woman said.

"Well, thank you. I appreciate your help," Stormy said.

"May I ask what happened?" The woman said.

"I'm not at liberty to say, just yet. We need to speak with Mr. Taylor first," Stormy said, smiling and walking to his car.

****

Stormy arrived at the office and was walking to the Captain's office when his phone rang.

"Hello, Jack Storm here," he answered, noticing that the number calling was unfamiliar to him.

"Mr. Storm, this is Ronald Taylor. I called the office where I live and they advised me to call you at once. Whats this about? Is there something wrong with my wife...I've been trying to reach her for nearly two days now."

"Mr. Taylor, I'm afraid there's been an accident. Where are you now?" Stormy asked.

"I just got back in town. Do you need me to come by your office? Oh my God...is Stefanie alright, can you tell me anything?"

"Yes sir, please come straight to my office on LeJuene Road. I'll explain everything when you get here," Stormy said, cutting the connection before Ronald Taylor could ask further questions.

Chapter 10

Three days earlier

MARC BUTLER SAT QUIETLY in his car in the parking lot in front of Westland Mall. He figured he would have to wait for an hour at least. He had followed his target to the mall and had parked next to her. She exited her car and began walking to the mall to do some shopping. She never once looked over at him as he sat in his car. As he waited in the dark, his thoughts ran rampant. He was going over what had brought him to this point in his life.

Marc had moved from Georgia to the Miami area six years earlier. He came from a small town that held no job future for him. While in Miami he worked many dead-end jobs, moving from job to job. Most of the time it was because of his temper, which could erupt over the most minor of things. He never became physical, but his mouth was his worst enemy. He had no friends in the area and spent most nights watching television. He loved the CSI shows and decided he wanted to work in that field.

He became determined to go to Dade Community College and managed to get a night job which allowed him to attend classes during the day. He graduated with an Associates Degree in Criminology and set out to apply at various police departments. He was turned down by the first three he applied to – Miami Police, Miami Beach Police and Metro-Dade.

Becoming discouraged, he moved inland and applied at the Hialeah Police Department. To his delight he was accepted and told he would be working in the CSI unit. His supervisor would be Linda Ward.

When he reported to work he was issued the standard CSI uniforms but was told he would not be issued a take-home car until he completed probation, which was six months.

Linda made sure she worked cases with him, a practice she used with all new personnel. She was a stickler for details and made sure he collected and logged evidence correctly. The first couple of weeks went fine, but she began to see that Marc was beginning to take some shortcuts, overlooking vital procedures that needed to be followed. Before long Marc's personnel file contained several letters of reprimand from Linda, detailing his failure to follow standard operating procedures and various other infractions. It seemed that he thought he was already a top-notch crime scene investigator, when in fact, he was below par.

Two weeks before Marc's probationary period was up, Linda recommended that he be terminated. The final straw was the improper logging of some evidence that caused a major case to be dismissed. Marc was called in and advised that he was being terminated. He was furious and demanded to know why. He was read several of the complaints Linda had filed and told that he was to turn in his badge and uniforms. Marc handed over his badge and said he would bring in the uniforms later, then left the building in a furor. He had landed his dream job, and now Linda Ward had ended it in a flash.

For the next few weeks he was in a foul mood and was determined to get even. That was when he formulated his plan, a murderous one that there was no coming back from once he started.

For the next several days he followed Linda, learning where she lived and her routes to work. One day he followed her to a cafe and watched as she had lunch with another woman, one who resembled her. He overheard her say, "goodbye, Sis, see you next week" and knew that he had found the perfect way to get to Linda. He followed Linda's sister to her apartment, and checking the mail box, found out her last name was Taylor. He watched her for a couple of days and found out her name was Stefanie Taylor. He had what he needed now and implemented the first step of his plan. He killed victim number one.

Marc snapped himself out of his thoughts and looking around the parking lot, observed that there was no one near. He exited his car and knelt down, pulling out the K-bar knife he had brought along. He checked once again and, seeing no one around, quickly sliced the right rear and front tires of the car parked next to his.

The air rushed out of the slashed tires quickly, and Stefanie's car leaned to the right slightly as the tires went flat. He returned to his car and checked that the duct tape he had brought along was covered under a shirt on the back seat, in case he needed it.

He walked to the front doors of the mall, where he lingered just inside as he waited for her to approach. Within thirty minutes he spotted her walking towards the exit doors. As she walked out, he did also, walking about twenty feet behind her. He didn't want to alarm her by following too closely. He had his phone out and pretended to be looking at it as he walked. Stefanie glanced back once, and he kept his eyes on the phone.

"Oh no, that's just great," he heard her exclaim as she reached her car.

"What's the matter?" Marc asked, as he reached his car also, parked next to hers.

"I have a flat tire," she said, pointing down at the rear tire.

"I can change it for you if you like," Marc replied.

"Would you? That would be great and I'll pay you. I have no clue how to change a tire," she said.

"It's no problem at all. And no, you don't have to pay me," Marc said with a short laugh.

Stefanie opened the trunk and showed Marc where the spare tire was. Playing along, he took the tire out of the trunk and then said, "I don't think this is going to work...you have two flats."

Squatting down and pretending to study the tires he turned and told her, "Someone cut your tires. Some punks out having what they determine is fun, I suppose."

"Hey, don't I know you?" Marc suddenly exclaimed.

"I don't think so," Stefanie replied.

"Yes, now I remember. You're Linda Ward's sister," Marc said.

"How...but how do you know. I've never met you," she

said, puzzled.

"Oh, we've never met. I work with her at CSI. I've seen your picture on her desk, and she talks so much about you."

"Really! What's your name?" She asked.

"Marc...Marc Butler," he replied.

"Oh, I've heard her mention someone by that name. You're the new tech at CSI, aren't you?"

"Yep...that's me. Well, I know you don't have two spares, so if you like, I'll give you a lift home," Marc said.

"Oh, you don't have to do that. I'll just call a taxi."

"You really think that Linda would forgive me if I let you call a taxi?" Marc said. "Come on, I don't mind at all," Marc said, holding his hands out, palms up.

"Well, if you really don't mind, I suppose it'll be okay. Besides, I wouldn't want Linda to chew you out, you being new and all," Stefanie said with a laugh.

Marc put the spare back into the trunk and opened the passenger side door of his car for Stefanie. She got into the front seat. Marc walked around to the front and got into the driver's seat.

"Okay, buckle up, lady," he said, with a chuckle.

Stefanie reached over and grasped the seat belt, pulling it loose. Suddenly, Marc lunged over and grabbing the loosened seat belt, quickly wrapped it around her neck. He pulled tightly as she struggled and kicked the dash. Within fifteen seconds she slowly relaxed her grip on his arms, but he maintained his grip until he was sure she was dead. He released the belt and she semi-slid down into the seat, her head lolling against the seat back. He straightened her up and buckled her in, giving the appearance of a sleeping passenger.

Marc quickly backed the car out and began driving towards Okeechobee Road, heading to Miami, getting out of Hialeah. He soon reached the area where he had planned to dump the body, near downtown, in the Miami River. He ripped her clothes, pulled her top up around her head, jerked her bra down, exposing her breasts, and made sure her shoes were still on her feet. He didn't want to leave any evidence in his car.

Once he thought it was clear, he opened the door, and dragging her body to the edge of the embankment, he quickly rolled it down towards the water. In the dark he barely saw the tall cattails lining the edge of the bank, but he did see her roll to a stop, her body half in the water.

Looking around and seeing no traffic or anyone in the area, he quickly made a U-turn and headed back to his houseboat.

Chapter 11

RONALD TAYLOR HAD SHOWN UP, and in the confines of the Captain's office, for privacy purposes, Stormy had broken the news to him about his wife. He had taken it badly and blamed himself for being out of town so much. Stormy had assured him that it could have happened even if he had been in town. Dakota volunteered to take him to the Medical Examiner's Office to make an identification of the body. Stormy asked her if she wanted him to go with her, but she told him to go home, to be with Shaunie and get some rest.

Stormy decided to take her advice. When he got home, he parked his car next to Shaunie's and walked into the house. He took his badge and weapon and placed them on the vestibule in the hallway.

"Honey, I'm home," Stormy called out, walking to the kitchen to get a cold drink.

"Hey babe, I'll have dinner ready in just a few. How did your day go?" Shaunie called from the kitchen.

"Another day in the big city," Stormy replied, postponing telling her about Linda's sister until after dinner. Bad news had a way of ruining meals.

Shaunie *waddled* over and gave Stormy a kiss, her pregnancy almost at an end. She told Stormy to get his drink and take a seat, that dinner was almost ready.

"You sure you're not having twins?" Stormy asked as he rubbed her swollen belly.

"Would you have a problem with that?" She asked smiling.

"Not at all...one of each would be good," Stormy said.

"Yeah, easy for you to say," Shaunie said with a big grin.

"What wonderful delight have you prepared for us tonight?" he asked as he took a sip of his beer.

"Tonight, dear, we're having a gourmet meal – meatloaf and mashed potatoes and peas," Shaunie said with a melodic laugh.

"Good, my kind of comfort food," Stormy said, smiling up at his wife.

Due to her pregnancy he had tried to get her to hire someone to come and do the cleaning and cooking. She had refused, saying she was fine but she *did* give in and agree to have someone over for a couple of weeks after she had the baby.

When they had finished eating Stormy told her go sit in the living room while he cleared the table and cleaned the kitchen. She didn't protest, instead telling him she was going to soak in the tub for a while. When he had finished cleaning the kitchen he pulled another beer from the fridge and walked into the living room. Kicking his shoes off and picking up the remote, he switched on the television and plopped down on the couch. He watched as the news continued to talk about the recent body pulled from the Miami

River, speculating on whether or not the three women were connected somehow, or if possibly there was a serial killer loose in the area. So far, the Miami Police Department had been reluctant to admit that a serial killer was a possibility. It was only a matter or time, "Stormy thought to himself." As the local news went off and the national news came on, Shaunie walked into the room, already in her robe and pajamas. She stretched out on the couch and put her feet in Stormy's lap, indicating she wanted a foot massage.

"I hate to be the bearer of bad news," Stormy said as he massaged her feet.

"What? Rough day at the office?" Shaunie asked.

"No, worse than that. Have you been keeping up with the news about the women Miami P.D. has pulled from the river?"

"I've seen some of it. Those poor women. I can't imagine what their families are going through," Shaunie replied. "What about it?"

"The last body they pulled out was Linda Ward's sister," Stormy said softly.

"Oh my God! That poor girl. How is she taking it? Never mind, that was a dumb question, she has to be devastated," Shaunie said, tears welling in her eyes. She sat up and put her arm around Stormy.

"She is. Dakota is her shoulder to lean on, for now," Stormy said.

"When can I see her or call her?" Shaunie asked.

"I would give it a day or two," Stormy replied.

"I didn't know her sister, but Linda is such a sweet person," Shaunie said, reaching for a tissue.

"I had to break the news to her husband just before I

came home. He didn't take it too well. Dakota was taking him to the morgue to identify the body."

"That poor man. Did they have any children?" Shaunie asked.

"Not that I know of. I've been assigned to work the case with Leo," Stormy said.

"What? It's a Miami case, so why would you be helping them?"

"Leo wanted me to follow up on Stefanie's, that's her name, movements for the last few days to see if anything sticks out. We have to find out who did this to her, and the others."

"You find out who did this Stormy. For Linda's sake," Shaunie said.

After retiring to bed, Stormy listened as Shaunie softly sobbed. He put his arms around her and tried to give her comfort, and soon she fell into a restless sleep. Stormy listened to her breathing and tried to get some sleep also. It was probably an hour before he could finally drift off, his also a restless sleep.

Chapter 12

CONSUELO LEFT THE PRINT SHOP with the bogus business cards. They were essential in her getting to The Scorpion in jail. She had no way to contact him with the change in demands other than pretending to be an attorney. It was a risky gamble, but one she felt confident that she could pull off. As the Uber driver she had called drove her to the Criminal Justice building in Miami, she placed a call to Pepe.

"I will be calling you again in a few hours...after I make contact with the party we discussed," she said when he answered.

"I'll be waiting for your call, but be advised, time is of the essence. A lot of planning and money has to go into this in order for my crew to pull it off successfully," Pepe replied, severing the connection.

The Uber driver let Consuelo out in front of the Criminal Justice building. After she paid him she clutched her briefcase, which she had also bought for this meeting, and headed into the complex.

When she approached the clerk, she smiled and said, "I'm here to see my client, Juan Castro."

After producing her phony identification and a business card, she was allowed to go into the waiting area, but only after being scanned with a wand, walking through metal detectors and a thorough search of her briefcase. She kept a slight smile on her face as she waited, trying not to exhibit any nervousness. She figured at any minute she could be arrested if the clerk or anyone else had bothered to check out the bogus address she had given as her law office.

Finally, after about a fifteen-minute wait, a corrections officer approached her and told her to follow him. She was led into an interview room, bare except for two chairs and a metal table which was bolted to the floor.

"I expect the respect of client/attorney privilege, sir. No video or taping our conversations," Consuelo said, still maintaining her smile to keep up appearances.

"We know the law, Counselor," the officer replied.

He left the room and Consuelo took a seat, placing her briefcase on the table. She only had to wait for a couple of minutes before the door opened and a guard led Raul, AKA The Scorpion, into the small room. He was cuffed with his hands in front and leg irons with a short chain on his ankles. He shuffled slowly to keep from falling as he rounded the table and took a seat. The guard fastened his cuffed wrists to an eye bolt on the table in front of him. The guard then stepped to the wall and crossed his hands, not leaving the room.

"This is an interview with my client. You are not allowed to be in the room, sir," Consuelo said, glaring at the guard.

"I was told to wait in here with the prisoner," the guard replied.

"I suggest you get your supervisor in here ASAP.This will not do. This is a privileged conversation between me and my client, as allowed by law," Consuelo said.

The guard reached for the phone on the wall by the door and waited for someone to answer. In a second he told the party on the other end what Consuelo had said. He hung up the phone and told her, "The Captain will be here in a minute."

Within two minutes the door opened and the Captain walked in.

"We have our rules here, Counselor, there is to be a guard inside with violent inmates," the Captain said sternly.

"You really think that he's going anywhere, or doing anything to me, with all those cuffs and restraints?" Consuelo said, standing and facing the Captain. "I have important business to discuss with Mr. Castro, mainly in reference to an appeal when his sentence is handed down. If I have to I will call the Governor's office this very minute, I'm sure Ted, my friend the Governor, will have something to say about this," Consuelo bluffed, hoping the Captain wouldn't call it.

"Very well, but the guard will be just outside the door," the Captain replied, then turned and left the room, the guard trailing behind. Once the door closed, Consuelo sat back down and faced The Scorpion.

"Do you want to talk in English, or do you prefer Spanish?" Consuelo asked Juan.

"Spanish, my English is not the best," Juan replied. "Who are you?" He asked.

"Why, I'm your attorney," Consuelo said, with a slight

grin.

Before he could respond, she pulled out a legal pad and wrote, "I'm the person you called yesterday in reference to a problem you need help with. Do not use my name in here!"

"You have some real cojones, senorita," Juan said with a big smile.

"You have no idea, Mr. Castro, you have no idea," Consuelo said.

"The problem you need help with is more expensive than you thought. Three times more. Special needs have to be purchased, and a lot of last minute planning," she said.

"But no guarantee of success," Juan said, his mind racing a mile a minute. He could afford the three million she referred to but wanted some assurances. She showed she had the guts to follow up on this problem just by the way she made it here. He decided to trust her. "Done! Half now and the rest when the problem is resolved," Juan said.

"How good are you at memorizing numbers, Mr. Castro?"

"I have a knack for such a thing. Why?" He asked.

Consuelo turned the pad around, lifted a page and showed him a string of numbers. She wrote underneath the line, 'wire one and a half million to this account number.' You can use the phone you called me with yesterday.

Juan studied the numbers for about thirty seconds and nodded his head. Consuelo took a marker and blacked out the numbers, then she replaced the pad in her briefcase.

"In two days time you will be transported from here to a holding facility in South Miami. Be prepared for anything between here and there. Do exactly as you are told, and don't ask questions of the people involved. Do you understand?" Consuelo stated.

"Yes, I understand," Juan replied.

"How soon before the compensation will be transferred?" She asked.

"As soon as I am back in my cell...give me thirty minutes."

"That will work out fine. As soon as I see it has been transferred, I'll set things in motion," Consuelo replied, as she stood and took her briefcase. She walked to the door and tapped once. The guard opened the door and stepped inside.

"We have finished our business, for now," she said. "But, when I return for another meeting I don't expect to have to go through the same concerns as before, okay?"

"Lady, I just work here. I do what I'm told. If they tell me to stay in the room the next time, then you'll have to work it out again," the guard replied as he walked over to unshackle The Scorpion.

Thirty minutes later, as Consuelo exited the Uber driver's car, her phone beeped. She looked at the text and smiled. The money had been transferred to her account. She paid the driver and as she reached the front doors of her hotel, she stopped and dialed Pepe's number. All she said was, "It's a go."

Smiling, she entered the hotel and diverting to the lounge she ordered a drink. She deserved it, and she was going to enjoy it.

Chapter 13

STORMY EXITED THE SECOND-FLOOR ELEVATOR and walked into the squad room of the Homicide Division at Miami P.D., holding two boxes with one hand in a juggling act of sorts. He walked over to Leo's desk and gently set the boxes down.

"My God! You came through the front door of a police department, with Krispy Creme doughnuts! Are you trying to destroy the reputation of police officers," Leo exclaimed, looking at the marked box and laughing at Stormy.

"You really care if people associate cops with doughnuts?" Stormy asked, also laughing. "I happen to like donuts and I'm not going to stop eating them just because of some stigima attached to the two."

"I do too...just busting your chops, pal," Leo said, as he took a glazed doughnut from the box.

"So, anything turn up at your end?" Leo asked as he licked the glaze flakes off his fingers.

"I contacted Stefanie's husband. He's an over-the-road truck driver and was in Georgia when she was killed. I had to break the news of her death to him...which he didn't take very well, which is understandable," Stormy replied, also reaching for a doughnut.

"That's tough man. Wouldn't want it to happen to me," Leo said. "Anything else?"

"No, not yet. I had Dakota take him to the morgue to make a positive identification," Stormy said, "Anything on your end?"

"Well, so far we haven't been able to connect the three victims to each other, and the way it looks they didn't know each other. Let's hope we don't have another one anytime soon. We have to catch this guy, and quick. The news media wants us to declare a serial killer is on the loose. We don't need that kind of panic, but if another body shows up we may not have a choice," Leo said.

Grabbing a cup of coffee, the two of them went into Leo's office with the remainder of their doughnuts. Leo took a seat behind his desk and stormy sat in an easy chair by the door.

"Okay, so far we can't find a connection with the three victims. They were not sexually molested according to Doc Davis, although their clothes were deliberately ripped to make it appear that an assault took place. And, all of the vics were dumped into the Miami River," Leo began. "Let's eliminate the first thought, for now. We may still find out later that they had a connection. Now, about the lack of a sexual assault on any of them..."

"As far as the lack of sexual assault. Maybe the perp just gets off on killing women. It seems that ripping their clothes is an act of frustration. I can't believe how he manages to *not* leave some evidence at the scene. I mean nothing! That takes meticulous planning, something someone would have to have the knowledge of how to clean a crime scene. Maybe a professional? But to what purpose? And, we still have to determine that the same person is responsible for all three murders," Stormy said, draining the last of his coffee.

"Well, I think it's the same person responsible. Wanna know why?" Leo asked.

"Why, you have a crystal ball or something?" Stormy said with a chuckle.

"No, although that would be great. But I do think that it's no coincidence that the victims are all dumped into the same river. This guy has a knowledge of the right places to dump and flee, without detection. Deserted areas, areas that he seems to have scouted ahead of time. I think he lives near the river and that affords him the opportunity to get home before any kind of dragnet can be put in place," Leo said, smugly.

"Damn Leo, you sound like Columbo," Stormy said with a hearty laugh.

"Who is Columbo?" Leo asked.

"I know you're kidding me, right? Columbo...TV detective!"

"Stormy, I'm not a television man...news only, when I do want to watch. I'm a reader," Leo said, grinning. "You should try it sometime."

"You're lying, Leo Sharp," Stormy said. "Anyhow, what you said makes sense. How are we going to handle this? We could set up surveillance along the river, but it could be days or months before it happens again, if it happens again."

"Yeah, that would be out of the question, for now at

least, unless we received a tip or other info that would warrant it. So, what you gonna do now, Stormy?"

"I may follow your premonition and do some leg work along the river," Stormy said.

"Let me know if you find anything," Leo said, as Stormy arose and headed out the door.

"And Stormy!" Leo said, causing Stormy to stop and turn around.

"Yes?"

"Thanks for the doughnuts...next time hide them in an unmarked bag," Leo said, grinning.

Stormy smiled and shot Leo a bird as he walked to the elevator.

Chapter 14

LINDA CLOSED THE DOOR behind Dakota. She had arrived an hour earlier to visit and check on her. Dakota was such a sweet person, and Linda really like her. After a light lunch, which Linda prepared, Dakota talked with her for a while and soon ran out of things to say. She bade her goodbyes and told Linda that she would visit again in a couple of days.

In the kitchen she began to clean up from lunch, rinsing and putting dishes in the dishwasher. When she had finished she took a bottle of Voss water and sat down in the living room. Voss was the only water she would drink. She imagined that it tasted as fresh and clean as a mountain stream, even though she had never drunk from a mountain stream. She didn't turn on the television, just sat and cried some more. She had gone through two boxes of tissues, and she was just about cried out.

The loss of her sister had hit her hard. She could still see her smiling when she and Dakota had gone out to lunch. Now, crying time was over. Grieving could come later. She was mad and furious at whomever had murdered her sister. She thought about calling Stormy to see if he had any leads, but she held off, knowing he would call if and when he had anything.

As she sat thinking and rocking in her lounger, her eye caught the blinking light on the answering machine. She was still one of the last holdouts that had to have a landline and answering machine. She debated on getting up and playing back the messages, but she had done that the day before and nine out of ten were friends and family extending their condolences. Of course, there was the one or two that were telemarketers or scammers. They could always be counted on to call once or twice a week.

Finally, as she finished a swallow of water, she got up and walked over to the answering machine. She picked up a pen and pad lying on the table in preparation for writing down any numbers she would have to call back. She saw the counter on the machine and it said she had thirteen missed calls. Thirteen! Unlucky number. She was tempted to just erase them all, not in the mood to listen. Instead, she hit the play button and had her pen poised to write if necessary. As she had thought, ten of the calls were condolences, two from someone trying to sell something. The last one, she noticed, had come in only a couple of hours earlier. When she hit the play button, the message started.

"I know who killed your sister," the voice said. Then the call ended. That was the only message the unknown caller left. The voice was disguised but had a familiar ring to it, she just couldn't place it.

She was in shock at hearing the message. Tears began to well up in her eyes, but she quickly wiped them away. She was done crying for now. That could come later. Right now she wanted to know who had placed the call and why they had hung up. She played the message over and over, in the process trying to identify the voice. She just couldn't but knew that it had a familiar ring to it.

She had to call Stormy. She took great care to not erase any messages now...not wanting to accidentally erase the one that she had just listened to. It could be a crank call, but something told her that it wasn't.

Linda went to the kitchen where she had left her cell phone. Stormy was on speed dial so she quickly picked it up. Just as she was ready to punch in his number, the house phone rang. Exasperated, she lay down the cell and went back to answer the landline.

"Hello!" Linda answered on the landline.

"I know who killed your sister," the disembodied voice said, repeating the message Linda had just listened to minutes earlier.

"Who is this? What do you want? Why haven't you called the police with this information?" Linda asked in a rush.

"NO POLICE! Do you understand. What do I want? Money! Five thousand dollars and I will tell you who killed your sister," the voice said.

"Five thousand dollars! How do I know you have the name of the murderer? You could just be someone trying to take advantage of someone's tragedy," Linda said.

"AH...my dear Linda. I'm legit. I'll call tomorrow with where you can drop off the money. Don't call the police or you will never hear from me again...and trust me...I really know who killed her," the caller said and then hung up the phone.

Linda held the phone in her hand, just staring at it. The

man had called her by name. Sure, he may have pulled it up from the phone book, but he used it too freely, as if he knew her personally. She had to call Stormy...but the caller had insisted no police were to be notified.

Linda was in a quandary – to call Stormy or not. If she did and the caller found out, she might never know the name of who killed her sister. But, then again, Stormy was the best investigator she knew. She had to tell him. Maybe he would be able to find the caller. But, did she want to take that chance. For now, she decided to wait for the call tomorrow. One thing she did do was to set the machine so that every call was recorded. Who knows, it could come in handy later.

Chapter 15

MARC BUTLER SMILED as he severed the connection with Linda on his phone. It was a burner phone and although would be hard to track, he still took the sim card out and smashed it to pieces. He had several other burners, and he didn't intend to make a stupid mistake like allowing someone at the police department to track his call.

Marc pulled a coke from the fridge and went out onto the deck of his houseboat. He took a seat under the overhead deck, out of the sun, and thought as he sipped his coke. He didn't care about the money. It was just part of his plan to get his hands on Linda Ward, but she didn't know that. He had used a voice distortion module he had picked up at one of those *spy* shops. He was surprised how well it worked. He knew that his distinctive Georgia accent would have given him away immediately. So, he looked until he found a shop that sold all kinds of spy and surveillance gear.

He thought back on the conversation he had just had with Linda. At first she seemed belligerent, then quickly changing to hopeful. He would let her stew for a day until he was ready to call with more information. First, he needed to figure out where he was going to lure her and how he would restrain her. He knew from working with her she was only about a hundred and ten or twenty pounds. She wasn't tall either, probably only around five feet and four or five inches in height. He didn't see any problem in handling her, physically. He just needed to make sure that when she arrived wherever he told her, that the advantage would be his. Hell, the girl carried a firearm, and he was determined to make sure she didn't bring it with her. That would have to be part of his planning when he told her where to go.

There were several rundown and abandoned boathouses along the river, but they didn't afford the privacy he needed. Two vehicles parked at an abandoned boathouse would prompt a roving patrol officer to stop and check it out. No, he needed to find somewhere that he would be able to do what he planned to Linda Ward without anyone being able to hear talking or screaming or to see them. He had to begin searching for just the right place, and now was as good a time as any.

He began driving aimlessly around the area, not too close to his houseboat, but near enough to get back home quickly. Driving through an area that held small warehouses, he decided that they were too populated, too many eyes, and more than likely some worked there at night. He crossed off those areas from his search and kept looking. Driving further west on Okeechobee Road he was soon leaving Hialeah and the area became less populated. He had told Linda he would call tomorrow, and he needed to have a place to send her. So he kept driving.

When he reached the Hialeah Gardens area that abutted

Okeechobee Road, he spotted a small strip mall, probably no more than six or seven stores, on the south side of the road. It appeared to be abandoned, so he made the first turn he could and wended his way back to the strip center.

When he arrived, he noticed there was a sign that said *No trespassing*. Further down the strip was a sign on one of the doors, and he could see in red letters, *Foreclosure*. He exited his car and carefully strolled past the half dozen stores, all empty and boarded up. He didn't worry too much about the no trespassing sign, he would simply tell anyone who stopped and questioned him that he was interested in acquiring the property from the bank.

The front of the strip mall faced the highway and anyone passing could see the front of the buildings, and, whatever vehicles were parked there. Marc walked around the rear of the center and checked each door, finding all but one securely fastened. That one was on the west end of the center and had a rear window and bay door. He attempted to lift the bay door, but it was fastened from inside. There were no bars on the window, but it was locked also.

Looking around and seeing that there were no houses visible from the rear, Marc picked up a palm-sized rock from the ground and gave a sharp tap just above the inside lock on the window. The glass broke and left a hole above the lock with just enough room for him to flick the latch up with his forefinger. He lifted the window, listening for any type of alarm. He was hoping that there wasn't a silent alarm that went to a monitoring company.

He carefully climbed in the window and dropped to the floor. Once inside, he closed the window and looked for was an alarm box. There wasn't one, so he continued walking through the building. The store evidently was originally an auto parts store, with a bay for inventory to be stored. There were still rows of steel shelving, some with a few boxes still sitting there. Marc walked to the rear and opened the door leading to the storage area.

Inside there was room to park a vehicle, a bunch of boxes piled up against the wall, and a table and chairs. Other than that, there wasn't much else. He studied the area for a few minutes and decided that this would work. He would have to add a few things to aid in what he had planned. He would make his call to Linda as planned but would delay her bringing the money until he had made the additions here that he would need. Before he left, he busted the inside lock on the overhead door, leaving it free to open. He would park inside once he returned. It would eliminate the chance of a patrolling cop or anyone else becoming curious about his car parked outside.

Marc drove to the nearest Ace Hardware Store and began gathering the things he would need. He picked out a battery-operated heavy-duty drill, an extra battery, two battery chargers, concrete drill bits, several u-bolts and twenty-five feet of heavy chain. He also picked up a bag of quick-set cement. He grabbed a coke from the box by the register and wandered the aisles, his mind running through what else he would need. In one aisle he rolled out ten feet of black plastic, for covering the window in the bay area. He didn't want someone looking inside the window and seeing what he was doing. He spotted sleeping bags on a shelf and grabbed one. On the way to the register he suddenly thought of the need for a flashlight. After picking one from the shelf, he went to the register to check out.

After loading all the items in his car he drove to his houseboat, and once inside, he plugged in the two battery chargers he had purchased. Inserting the batteries, he knew he would have to wait for about two to three hours for a full charge. While they charged, he decided to go grab some lunch and think if there was anything else he would need.

Marc stopped at a Burger King and ordered a Whopper with cheese, fries and a large coke. As he slowly ate his lunch he used a napkin and jotted down other things he thought of that he would need – a water bottle with a plastic straw, two gallons of water, a five-gallon plastic bucket, energy bars, and toilet paper. He also added two pairs of handcuffs, which he would pick up at a gun shop. He still had his CSI identification card, so he shouldn't have any problem there. Finishing his lunch, he dumped the trash in a receptacle by the door and returned to his car.

From there he drove back to his houseboat. He would still have to wait about an hour or two before the batteries were fully charged. He decided that while they charged he would go to a gun shop and pick up the handcuffs. By the time he returned home the batteries should be charged up enough for him to perform the tasks he had to do.

Chapter 16

PEPE LOPEZ HAD A REPUTATION throughout South Florida as "the man to go to." He had committed almost every crime you could think of and had served time for some of them. He had learned from those mistakes that had gotten him caught and for the past ten years had escaped the clutches of the law. He had an entourage of ten hard core men that he used regularly, men that he trusted, as much as he could trust anyone. The main reason he had been jail free for the past ten years was that he did the planning for the jobs, and his men carried them out.

Pablo, a man he didn't completely trust, had called him with the chance of a big payday. He didn't trust Pablo, not because of any particular reason, but because of rumors, persistent rumors, that he was a C.I. for some detective. So far no one had produced any proof of that claim, but Pepe wasn't one to take a chance, even if it was just a rumor.

Of all the various crimes Pepe had committed, and the list was long, he had never had to break anyone out of jail. He had called the woman, Consuelo, and agreed to take the job, if she agreed to the price. He had heard of her but never met her. Her reputation was whispered in the circles he ran in but not in tones as reverent as those of the man he was to spring from jail, *El Scorpion.*

Pepe hung up the phone and faced his men sitting around a large table in his warehouse. He had just gotten off the phone with his cousin, who worked with the transportation division for the Dade County jail. His cousin, Jorge Sanchez, had access to transportation records and had provided him with the route they would be taking to the Metro holding facility in South Dade County. He would call later when he found out the exact time the transport would be leaving.

Pepe had thought long and hard for hours after receiving the *go* signal from Consuelo. He knew that any success of breaking The Scorpion out of the Dade County jail would be nearly impossible, so he dismissed that idea. Then it had hit him suddenly. His cousin would play a crucial part so he had made the call. Now, he had a working plan and had summoned his men to the warehouse where they would go over it. Mentally patting himself on the back, he knew his forte was in planning hard to do jobs, and this one would be the crown jewel for him, not to mention his biggest payday yet. He didn't have a lot of time, only two days, and it had to be perfect. Stroking his ego, he knew it would be perfect.

"Alright, listen up, guys. I'm going to lay out the plan, and I need your input on any changes that we need to consider. We're not leaving here until we know we have a plan that will work," Pepe said to the group of gathered men.

For thirty minutes Pepe laid out his plan, adding and changing as he went along. Finally, he had what he figured was a workable plan and opened up the table for discussions.

"Okay, we have the route, but what about the time they will be taking it?" asked one of the men.

"My contact will provide that by tomorrow," Pepe replied.

"What about we have someone further up the route that will radio us when the transport is near?" another asked.

"A great suggestion, Mario. I hadn't thought of that. We will use Manny since he has a bad leg," Pepe said.

"My leg won't get in the way of our job," Manny replied, almost whining. Manny was the oldest of his men, approaching sixty now, and he needed a knee replacement, badly.

"I know you can hold your own, Manny. But being able to alert us when the transport is approaching will be the most important part of the job. I'm counting on you," Pepe said, in an attempt to placate Manny.

"Okay. If it's that important, I'll do it."

"So now we will all have walkies-talkies. Once Manny alerts us we can put them away," Pepe said.

"Juan, you were a welder so you will be responsible for going to the manhole and welding the chains in place. You'll need to dress up the van with a city sign and take a hard hat. The people in the neighborhood will think you're just doing work for the city. Once that is done, close up the manhole and get out of there," Pepe said.

"I'll get it done today, boss," Juan replied.

"Now, one of you find a walker to take with us."

"What kind of walker?" one man asked.

"How many kinds of walkers are there, dummy?"

Manny replied.

"Well, taking your age into consideration, maybe you have one," the man said, laughing.

"Just so you know, funny man, I do have one. My wife used it after her surgery," Manny said.

"Great! Bring it in tomorrow, Manny," Pepe said.

After discussing the plan for a couple of hours, they concluded that it would probably work, in fact, they could see no reason it wouldn't. Pepe dismissed them and reminded Manny to bring in the walker, to the grins of the other men. He had Juan stay behind, needing him to purchase or find things they would need. The walkies-talkies, heavy-duty chain, welding equipment, and other stuff.

Once Juan left, Pepe stayed at the table, his thoughts making sure that he had covered everything. He couldn't find any fault with the plan, so he pushed back his chair, stretched, and returned to his office. Yep, he decided, this would be the best plan he had ever put together.

Chapter 17

STORMY PARKED HIS CAR just off Okeechobee Road, on the river side. He got out and walked down to one of the locations that Leo had provided him, near where the first body had been discovered. He walked the bank for several hundred yards before turning and walking the same in the opposite direction. He didn't know what he was looking for, but if something jumped out he would be ready.

Seeing nothing of value he got back into his car and drove to the next site, where the second body was found. Performing the same task, walking in both directions, he found nothing that could be possible evidence. There was only one site left, the one where Stefanie's body was found, and he wasn't looking forward to it. But it had to be done.

Stormy carefully walked and half slid down the embankment at the site where Stefanie's body was found. He parted the cattails carefully and let his eyes scan the area, including the cattails. He still found nothing of value. Obviously, the killer had taken great pains to ensure he left no evidence connecting him to the crime.

Stormy climbed back to the top of the embankment and stood there for minutes, looking around, trying not to miss a square inch. He carefully scanned the ground around him, seeing dozens of footprints. No doubt, all of them were left by the police that responded, the kids who found Stefanie, and the CSI personnel. If the killer left a footprint it was contaminated now by the intrusion of everyone who had been at the crime scene. He searched yards in both directions for tire impressions but there were too many, probably by the CSI and police vehicles.

He returned to his car and sat for a few minutes, the air blasting full force, cooling the sweat he had worked up climbing up and down the embankment. He tried to put himself in place of the killer, trying to figure out how he dumped the body, how he managed to avoid leaving any trace of his presence.

After several minutes Stormy concluded that the killer had pulled up on the embankment, probably very late at night when traffic was at a minimum, quickly opened the door and rolled the body down the embankment. It seemed to be the only answer. He put his car in gear and drove back to HPD to check with Dakota and see how Linda was holding up.

Stormy arrived at the Bureau and found Dakota working at her desk. He grabbed a cup of coffee before taking a seat across from her. She looked up just as he took a sip of the coffee, his face suddenly screwing up, causing him to lean over and spit the coffee into the trash can.

"Sorry, I couldn't swallow that swill. Who made it and when, yesterday?" Stormy said as he wiped his mouth with the back of his hand.

"Now you see why there is not a cup on my desk. I don't know who made it, but they must have put half a pound of coffee in the pot. It could walk out of here," Dakota said, laughing at Stormy.

"When was the last time you saw or talked with Linda?" Stormy asked.

"About an hour and a half ago. She seemed a lot better, chomping at the bit to come back to work."

"That will be up to the Captain. Probably another day or so I would imagine," Stormy said.

"Anything new on what you're working on with Leo?" Dakota asked.

"I've spent most of the morning walking all three crime scenes. This guy is covering his tracks pretty good. Couldn't find a damn thing we could use," Stormy replied, still wiping his mouth.

"Well, he can't be that good forever. Sooner or later you'll come up with something."

"Hopefully before he dumps another one," Stormy said.

"How's Shaunie doing?" Dakota asked, changing the subject.

"I think she's gonna bust any day now."

"That's an awful way of putting it, Stormy."

"I know. It's just that she is so close to having the baby, and she has gotten so big."

"Maybe you should go home and check in on her," Dakota said, raising an eyebrow.

"Yeah, I guess I should. If the Captain asks, tell him I went home to check on her," Stormy replied. "I'll be back in an hour or two."

As Stormy was leaving the squad room, Dakota called out, "Tell Shaunie I said hi."

Stormy waved a hand without turning around and headed for his car.

Chapter 18

BRENDA SKIPPER SAT at her desk, intently studying her computer screen. Almost without a conscious thought, she brushed back a lock of her dark hair that had dropped down across her forehead. Suddenly, she let out a yell...the picture on her screen popping up after an hour of her staring at it. She had been running the FBI's facial recognition program, pulling up comparisons from around the country to the photo she had put into the system. Finally, she had a hit. The subject of her search had been found on a camera at the Miami International Airport baggage claim area. Consuelo Alvarez could be seen picking up a small suitcase from the luggage carousel, then walking out and getting into a taxi.

Brenda had been with the FBI for a dozen years now and stationed at the headquarters in Washington, D.C. for most of her career. She hadn't been a field agent in all that time, her skills needed at the office performing analytical work for most of the other agents. She had a knack for steering some of the agents in the right direction and getting the right information for them when they asked for her help.

Several days earlier, the AIC, agent-in-charge, had dumped a case on her desk. It was a file forwarded to them by the Miami and Hialeah police departments. Normally, the FBI didn't work local homicides, but this one had crossed state lines, several in fact. The victim had been found dead in a hotel room in New Orleans, his death ruled a heart attack, but a closer examination ruled otherwise. His heart had shown no signs of disease that would have led up to a heart attack. He had been a suspect in several murders in the Dade County area. It was also noted that he was an ex-police officer of the Hialeah Police Department. He had been supposedly killed when the detective in charge of the investigation had a showdown with him on an abandoned freighter. His body had never been recovered and had been presumed washed down the river and possibly out to sea. A tip from an anonymous caller had prompted the AIC to at least look into it. The caller had given him Consuelo's name and some details into her profession, touting her as a hired assassin. Not giving much credibility to the information, the AIC decided to pass the case on to Brenda, not really expecting her to find anything of value. He decided she could work with the case when she wasn't helping other agents.

Brenda grinned with glee and leaned back in her chair, planning how she could convince the AIC to let her run with it. As she sat thinking, she looked at the picture of her daughter, Sheila, smiling from a silver frame on her desk. She was proud of Shelia. She had also entered the law enforcement arena by taking on a job with a police department in Central Florida. She had only been an officer two years when she got the opportunity to become a homicide detective. Her attention to detail, professional report writing and overall professionalism had caught the attention of the brass. She jumped at the chance to become a homicide detective and had not disappointed those who had placed their faith in her and given her the chance. Yes, she was proud of her daughter and if she could snag this case and run with it, Shelia would be proud of *her* as well. Not that she wasn't proud of her mom, but becoming a field agent would certainly make Shelia smile. Now, if she could convince the AIC to let her handle the case, maybe she could kiss this office and all the mundane paperwork and filing goodbye.

Brenda performed one more task; she contacted the FBI agent assigned to New Orleans and had him run camera footage from the night Rolando had died. Sure enough, the agent got a hit and after comparing it to the photo Brenda had faxed him, was sure it was the woman she was looking for.

****

"Sir, I would like to follow up on this case. I managed to track down Consuelo Alvarez in Miami," Brenda said. "Also, I used resources in New Orleans and found camera footage of her on the street outside the hotel Rolando had been staying in when he died. That puts her in the area at the time of his death.

Brenda had been allowed to see the AIC through his secretary. Now, she was nervous in his presence, knowing how little patience he had. Several employees had mentioned how he was impatient and had a habit of cutting off conversations with the lower echelon. She knew that she had to make her case fast, meaning few words and being concise in her findings.

"What makes you think this... Consuelo person is in Miami?" Asked the AIC.

"Based on the information you supplied me and doing a search, I found a passport picture of her, taken about ten years ago. Then I ran her through the facial recognition program and got a hit from one of the cameras at the Miami International Airport," Brenda replied.

"How long ago was she there?"

"Sir, the camera time-stamp shows she was there two days ago. She has to be there for a reason and given her supposed profession, we know what the reason could be. Someone has probably been marked for elimination," Brenda said, trying to get out all the information she could before the AIC decided he wasn't satisfied.

"Sir, I really would like to follow up on this. It would be my chance to do some field work and show you that I am ready. Also, maybe we can connect her to the homicide in New Orleans," Brenda said, trying not to sound like she was begging, which she actually was. This was her chance and she had to sell it to him.

"I don't know, Brenda. Do you think you're ready for the field?" The AIC asked, steepling his hands under his chin.

"Yes, sir. I really do."

"Well, I think you are too," the AIC replied, much to Brenda's astonishment.

"You do? Thank you, sir, I won't let you down," Brenda replied, her cheeks turning slightly red.

"Do your research and then take the Bureau's Gulfstream to Miami. I'll have one of our agents there meet with you. Don't worry, I'll advise him you're in charge of the investigation," the AIC said, signaling the meeting was over.

Brenda arose from her chair, her heart slightly pounding, and left the office. When she reached her desk, she placed the file on top and went to the ladies' room. When inside, she made sure she was alone, then looked in the mirror and gave out a loud whoop. Finally, she was going to do some field work. When she finished, she washed her hands, brushed back her hair, and went to her desk to go over the file again, her smile even bigger.

When Brenda had read over the file for almost an hour, she packed it away and called the transportation office to arrange for her flight to Miami. She was told she would be leaving at nine in the morning and could expect to arrive in Miami around eleven a.m. She took the photo, and the case file and headed home, but not before touching her forefinger to her lips and then touching the photo of her daughter.

****

After a short holding pattern, the FBI's Gulfstream G650 landed at Miami International Airport. Once it had taxied to the private hangar reserved for the FBI, the steps were lowered and Brenda stepped off. She was greeted by Lawrence Foresman, an agent attached to the Dade County office. He helped her with her carry-on luggage and escorted her to the black GMC parked just inside the hangar door.

"It's a pleasure to meet you, Agent Foresman," Brenda said, extending her hand.

"Likewise, Agent Skipper," Larry replied. "What hotel will you be staying at?"

"The Marriott, downtown," Brenda said. "But, before we leave I need to go to the communications department of the airport. I want to have their techs access the video of the luggage pickup area. I'm looking for someone in particular, and it relates to the case I'm working."

"No problem. I'm familiar with the tech's there, and we should have what you want in no time," Larry replied.

Chapter 19

MARC BUTLER WALKED OUT of the gun shop after purchasing the handcuffs. He didn't even have to show his identification. He grabbed a Cuban coffee from a small cafeteria next door to the gun shop and returned to his car.

When he walked into his houseboat, he glanced at the light on the charger and saw to his delight that the light was green. It didn't take as long as he thought for the batteries to charge. Probably they had a partial charge from the factory. He unplugged the charger, and taking the batteries, he went back out to his car. Once he was sure he had everything he needed, he headed back to the strip shopping center.

As he approached the abandoned strip mall, he made sure there were no vehicles there. He drove in and around the back quickly. Getting out of his car he swiftly opened the roll-up door, drove his car inside, and quickly pulled down the door. As a precaution, he wedged the broken lock against the track ensuring the door couldn't be opened by anyone from the outside. He unloaded the purchases from his car and prepared to get to work. He wanted to be finished before darkness fell.

Taking the drill, he attached the battery and began drilling four-inch holes in the concrete in one corner of the bay. Once he had finished one side, he spread out the bedroll and placed it next to the holes, figuring out the spacing he would need to drill the other side. After completing the drilling, he took the u-bolts and placed one in each hole. Using a small empty paint can he found in the area, he mixed the quick-set concrete. Holding the bolts up straight, he used his hands and packed the concrete in and around the bolts. Once he was sure they would stand up straight, he turned to the next chore. He took the chains, each three feet in length, and attached one to each bolt. Once the concrete was set the chains would be tightly affixed.

Standing back, Marc looked over what he had done. Satisfied with the results, he opened one of the bottles of water, took a long swig, and recapped it. He left the bedroll laying on the concrete floor between the two affixed chains. He placed the five-gallon bucket nearby and attached the handcuffs to each of the chains. He took the energy bars and placed them on the bedroll. Now that he had finished his preparations, he removed the busted lock, opened the door, and backed his car out. He rolled the door down and headed back home. He had one more stop to make and then a call to make.

Marc pulled into the parking lot of Dr. Ignacio Morales, an aging man who was planning to close his practice within a few months. Dr. Morales' wife, who was not in the best of health, wanted for them to travel some before they became too old or had health problems that prohibited them from doing so. Dr. Morales was only sixty-six years of age, but his wife was a couple of years older than him. He loved her with all his heart and their forty years of marriage was a true testament to their devotion to each other. Therefore, he was closing shop after more than thirty years of practice.

Marc had met the doc a year earlier when he had moved down from Georgia. He had caught a flu bug, and Doc Morales was the first office he had gone to for treatment. They had struck up a minor friendship that developed quickly. He had even been to the doc's home for dinner once. Marc turned off the ignition, stepped out of his car, and went into the office. He told the receptionist that he needed to speak with the doc. There weren't any patients waiting in the office at that time, so she told him to wait a minute. She went to the back and in thirty seconds returned and told him to go on back, that the doc was in his office doing some paperwork but would take time to see him.

"Hey, Doc. Thanks for seeing me," Marc said as he stepped into the small office.

"Hi, Marc. Always time for you, my friend," Doc Morales replied, as he stood and held out his hand. "Take a seat and tell me what's on your mind," The doc said motioning to the seat in front of his desk.

Marc took a seat and looked around the office at the boxes stacked against the walls.

"You moving, Doc?" Marc asked, raising his eyebrows.

"No, I'm retiring and closing shop. Wife wants to travel some before we get too old," Doctor Morales replied.

"Wow, congratulations. That's great, Doc, I wish you the best," Marc said, with sincerity.

"Thanks, Marc. To what do I owe the pleasure of this visit?"

"I have a favor to ask of you. You can say no and there will be no hard feelings," Marc began.

"What is the favor? You know I will do it if possible," Doc Morales replied.

"I have a problem with wild critters around my houseboat. I'm not a cruel man, so I don't want to use cruel methods to *kill* them. I was wondering if you have any ether that you could sell me a small bottle of. I plan to trap the animals but want to give them a humane death," Marc said, holding his breath, hoping the doc would buy the lame story.

"Gee, Marc. I would have thought that a farm boy from Georgia would be used to hunting and killing animals," Doc Morales replied, smiling.

"Well, my dad took me hunting once or twice, but I cried like a baby when I killed my first deer," Marc said, hoping the lie would be believable.

"Really? Well, I know some people like that. They hate even killing bugs," the doc said, giving out a hearty chuckle.

"Normally I wouldn't do this...legality's and all...but, since you work with HPD I trust you will use it as you say," the doc said. "But I have no ether. It isn't used that much anymore. Most doctors and dentists use chloroform. But there is something else even better; it works like chloroform but is safer. It's called halothane. I happen to have some and you are welcome to it. It should do the trick for you.

Marc sat still, holding his breath, not revealing that he

didn't work with HPD any longer.

"Hang on a minute," the doc said, as he arose and left the office.

"Here you go, Marc," the doc said as he returned, holding a small bottle with about five ounces of a clear liquid inside.

"Hey, Doc, I really appreciate this. How much do I owe you?" Marc said, holding his hand out for the bottle.

"Nothing, my friend. Since I'm closing shop I don't really need it. Just make sure you cover your nose when you use it, or you're likely to take a quick nap," Doctor Morales said, laughing loudly.

"I really appreciate it. Give Cecilia my best, and if I don't see you before, have a great trip," Marc said as he rose and held out his hand for a shake.

After promising to keep in touch, Marc left the doctor's office and got into his car. He carefully placed the small bottle into the glove box. He backed his car out and began the drive home. He still had a phone call to make.

****

Linda was placing the dishes into the dishwasher when the phone rang. She had just finished her dinner and was preparing to watch some television before retiring for bed. She glanced at the clock on the kitchen wall, noticing it was seven forty-five, fifteen minutes before the next episode of NCIS was scheduled to come on.

"Hello," she said, as she answered the phone.

"Hello, Linda. Do you know who this is?" the distorted voice replied.

Linda felt her heart skip a beat. She had been waiting for over a day for the next call from this creep.

"I do. Are you ready to tell me who killed my sister?" she replied.

"Do you have the money?" the caller asked.

"I do. Where do you want me to take it?" she asked.

"Not so fast. There are some ground rules you must follow," the caller said.

Linda slowly reached over and switched on the recorder, she needed this call recorded to go along with the others.

"What sort of ground rules? You told me to get you the money...I did. Now you're changing the game? Come on, man, quit jerking me around," Linda responded, the anger evident in her tone.

"Don't cop that attitude with me, Linda. I have the information you want and I have no intentions of you setting me up and getting me busted for extortion or whatever. So, are you willing to follow my rules or not?" the caller asked, somewhat calmly. He knew he was in charge of the so-called game and wasn't worried that she would hang up.

"Alright, I'm calm. What are your rules?"

"That's better. I want you to meet me tomorrow night at Triangle Park across from City Hall on Palm Avenue. That should make you feel safer meeting with me. I sure wouldn't try something in that area where the police come and go all the time. After all, it is a public place, plenty of open space. Plus I will be able to spot if you have anyone watching me...and if you do, you'll never hear from me again and will not get the name of your sister's killer," Marc said.

"What time? And where in the park?" Linda asked, somewhat subdued but still seething inside.

"Meet me at nine o'clock in front of the War Memorial. Remember, if I see someone watching, I **will** disappear and you'll never get the name," Marc replied, ending the call.

Chapter 20

STORMY LEFT HOME and headed back to Hialeah. He had spent an hour with Shaunie, and she had assured him that she hadn't had any pains yet and that the doctor had told her that she still would have maybe a week before labor started. Stormy wanted to stay, but she insisted that he return to work and not worry about her. She told him she would call immediately if she had any signs or pains start up. He gave her a kiss and left.

As he drove towards the Bureau his mind was racing. He was missing something and couldn't figure it out. Then it hit him! He needed to hit any bars near the dump scenes and show photos of the victims. Maybe, just maybe, he would get lucky and someone would remember seeing one or more of the victims.

When he reached the Bureau he exited his car and began walking towards the back entrance. As he reached the door, it opened and Dakota stepped out, a blonde woman walking with her. The blonde looked to be in her mid-twenties, slim and about three inches over five feet tall.

"Hey, Stormy. This is Nickie Allen. She just got transferred to the Bureau. The Captain wanted me to take her under my wing until you finish with helping Leo."

"Hi, Detective Storm," Nickie said, smiling. "I'm kinda surprised."

"What do you mean you're surprised?" Stormy asked.

"Well, from all the stories of your escapades, I thought you would be wearing a cape or something," Nickie replied, a grin on her face.

"I like her already," Stormy said to Dakota. "And, you can call me Stormy, Nickie."

"Have you come up with anything useful yet?" Dakota asked.

"Not yet. I'm getting ready to canvas the area and show some photos. You girls want to ride along or do you have something else going on?"

"Nah, nothing that won't hold. Sure, we'll go with you," Dakota replied.

"Give me a few minutes...I have to pull the photos from my file. I'll be right out."

Stormy continued on into the Bureau, stopping at his desk and pulling out the file that Leo had given him. He hoped there were photos of the victims inside. He opened the file and true to form, Leo had anticipated the photos may come into play. He took the file and walked over to the Captain's office. Tapping lightly on the door, he waited until he heard the Captain say, "Come in."

"Hey Captain. Just checking in with you," Stormy said, as he opened the door and stepped into the office.

"Hey, Detective Storm. You or Leo come up with anything yet?" He asked.

"Not yet...but I'm heading out to show some photos of the victims at the bars along Okeechobee Road. Maybe I'll get lucky, but I'm not holding my breath," Stormy replied.

"Okay, just be careful and keep me updated," the Captain said.

"Oh, and I'm taking Dakota and the newbie with me, if that's okay with you."

"If she doesn't have anything pressing, I'm okay with it."

"Thanks, Captain. I'll let you know if we get a hit," Stormy replied as he turned and left the office.

Stormy walked out into the bright sunshine and quickly put on his shades. After all these years he still couldn't get used to the bright sun and wore the shades most of the time. Dakota used to tease him, telling him he was trying to look cool. He would always reply to her, *"I am cool."*

"You girls ready for a ride?" Stormy asked as he approached them.

They were standing next to his car, chatting away, neither wearing sun glasses. He just shook his head.

"Yeah, Nickie will take the back seat. She's a little smaller than me and that Camaro of yours isn't all that roomy in the back."

They all got into the car, and Stormy pulled out from the parking lot, heading for LeJuene Road. Once on the road he headed south towards Okeechobee Road.

"So, Nickie, how long you been on the force?" Stormy asked as he began driving.

"I've been in patrol for three years now," Nickie replied from the back seat.

"Wow, you must have done outstanding to make detective so soon."

"I was told that my report writing was above par and

that my ability to handle myself was also taken into consideration when I applied for the Bureau," Nickie said, no sign of an ego in her voice.

"Yeah, they do like good report writing. Just stick with Dakota, observe and remember how she does things. You'll do just fine," Stormy said.

"I will. Maybe someday I'll get a cape, also," Nickie replied laughing. Dakota started laughing and then Stormy joined in.

The first bar along the canal leading to the Miami River was right on Okeechobee Road. They parked the car and looked at the dilapidated sign above the entrance, *The Blue Moon*. Not very original but patrons usually cared more for the libations inside, not the name. You could probably go inside and ask anyone the name and they wouldn't even know.

Stormy took the file folder containing the photos and the three of them walked into the bar. It was dark inside but not so much that they couldn't see everyone inside. There were only about six or eight patrons sitting around inside. Most of them were apparently regulars and sat together at tables. They, for the most part, looked like day laborers, just waiting to get some work or having just gotten off of a job. Several had dust on their clothing, most likely from the local sand mine several miles west just off of Okeechobee Road.

Stormy approached the bar and a Latin man walked over to him.

"What can I get you, mister," the bartender asked.

"I'm Detective Storm with HPD. I would like to show you some photos and see if you recognize any of them,"

Stormy said as he laid the file on the bar top.

"Sure, Detective. Always glad to cooperate with the law."

Stormy spread the three photos out on the counter and turned them around for the bartender to see. He leaned over and scanned the photos.

"I don't recognize any of them. They are all dead?" he said.

"Yeah...and we really need to find out who did it. Could you please take another look?" Stormy asked.

The bartender pulled out a pair of glasses from his shirt pocket, took a second to put them on, and leaned over the bar to take a closer look.

"I'm sorry, Detective. I just don't remember ever seeing any of those three in here, ever. I wish I could help, whoever did this deserves the chair," the bartender said, as he straightened up and took his glasses from his face.

Stormy could see in the man's eyes that he was disturbed by the photos and was telling the truth. He gathered up the photos and returned them to the file folder.

"I appreciate your help, sir. Have a nice day," Stormy said, turning and leaving the bar, Dakota and Nickie right behind him.

They only had to drive about a half a mile before finding another bar. They exited the car and walked inside, the lighting a little better than the previous one. Stormy walked to the bar where three men sat, smoking and sipping their beer. One glanced over at Stormy and whispered to the others, "*El policia.*" The men rose from their seats and walked over to a table. Stormy watched in amusement and continued on to the bar. The men at the table could be overheard whispering about the two women with Stormy. Evidently one of the men said something derogatory and Nickie flipped him a bird, causing the men to laugh out loud. Dakota gave her a look that said, *not cool.* Nickie shrugged her shoulders and smiled at the men.

Stormy approached the bar and once again summoned the bartender over. After explaining that he wanted him to look at some photos the man agreed. Again, the same results – the bartender claiming he had never seen the women in the bar.

Feeling frustrated, Stormy slammed the car door. He knew better than to let it get to him, having done this hundreds of times in the past. Still, it aggravated him that he was no closer to gaining any more clues than before.

Starting the car, he drove further down Okeechobee Road towards Miami. At the city limits sign he saw another bar, sitting back further from the road, right on the water. They pulled into the parking lot, which was empty but for one car, which probably belonged to one of the employees.

As they approached, Stormy glanced up and saw a security camera over the door on the outside. Looking down the side of the bar he saw another one affixed to the rear corner of the building. They continued on inside the building. The only person present was a young man, probably in his mid-twenties, stocking up the cooler behind the bar. He rose up and smiled at Stormy and his entourage as they walked in, but the smile quickly faded as he spotted the badge hanging on Stormy's belt. Stormy noticed and once at the bar, introduced Dakota and Nickie and then presented the same spiel as before at the other bars.

The young man, seemingly relieved that he was not in

trouble, introduced himself as Manuel and agreed to look at the photos. Once they were spread on the bar top he leaned over and studied each one carefully. Pointing at one of the photos he smiled and said, "She was here a night or so ago. Actually I've seen her in here several times in the past."

Stormy could feel his Adrenalin beginning to pump up. At last, he had something to go on. He told Manuel he had seen the security cameras outside and wanted to know if there was a chance he could view the footage. Manuel smiled and pointed to the back of the bar to an open door. Stormy followed with the girls tagging along behind. Manuel couldn't keep his eyes off of Nickie, smiling broadly at her whenever he caught her eye.

After Manuel showed Stormy where the playback button for the cameras was, he allowed Stormy to sit at the desk, and he began rewinding the tape back two days prior. Stormy told Manuel that he could continue stocking the bar as it would probably take a while to go through the footage. Manuel smiled and told Stormy to take his time, that his customers probably wouldn't start coming in for another hour or two.

Dakota took the only other available seat and pulled it alongside Stormy. Nickie stood behind them, watching as Stormy began playing the tape. Nickie smiled as she realized that the security camera system was of the old tape type and not a current digital model. Stormy fast forwarded through the tape until he saw the time-stamp at about six in the evening. At this point he slowed the tape down and sat back to watch, prepared for a long wait.

As he waited, he opened the file and read the report on

the girl that Manuel had picked out. Her name was Lilly Sanchez, twenty-two years of age, single and had been living at home with her parents prior to her demise. He was so caught up in reading the file that he almost jumped out of his chair when Nickie yelled out, "Stop! There she is!"

Stormy rolled the tape back until Nickie told him to stop. He put it on slow forward, and once he caught sight of Lilly entering the bar, he froze the image. Pulling out the photo he compared it with the image on the monitor. It was one and the same.

"Nickie, go out and ask Manuel if there are cameras inside the bar," Stormy said.

When she returned, she shook her head, "No cameras inside...only on the outside in case of a burglary."

"Damn. Oh well, we can play the tape and watch to see when she comes out and if she is with anyone," Stormy replied.

He played the tape in the fast forward mode until he could see someone exit the bar. Then he would stop the tape, rewind it, and not seeing Lilly, begin playing it on fast forward again. This went on for almost twenty minutes until he finally stopped it upon seeing Lilly leaving the bar, holding onto a man's arm. He put the tape in slow motion, the movements jerky at best, hoping the man in the picture would turn around for a facial shot. It never happened, almost as if the man knew the cameras were there and refused to allow his face to be recorded. The range of the cameras on the outside of the bar was limited. They had been installed strictly for observing anyone trying to break *into* the building. The parking lot was hardly covered at all.

Just as the couple walked to the far edge of the cameras

coverage, Lilly spun around, still holding onto the man's arm. Her actions caused him to turn slightly towards the camera at the rear of the building. It was only a partial side view, very grainy and kept the man's face mostly in shadow. It was probably going to be almost impossible to identify the man from this shot. It was the only one that had captured him, so Stormy asked Nickie to have Manuel come back to the office.

"Is there any way for you to make a copy of this picture for me?" Stormy asked.

"Sure, *amigo*. My printer is set up for that...I only have to connect a couple of cables and we're good to go."

Once Manuel had set up the printer, Stormy had him print out several pictures, mostly of Lilly as she entered the bar from the outside. He also had him copy several of the unknown man from the time he walked out with Lilly until the side shot appeared.

To his credit, Manuel didn't ask if the man was the one responsible for the girl's death. He was too preoccupied with staring at Nickie. Stormy thanked him for all his help, and they left the bar. Nickie was not able to resist turning and waving at Manuel, who turned all shades of red.

Chapter 21

AGENTS BRENDA SKIPPER and Larry Foresman stood inside the security tech center of the Miami International Airport. Brenda quickly took in the highly advanced tech center, from the multitude of monitors relaying continuous pictures of areas all over the vast airport. There were no less than a dozen workers in the center, all paying close attention to their individual tasks.

"Agents Skipper...Foresman...I'm Carl Rogers, supervisor. What can I do to assist you?"

"I have a photo of a woman and would like for your people to check back a week and see if she showed up at the baggage claim area." Brenda replied.

"No problem. I'll put Stan on it...he's pretty good at picking out people." Carl said, as he led Brenda over to a work station near the back of the room.

"Stan, these are FBI agents, and I'm leaving them with you. They will tell you what they need. Please see to it." Carl said.

"Stan, I'm Brenda Skipper, and I need your expertise in spotting someone who may have been in the baggage claim area. Here is her photo." Brenda said, handing a full face photograph of Consuelo Alvarez. “You may want to start your search back a week.”

“I’ll get right on it, Agent Skipper. With our facial recognition program it shouldn’t be a problem. You may want to grab a cup of coffee or something. This may take an hour or so, unless I get lucky right off the bat.” Stan replied.

“We’ll run down to the concourse and find a bite to eat. Here is my number...please call if you get a hit while we’re gone.” Brenda said, handing Stan a business card.

Brenda and Larry left the room and headed down the elevator to the concourse. Once there they quickly found the food court area and opted for some fast food, just in case Stan called while they were eating.

“What are you hungry for, Larry?” Brenda asked. “I’m buying, so let’s grab some food.”

They both decided to go for the Chinese food, Brenda selecting sweet and sour pork and fried rice. The smell assaulted her senses, and she realized she hadn’t eaten anything since leaving Washington. Larry chose won ton soup and a couple of spring rolls. Brenda paid for their meals at the register, and they took their trays to an empty table near the open concourse.

As the two of them ate, they made some small talk, but mostly settled for enjoying the meal. They watched the travelers scurrying like disrupted ants to and fro on the concourse, some looking harried, others relieved to have arrived without incident and happy to be at their destination. As Brenda delicately picked up a small piece of pork with her chop sticks, her cell rang. Placing it back onto the plate, she retrieved the phone from her purse and answered.

"Hello, this is Agent Skipper."

"Agent Skipper. I found your girl. She did pick up a bag from the baggage claim area." Stan said.

"Great! We'll be right up." Brenda replied, as she severed the connection.

"That was Stan. He got a hit on the party I was looking for."

"I'm finished. So if you're ready, we can go." Larry said.

They picked up their trash and deposited it in the bin on the way out. Wading through the busy concourse, they made their way to the bank of elevators. When the elevator reached their floor they exited and walked down the hallway, entering a door that had a sign on the outside that read, *Warning, Security Personnel only.* Once inside they walked over to Stan's desk and waited patiently until he finished a phone conversation.

"Hey, Stan. What do you have for me?" Brenda began.

"I went back a week as you requested, and three days ago I picked up this image approaching the bag carousel. I ran the facial recognition app against the photo you gave me...and it was a match." Stan replied.

"Can you play it back for me, please." Brenda asked.

Stan typed in a command and the program automatically rewound to the frame he had discussed. He set it on slow motion, frame by frame until a woman walked over to the bag carousel and picked up a small suitcase.

"Back it up two frames and freeze it, please." Brenda asked.

Stan complied and once the frame was stopped, he zoomed in and the facial features, although not crystal clear, it was apparent that the woman Brenda was looking at was indeed Consuelo.

Stan resumed the forward motion of the images at Brenda's urging, and they watched as she exited the double glass doors leading outside to the taxi area. They watched as she entered the rear door of a taxi and watched as it drove away.

"Are you able to pull up the image of the taxi and obtain the vehicle number for me?" She asked.

"No problem. Give me a sec." Stan said.

Brenda and Larry watched as the tech wiz played with the camera, zoomed in and enlarged the number on the cab. Taking note of the name of the company, Brenda made a couple of quick notes, jotting down the number, time and company name.

"Thanks Larry. That was great work." Brenda said.

"Anytime, Agent Skipper." Stan replied with a smile, handing Brenda the photo and turning back to his work. Brenda wanted to also give thanks to Carl Rogers for his assistance, but he was nowhere in sight, so she and Larry left the room and headed to the elevators once again.

Once Larry and Brenda had left the main part of the building and reached Larry's vehicle, he asked her where she wanted to go next...hotel? Elsewhere?

"I would like to make a stop at the taxi terminal, if you don't mind."

"As a matter of fact, it's on the way to your hotel. So yes, we can stop there. What did you have in mind when we get there?" Larry asked.

"I want to find out where the taxi with this number dropped his fare off."

"They should be able to do that easily." Larry replied, starting the vehicle and driving away.

Only a few miles from the airport, Larry took an off-ramp from the expressway and drove along a service road for a mile before reaching the Metropolitan Taxi Company. After parking in the visitors' lot, they both walked into the front office and showed their FBI credentials to the receptionist, asking to see a manager. Within a minute of the receptionist making a call, the manager, Victor Longo, walked up to them, smiling and holding his hand out.

"What can I do for you, agents?" He asked, after shaking hands with them.

"One of your drivers picked up a fare several days ago at the Miami International Airport. His taxi number was A241. Here is a picture of the fare and the time-stamp of when he picked her up. We need to know where he dropped off this fare." Brenda replied.

"Of course, we are always happy to assist all law enforcement agencies. Give me a minute and I 'll check our records." Victor said, walking back to an office nearby.

In about two minutes Victor returned and smiling, told them that the fare was dropped off at the Loews Hotel on Miami Beach. Brenda thanked him as she and Larry turned and left the office.

"I suppose you want to go the Loews Hotel now." Larry said, grinning at Brenda.

"If you wouldn't mind, I would love to get this wrapped up as quickly as possible. If she is there, I'll place her under arrest, and there will be no need for you to take me to my hotel.

"No problem. I'm here to assist you however I can.

We'll head that way now, but it'll take about thirty minutes due to the traffic." Larry said as he started up the car and flipped on the air.

Chapter 22

A FEW HOURS BEFORE Agent Skipper had found out that Consuelo was staying at the Loews Hotel on Miami Beach, Consuelo had checked out. She never stayed at any one hotel any longer than two to three days at a time. In her line of work and adhering to her tradecraft, she made sure to cover her tracks. She always used aliases, moved around and watched for cameras. Too many people wanted her, either dead or arrested, for a vast number of reasons.

Consuelo had called an Uber driver from inside a parking garage she had been dropped off by a taxi she had flagged a block from the Loews Hotel. Her appearance was that of an older woman with a cane, the transformation taking place inside the garage. She had him drop her off a block from the hotel she was checking into. She traveled light, having left the small suitcase in the garage. She would buy a new suitcase and wardrobe later. She had walked the block to the Setai Hotel on Collins Avenue, discarding the wig and cane on the way, enjoying the salt air. The hotel was only a block or so off the beach, and if she were able, she would select a room with an ocean view.

When she walked up the circular drive and past the attendants outside, she was mindful of their stares. She entered the lavish lobby and made her way to the registration desk. Using a credit card under her new alias, Hedy Albert, she produced her passport for identification in the same name and rented a mini-suite for three days. Hopefully, before the end of the week, she would be long gone and out of the country again. It was pricey, over a thousand dollars a night, but she could afford it and loved to indulge herself with the finer things in life.

After taking a long, hot shower, she switched the water to icy cold and stood under the rain head for several minutes. After getting out of the shower, she slipped on the plush robe furnished by the hotel and settled in a seat overlooking the Atlantic Ocean. She felt the sun's heat radiating from the large window; it felt good after the drenching from the cold water. She stood and walked over to her suitcase lying on the bench at the foot of the California King bed. Opening it she retrieved one of the many burner phones inside. Taking all the necessary precautions, she never used her phones more than a few times – they were not as easy to track as a regular cell phone, but they could be, if given enough time.

Returning to the seat by the window, she dialed Pepe's number from memory. She watched the sunbathers on the beach as she waited for Pepe to pick up. If only those foolish women and men realized what damage their long exposure to the intense sun, day after day, did to their skin, they would think twice about their actions. Just as she thought Pepe wasn't going to answer the phone, he picked up.

"Who is this?" he asked, without revealing his name.

"Hey, Pepe. This is the party you are doing a job for in the next day or so," Consuelo replied.

"Oh, hey. *Que pasa*?" He responded.

"Just wondering how the plans were going," Consuelo said.

"In just under two days it will be carried out. My contact has given me the time and route. I'll contact you a few hours before since you told me you needed to be there to take charge of the package," Pepe said. "Is this a good number to call back?"

"No, I'll call you," Consuelo said, hanging up the phone.

Consuelo stared at the phone for a few seconds. Pepe was a man of few words, but it appeared that everything was on track and that was all that mattered. Picking up the room phone, she dialed the front desk and asked for a good bottle of wine to be sent to her suite. She had no plans to go anywhere until dinnertime. After that she had to take a trip to South Miami to see an old friend. She had a few more purchases to make before picking up Juan, that is, if the breakout was a success. The man she was meeting in South Miami was the best she knew at making false passports. She would need to have one made for herself and Juan. She had taken a photo of him on her cell phone when she had paid him a visit at the jail. The necessary money had been already transferred to her account by Juan and she would be transferring what she owed to Pepe within hours.

Consuelo took an Uber to the Alloy Bistro Gourmet Restaurant in South Miami. When she arrived, it looked as though she had been transported to somewhere in Europe. Although the Bistro was fairly small, she was given a good seat. She had heard about this five-star restaurant and now had the chance to form her own opinion about the fare.

A good red wine was ordered first, and she delighted in the fruity taste as she perused the menu. The waiter explained to her that the chef made the pasta fresh for each order, if she decided to get the ravioli, which she did finally settle on.

The ravioli was definitely the best she had ever eaten. It came, as promised, from fresh pasta and stuffed with pistachio and ricotta cheese. Although the portion was ample, she finished everything on her plate. Finishing her wine and forgoing dessert, she paid the check and left a more than handsome tip. The meal was fairly pricey but well worth the cost. She called for another Uber ride and waited outside for only two or three minutes before the driver pulled up to the curb. It turned out to be the same one that had dropped her off an hour earlier. She got into the car and gave the driver the address where she wanted to go. When they arrived at the house in South Miami, she asked the Uber driver if he would wait and that it would probably be at least thirty minutes before she was ready to leave. With the promise of a hundred-dollar tip he was more than willing to wait.

As she walked up the double drive, she observed that the house was not overly large in comparison to some of the others on the street and had the bars on the windows that were prevalent in South Florida. The yard was well tended and the house appeared to be well kept. She walked up to the door and rang the bell. Within thirty seconds the door opened and a frail looking man, wearing bifocals, looked at her.

"I'm Consuelo. I called earlier," she said.

"Please, come in," the man said, looking over her shoulder and scanning the street. "Is that your car?" He asked, pointing at the Uber driver.

"Yes, my driver will wait for me, if that's okay," she replied.

"It will be no problem, but better if he pulls into the driveway. The neighbors get annoyed if someone is parked on the street."

Consuelo walked back to the car and asked the driver to pull into the driveway. Walking back to the house, she entered and the man closed the door behind her. Following the little old man, she walked to the dining room and took the seat that he motioned to her. He sat down opposite her and began opening some folders.

"I believe you said you needed two passports. Where is the other party?" he asked, slightly raising his bushy, gray eyebrows.

"I have his photo with me. It's on my phone and hopefully you have the ability to download it," Consuelo replied.

"I do. But this will cost extra since I was expecting there to be two of you here."

"I can pay the extra fee," Consuelo said, giving a slight smile at the man, knowing he was going to gouge her as much as he could. But, he didn't know her and would have thought twice about gouging her for extra money if he had known her occupation.

"What will be the names on the documents?" he asked.

Consuelo pulled a sheet of paper from her purse, unfolded it and placed it on the table in front of the old man.

"Miguel Soto and Felicia Maria Soto," the man read from the paper, also noting that she had already provided phony addresses and dates of birth to add to the documents. "And the photo you referred to?"

Consuelo pulled her cell phone, scrolled in her photos until she came to the one she had taken of Juan. She handed the phone over to him and watched as his eyes widened at the image. It was obvious he recognized the photo, probably from the news reports of the arrest and the trial. He looked over the top of his bifocals at her but said nothing. There was a time to keep your mouth shut, and this was most definitely one of those times. He stood and plugged her phone into a port on his computer and downloaded the photo of Juan, AKA The Scorpion. After asking a few more questions, and typing in the answers she gave, he told her that there was fresh coffee in the kitchen and to fetch him and her a cup while he finished up.

Consuelo sipped the strong coffee and waited patiently as he worked. In about twenty minutes he told her he was done, handing over the two passports for her to see. Consuelo went through each of the passports carefully, making sure they would pass scrutiny at the airport. Once satisfied, and she *was* impressed at the quality of the work, she passed an envelope to the man containing five thousand dollars. Opening her purse, she extracted another two hundred and placed it on top of the envelope, for the extra fee.

"I assume you recognized the man. Am I going to have to worry about you telling anyone or the police?" Consuelo asked.

"I wouldn't be in business for long if that were the case. No, you don't have to worry at all."

Walking back to the car waiting in the driveway, she smiled to herself, pleased at how smoothly everything was going. She gave the driver the address of a local nightclub several blocks from her hotel and settled back for the ride. She was being overly cautious, and if any law enforcement or other agencies pulled the records from Uber, they would only show where she was dropped off. If the records showed where she was previously, getting the false passports, that was not her problem. She would carefully make her way from the nightclub via a circuitous route to the hotel. She didn't get this far in her profession, and life, by becoming careless, and she didn't intend to begin now.

Chapter 23

MARC DROVE ALONG Okeechobee Road in the old black panel van, headed for Triangle Park across from City Hall in Hialeah. He had spotted the van in a driveway with a for sale sign on the window, e*ight hundred dollars*. He paid cash for the old panel van, black in color. He had made sure that it was after business hours for the Department of Motor Vehicles and promised the seller that he would do the transfer papers the next morning, of which he had no intention of doing.

The junker would serve the purpose for what he intended to do tonight and he would dump the van in a canal later, after wiping it down for prints. He was meeting Linda at the War Memorial at the park, she hoping he was going to provide the name of her sister's killer, he preparing to exact his revenge for her firing him from the one job he loved and for the embarrassment she had caused.

It was about seven thirty when he arrived and parked in the adjacent lot. There were a few cars parked there, but he figured that by nine o'clock the lot would be pretty much cleared out. He had arrived early to watch and see if any type of surveillance was set up, or for any other suspicious activity. He didn't think she would be so stupid as to do what he warned her against. But, she was law enforcement after all, and he couldn't take any chances.

He sat slumped down in the van, puffing on a small cigar, not really enjoying it, but allowing the smoke to curl up and drift away through the partially open window. He watched as two young boys used a skateboard in and around the concrete paths in the park. Hopefully, they would be gone by nine. Maybe they had a curfew on a school night. He hoped so since he didn't need someone watching what he had planned.

He had made some modifications before heading to the park. On one wall of the van he had bolted a u-ring and fastened a set of handcuffs to it, one part hanging down still open. He had considered putting a blanket or something on the floor for her to lie on, but he really didn't care if she was comfortable or not...besides, she would only be inside for fifteen or twenty minutes at the most before he would arrive at the abandoned strip mall. He had been meticulous in his planning and felt confident that everything would go smoothly. The only thing he had to worry about was some cop, with nothing better to do, who would pull him over. At least he had convinced the owner of the van to let him keep the tag...still, if he were pulled over he would have a problem with no registration to produce. He would cross that bridge if it came to that.

Time seemed to drag by one of the boys had left the park. The other was sitting on a bench fiddling with the wheels on his skateboard. Only two cars were left in the parking lot now and he observed a couple approaching one of them. They glanced at the van, but with the dark tinted windows he knew they couldn't see inside. So he continued to scan the lot for Linda. It was approaching nine o'clock now, and still she wasn't here. Had she decided to not come? He doubted it. She had been adamant about obtaining the name of her sister's killer. He allowed himself a chuckle as he thought about the look that would be on her face when he told her he was the killer.

Suddenly he glanced up and saw a uniformed officer approaching the lot. He felt his heart rate suddenly spike, his palms break out in sweat. He slouched lower in the seat and pretended to be asleep, hoping the cop would not stop at the van. He heard the man as his shoes slapped on the concrete when he passed the van. He risked a look in the side-view mirror and felt a sigh of relief when the cop got into the last car parked in the lot. He watched carefully as the headlights came on and the car backed out of the parking space. Only when the car had left the lot and was disappearing down Palm Avenue did he expel the breath he hadn't realized he had been holding in. The officer must have been at a meeting in City Hall across from the park. Now, his was the only vehicle in the lot.

He exited the van and slowly strolled over to the War Memorial, still not seeing Linda. It was ten minutes until nine so he would give her another fifteen to be sure something hadn't held her up. He patted his pocket and felt the folded cloth nestled inside. He had saturated it with the halothane prior to exiting the van. He stood at the plaque and pretended to read it but was actually letting his eyes scan the area. He noticed the skateboarder still messing with his board, obviously in no hurry to leave.

It was dark now, the sun having set forty minutes earlier, but there were still a couple of street lights burning around the park. He was mostly in shadows but still visible to anyone in the park. The boy was still there, showing no interest in him at all. As he turned to the parking lot, he saw a car pull in a couple of spaces from his van.

As the occupant exited the car he saw that it was Linda. He knew that she had espied him at the Memorial but was sure she couldn't recognize him in the shadows. She continued walking towards him and when she was ten feet away she let out a gasp, recognizing him immediately.

"Marc, what are you doing here?" she asked as she walked closer to him.

"I'm the one that has the name you want," Marc replied.

"But how...how do you know the name?" Linda asked, as she stopped within three feet of him.

"I read the news and since I used to be in law enforcement, somewhat that is, I did some investigating on my own. It was hard since you fired me, and I didn't have the necessary tools. But I got it done" Marc said, a phony smile plastered on his face.

"I have to call this in, Marc. You have to give all the information you have to the detectives," Linda said as she looked down to her purse and fumbled for her cell phone.

While she was searching for her cell Marc saw his chance and quickly pulled the halothane soaked cloth from his pocket. He stepped to her side, and in a flash he grabbed her and held the cloth to her face. Linda tried to scream as she dropped her purse. Her efforts were futile as the drug worked quickly and she slumped against him. He held her up as he leaned down and picked up her purse. Draping her arm around his neck, he half walked and half dragged her towards the van.

"Hey, mister! Is the lady alright?" the boy asked as he suddenly looked up at them.

"She's okay son, just too much to drink. I'm taking her home to sleep it off," Marc replied as he kept walking to the van.

"Are you sure? You want me to help you get her in the car?" The kid asked.

"No, I've got it...thanks anyway," Marc said.

Marc watched as the kid stepped on his skateboard and started out of the park, relief suddenly rushing through him. He really didn't want anyone to see his face, but it couldn't be helped. Maybe the kid didn't pay too much attention to him; he hoped so.

When he reached the van, he opened the side door with his free hand and then gently lifted Linda up and placed her inside on the floor. She was still out cold, but he put a gag over her mouth anyhow. It wouldn't do for her to come to and start screaming. He lifted her right arm and snapped the hanging cuff on her wrist. She slumped, unconscious and leaning against the wall of the van, her one arm slightly elevated as it hung from the handcuff mounted on the wall, her head drooped down onto her chest.

After checking to make sure she was breathing okay, Marc closed the door and took another look around the park to see if anyone else was there. Seeing no one he quickly shut the side door and walked around to the driver's side. Once inside he started the engine and backed out of the parking space and headed out onto Okeechobee Road. He began humming to himself as he drove the speed limit towards the abandoned strip mall. So far everything was going according to plan.

When he was approaching the strip mall he saw a Metro-Dade deputy's unit parked in front, his parking lights on. He noticed the interior lights illuminating the deputy sitting in the car, evidently doing some paperwork. He continued driving past the mall, cursing to himself. Of all times for someone to be there; he couldn't believe his bad luck.

He drove west on Okeechobee Road for about twenty minutes, hopefully giving the deputy enough time to finish whatever paperwork he was doing. He could hear Linda moaning in the back and after taking a quick look, saw that she was still out of it. He wanted to get to the mall before she came to and tried to resist. He still had the halothane-soaked cloth in his pocket but didn't want to use it unless he had to. He made a U-turn and headed back to the mall, anxious for the deputy to be gone. When he was about a quarter of a mile from the mall he saw the marked unit pulling out onto Okeechobee and heading back towards Miami.

Marc slowed down to give the deputy time enough to get further down the road before pulling into the abandoned strip mall. Once he felt that it was safe he turned onto the side road and quickly drove around to the back of the mall. He jumped out of the van and swiftly opened the roll-up door. After pulling the van inside he pulled the door down and secured it.

He walked hurriedly to the front of the empty store and peered out the window to see if the deputy had seen him pull in and returned. He waited and watched for nearly five minutes before he felt he had not been seen. He walked back to the rear of the store and into the bay where the van was parked.

Marc opened the side door of the van and climbed inside. He checked to see if Linda was still out, and saw that she was actually coming to. She stared at him groggily as he inserted the key into the cuff holding her in place. He released her hand and slid her over to the open door. As her feet touched the floor of the bay, she suddenly jumped down and slammed the door to the van shut. Marc began cursing...she had been faking being unconscious and waiting for the right moment to act.

He tried to open the door but she had shoved a table against it. As fast as he could he jumped over the console and into the front seat, exiting the passenger's door. Linda was not in sight but he saw that the roll-up door was still down so she had to still be inside the store. He ran to the front of the building and saw her holding a chair and watched as she smashed it into the plate glass window. The window shattered, and she began sprinting to the opening. She managed to get one leg up on the sill before Marc grabbed her waist from behind and pulled her back inside the store. Linda was still feeling the effects of the halothane but knew she had to get away. She began kicking and screaming as she tried to free herself. Then she felt a cloth pressed against her face, covering her mouth and nose. She knew that she wasn't going to make it out. She collapsed as the world went black, again.

When Linda came to she found herself secured with handcuffs on both wrists, lying on a blanket or bedroll, feeling the hard concrete beneath her. She was able to move her arms and even pull them close to her sides, but that was it, for now. She had just enough play in the chains to be able to plant her arms and hands on the covering. She could reach her nose to scratch it if she had to, but that wasn't her concern right now. She had no idea where she was and what Marc was planning to do to her.

Marc was fuming. He was so livid he almost punched her, but held off, for now. Now he had to go outside and sweep up the broken glass and figure out how to cover the opening. It definitely wouldn't go unnoticed if a patrol officer or deputy came around to check the area. Frantically, he grabbed the push broom he had seen leaning against the wall in the bay, opened the roll-up door and ran outside.

Once he arrived at the front of the store, he saw the scattered broken glass covering the pavement in front of the smashed window. He quickly began sweeping the glass up, all the while keeping an eye out for anyone driving into the area. He spotted a piece of cardboard on the ground beside the wall, and after retrieving it, carefully swept the glass onto it. He gently grabbed both ends of the cardboard and carried it to the rear, placing it into one of the several dumpsters that still had not been picked up.

As Marc headed to the open roll-up door he spotted just what he needed to secure the broken window. There were several sheets of plywood leaning against the wall of the store next to the one he was using. On the ground were several eight-foot two-by-fours, also. He took two sheets of plywood, one at a time, into the store, placing them against the wall in the front. Grabbing three of the two-by-fours, he carried them inside, also. He closed the bay door and secured it. Then he stood the two sheets of plywood against the opening where the window used to be, wedging the two by fours against the wood to hold them in place. It wasn't the best job of securing the window, but it would suffice for now. Later he would have to do a better job, but at least from a distance it would pass.

Marc walked back into the bay, glaring at Linda. She appeared to still be out, for now, but he would be careful about getting too close to her since he knew she could fake it. He grabbed a bottle of water from the small fridge and placed it within her reach, also getting one for himself. He had worked up a sweat sweeping the glass and securing the plywood to the open window. He sat down in a padded chair and leaned his head back, willing his heart to stop racing.

Now that he had her, isolated and secured, would he be able to go through with what he had planned. He had hated killing the other three women, but it had been essential to draw Linda out. He still felt sick to his stomach for what he had done, but there was no time for second thoughts now. He had crossed the line and was committed. He held the cold bottle to his forehead as he sat in the chair leaning back. After about fifteen minutes his adrenaline had subsided.

Marc eased himself out of the chair and slowly walked over to check on Linda, to see if she had come to.

As he warily approached her he saw that her eyes were open, watching him intently. He tossed a couple of energy bars onto the mat she was on. He made sure the bottle of water was close enough for her to reach.

"You almost made it, or so you thought. Just how far do you think you would have gotten before I caught up with you?" Marc asked, staring at Linda.

"What do you want? Why are you doing this?" Linda asked, her speech a little slurred as she hadn't fully come to yet.

"Oh, you'll see what I want soon enough," he replied.

Walking over to Linda he watched as she recoiled from him, but was restrained by the chains and cuffs. He reached down and in a swift movement he grasped the top of her blouse and ripped it off. Then he tore her skirt off, as well as her bra and panties, bundling them under his arm and walking away. As he turned, Linda's bra fell from under his arm, landing within her reach. She covered it with her leg and screamed at Marc, "You're not going to touch me, you creep!"

"Relax, Linda. I'm not a rapist, and besides, you're not my type. I figure that if by some stretch of the imagination you should escape, it will be a little hard for you to run down the road butt-ass naked."

"You don't have to do this. Just let me go, and I won't say anything," Linda said, although she silently feared the worst.

"No, I'm not letting you go, and you really think I believe you wouldn't say anything...please! Give me a little credit. There is water beside you, energy bars and a bucket for you to use to do your business. I'll be back in the morning, so you best get some rest. You're going to need it," Marc said, a cruel snicker erupting from him as he turned and left.

After Marc had gone, Linda tried and tried to jerk the chains free from the floor. The only thing she was doing was hurting her wrists, the chaffing already beginning to bleed. Finally, exhausted from the halothane effects, and her arduous struggles to free herself, she lay back and soon fell into a restless sleep.

It was a couple of hours before daybreak when she awoke. It took a minute for her to remember what had happened. She jerked the chains, but the pain in her wrists caused her to stop. Feeling a little better after a few hours' sleep, she began shuffling her legs back and forth, to get some feeling into them. Then she saw her bra lying on the floor by her leg, and an idea came to her.

Chapter 24

LARRY PULLED THE CAR into the circular drive of Loews Hotel on Miami Beach, parking in the valet lane. An eager young man ran over to the car, holding out a ticket as he opened the door for Brenda. Larry exited the driver's side, flashed his badge and told the man that they would only be a few minutes. He handed the young man a folded up five-dollar bill, and they walked into the spacious lobby of the hotel.

There were about a dozen people in the lobby, most standing at the check-in desk. Larry and Brenda walked up to the front of the line and asked the woman behind the desk if the manager was available. She punched in a single number and in a second advised the party on the other end of the line that there was someone who needed to speak with him. Brenda thanked her, and she and Larry stepped down to the end of the counter, away from the people checking in.

"I'm Charles Merritt, the manager. How may I help you folks?" the man who approached, asked.

"Brenda Skipper and Lawrence Foresman, Federal Bureau of Investigation," Brenda replied, as she held up her credentials.

"How may I assist the Bureau today?" Charles asked, plastering a forced smile on his face.

"We would like for you to look at this picture and see if you recognize her. She checked in here in the last few days," Brenda said.

Charles Merritt was a go-by-the book kind of guy. He had dealt with law enforcement in the past and most of the time he was able to provide what was asked of him. The one thing he was, he was a stickler for protecting the privacy of his guests. He looked at the picture carefully, and then he looked up at the two agents in front of him.

"I do believe I've seen her before," the manager said hesitatingly.

"Could you tell us what name she is registered under and the room number?" Larry asked.

"I'm afraid that without a warrant I can't do that, agent. We value our reputation for respecting the privacy of our guests."

"Could you at least tell us the name she is registered under?" Brenda asked, politely.

"Sorry, without a warrant I can't divulge any of that information," Charles stated, somewhat firmly.

"Mr. Merritt. I can obtain the warrant, and rather quickly with our resources. But let me make you aware. When the warrant arrives, and it will quickly, I will have a half a dozen agents bringing it. They will detain your guests in the lobby until it is served. Is that the scenario you want?" Brenda replied.

"I nor my hotel takes kindly to threats, agents," Charles responded in a huff.

"Oh, Mr. Merritt, that wasn't a threat, that was a promise," Brenda said sweetly, a big smile on her face.

Charles stood in disbelief at what he was experiencing. He stared at the smiling agent, then looked at Larry. Larry smiled and shrugged.

"Will you excuse me a minute, please. I will need to make a call," Charles replied. He turned and went into his office.

"You sure know how to make an entrance, Agent Skipper," Larry said, grinning.

"Not the first time, Larry. More than likely not the last," Brenda responded.

"I've conferred with our attorney, and he says I'm to give you the information you have asked for. But, he says that you will still need a warrant to enter the room," Charles said, as he returned to the front counter where both agents were waiting patiently.

"Mr. Merritt, I don't wish to cause a problem. However, this woman is most vital to a case we are working on, so could you at least tell us if she is registered here and the name she is using?" Brenda asked, a more sincere smile now on her face.

Charles Merritt went to a computer behind the desk and began typing. He suddenly smiled and looking up at Brenda, said, "I guess you won't be needing that warrant after all, Agent."

"What do you mean?" Brenda asked, although she already knew the answer.

"She checked out this morning and is no longer a guest here," Charles answered.

"What name did she register under, if you don't mind

telling me."

"She registered under the name of Roberta Estes," he said.

"I don't suppose you would let us review your camera tapes. We only want to see the footage from the outside," Larry said, after spotting cameras in the lobby and figuring there would be some on the outside.

"At this point, since she is not a guest here now, I don't see why not. Follow me to the security room," Charles said, as he turned and began walking to the end of the lobby.

In the security room Charles asked the employee monitoring the cameras to pull up the outside footage from eight o'clock this morning. They all watched and had the employee speed up the playback to save time. Suddenly Brenda saw a woman walk out and turn slightly towards the front of the hotel.

"Freeze that frame, please," she asked.

Brenda and Larry took the photo of Consuelo and compared it with the woman on the monitor. They both agreed it was definitely her. They told the employee to continue running the tape and watched as Consuelo casually strolled out onto the sidewalk and began walking away, pulling a small luggage bag on wheels.

"Smart! She knew there were cameras there and didn't take a taxi. Now she's out of range, and we have no idea where she went, or was going," Brenda said, noting the time-stamp of 10:45 am on the frame.

"Thank you very much for your time, Mr. Merritt. Please, have a great day," Brenda replied, turning and walking towards the front door.

"I figured she would use an alias; she's not a careless,

nor a stupid person," Brenda said to Larry, as they walked outside of the hotel and got into their car. "She exhibited her skills by not taking a taxi. Now we have to figure out where she went. I'm sure she has checked into another hotel by now...or maybe even flagged down a taxi and left for the airport."

"Well, there is another course of action we can take," Larry offered.

"Let me guess. We check the street cameras the city has up," Brenda replied.

"Nice guess. I have some favors to call in with the Miami Beach Police Department so let's head over there and see what we can come up with," Larry said, as he pulled out of the driveway.

They arrived shortly after at their destination and entered the building. After identifying himself and Brenda, Larry asked the desk Sergeant if Captain Fletcher was available.

"Let me ring back to communications and see," the desk Sergeant replied, as he picked up the phone and punched in a number.

After a couple of rings, the call was answered and the desk Sergeant relayed the request for Larry to see him. He advised he would be out in a few. The Sergeant told Brenda and Larry to take a seat, that the Captain would be with them shortly. Within ten minutes they were approached by a man dressed in slacks and a polo shirt.

"Larry, you old dog! What brings you to my bailiwick today?" He asked, as he pumped Larry's hand.

"Hey, Gerald, great to see you too. This is FBI Agent Brenda Skipper. She just flew down from D.C. on a case she's working," Larry replied.

"Great to meet you Agent Skipper, although I can't believe you're hanging with this guy," Gerald said, grinning, holding out his hand to shake hers.

"He was the best they could do on such short notice," Brenda said, grinning and playing along.

"Oh, you guys are killing me!" Larry said, in mock indignation.

"Seriously, what can I help you with today?" Gerald asked.

"Brenda is tailing a perp, and we just missed her at Loews, as she had checked out before we arrived. The video cams there showed her walking away, not taking a taxi. We hoped you could play the footage on the city cams there and see if she kept walking and where to," Larry said.

"Didn't take a cab, huh?" That tells me she was deliberately being evasive. Too darn hot to walk very far on the sidewalks so she must have either checked into a nearby hotel or flagged a taxi," Gerald replied.

"Our thinking exactly," Brenda said.

"Well, come on back to the *den*, and we'll run some footage and see if we can find her. What time did the timestamp on Loews' footage show?"

"It showed 10:45 on the frame we looked at," Brenda replied.

Gerald sat down at the bank of monitors and began typing in a date and time. He concentrated on cameras in the area of the Loews Hotel. His fingers flew across the keyboard and quickly he had the camera up he was looking for. He typed in the time Brenda had given him and was rewarded with an image of an attractive woman, pulling a piece of luggage on wheels, walking down the circular driveway of the hotel. The camera switched views and they watched as the woman, who was Consuelo, walk halfway down the block before stopping. A taxi pulled over to the curb when she had stepped down to the edge of the street and waved her hand. She placed her luggage inside and climbed in. The taxi continued driving southbound for a mile before turning into a parking garage.

"Why is she going into a parking garage?" Larry asked, slightly puzzled. "It's a public garage, not attached to any apartment buildings or hotels."

"I have a feeling she is dumping the taxi," Brenda replied.

They all watched and within five minutes the taxi exited the garage, turning back north towards the Loews Hotel.

"I'll bet dinner tonight she is not in that taxi now," Gerald said. "She will *have* to exit through the front; there is no exit at the rear."

Gerald, Larry and Brenda watched the front entrance to the garage intently, all the while observing several cars entering.

"Do you think she called someone to pick her up?" Larry asked Brenda.

"It's possible, but why not have them pick her up when she checked out. We'll watch for a while longer to see if she shows herself."

As they watched, a few cars drove out, but the grainy pictures and tinted windows wouldn't allow them to identify the people in the cars. Consuelo could have been in any of them, even lying on the floor out of sight. This wasn't working in their favor at all. Gerald switched camera views, but they didn't see anyone remotely resembling Consuelo walking down the street. They had to assume she had left in one of the several cars that had exited the garage.

"The only thing we can do now is get some of your people to canvas the hotels on the strip, in case one of the cars did pick her up and drop her off," Brenda said. "Larry, if you will take me to my hotel to freshen up, we can go to your office and make preparations for some old-fashioned foot-work."

They thanked Gerald and left the building, heading for the hotel where Brenda was registered.

If only they had watched for another thirty minutes they would have seen an old woman, walking with a cane, exiting the garage and heading south on the sidewalk. Consuelo had changed her appearance by putting on a gray wig and glasses and using a collapsible cane she had extracted from her suitcase. She was the ever consummate professional and was almost always prepared. The suitcase had served its purpose, and she left it abandoned in a corner inside the garage.

Chapter 25

STORMY STOPPED ON THE WAY BACK to the station and picked up subs and drinks for them. In the office they finished their meal and got down to business.

Nickie asked, "What's next?"

"I'm going to call a friend of mine at the FBI and see if he can run a facial recognition on the picture Manuel printed out for us. Maybe we'll get lucky and get a hit...or maybe not. Since it's not a frontal facial, it may not be any good for identification," Stormy replied as he lifted his phone and began dialing from memory.

"Well, that will have to wait for a while. Larry is out of the office with some agent from D.C. and won't be back for a few hours," Stormy said, hanging up the phone.

"If you girls have something to do, I think I'll swing by and check in on Linda. I'll give Larry another call after I leave her place...and then it's off to check in on Shaunie," Stormy said.

"No problem. Nickie and I can follow up on a case I need to close out. You make sure you give our best to Linda," Dakota replied.

Stormy gathered up his files containing the photos Manuel had provided and headed out the door. He got into his car, the heat already unbearable although they had only exited thirty minutes prior. It was going to be a long and hot summer, it seemed. Switching on the cold air, full blast, and cracking his window about three inches to allow the heat to escape, he started the car and pulled out of the lot.

Once on LeJuene Road he rolled the window back up and headed for Linda's house. He would call and let her know he was coming but wanted to surprise her. He stopped near her house and picked up a Starbucks latte that she liked so much.

Stormy pulled up in the driveway of Linda's house. It was a modest home with immaculate landscaping. The grass had been recently mowed and the sidewalk and driveway edged. Flower beds lined the front and neatly trimmed shrubs bordered the side. He didn't know if she performed the yard work herself or paid to have it done. In any case, it looked great and pleasing to the eye.

Stormy was out of the car and almost to the front door when he noticed her car wasn't in the driveway. He had been admiring the yard and completely missed it. He was about to turn and leave when he noticed that her front door was ajar. That was strange, since her car wasn't here. Setting the latte on the ground, he pulled his weapon out and carefully made his way to the door. Standing to one side, he carefully used his foot and pushed the door open enough to see inside. Seeing nothing untoward, he slowly entered the hallway, his gun at the ready. He moved slowly down the short hallway and stopped short of the living room.

Jerking his head quickly he took a fast glance into the living room. There was no one there, so he walked on into the kitchen.

After he had checked the bedrooms and found no one or nothing out of order, he decided that she must have left in a hurry and didn't pull the door closed by accident. That wasn't like her, but it happened. Stormy holstered his weapon and started walking back to the front door, then decided to leave her a note letting her know he had found the door open. He walked to the credenza on the far side of the living room to find a piece of paper and pen. As he approached he saw her phone off the hook, the message light blinking. Now, that was really strange, and the hair stood up on the back of his neck. Something wasn't right!

Stormy hung up the phone, and on a hunch, he pushed the playback button on the answering machine. As he listened to the messages, he felt a hollow feeling in the pit of his stomach. Someone with a distorted voice had called her claiming to know who had killed her sister. The last message, which apparently was left the night before, was telling her to go to the park by City Hall and meet with whomever had made the call. That meant she had been gone all night, and the door had been standing open. Now, more than ever, Stormy knew that something was very wrong. She hadn't returned home.

Picking up the phone, he called Dakota at the Bureau. She answered and was surprised to hear Stormy's voice.

"Hey Stormy, where you calling from? This isn't your cell phone."

"I think Linda is in trouble, Dakota," Stormy replied. "I'm calling from her house and she's not here."

"What do you mean she may be in trouble? And if you're there, how did you get in?" Dakota asked.

"The door was open, and her car was gone. I'll explain everything, just get over here as quickly as possible," Stormy said, hanging up the phone.

****

"We need to let the Captain know what's going on, Stormy," Dakota said, as she finished listening to the messages on Linda's answering machine. "You're right, something is not right and I'm worried."

"You and Nickie wait here. Call the Captain and have him come over and listen to the messages. I'm going to City Hall and check out the park," Stormy said.

"Okay, but let me know when you get there if you find anything."

Stormy left the house and set a speed record getting to City Hall on Palm Avenue. He parked in front and looked across the street at the park. There were about a dozen people there, so he walked across and wandered through the park. On a hunch, he walked over to the parking lot. There was her car! He ran to the car and looked inside. She wasn't there, but the driver's door was unlocked. He didn't touch anything, instead pulling out his phone and calling dispatch to send out Tech Services to process the car.

While he waited for Tech Services, Stormy walked around the park, not sure what he was looking for.

"Hey, mister. You a detective?" Asked a young boy on a skateboard, looking at Stormy's waistband where his badge hung.

"Yeah, I am, son. Why?" Stormy replied.

"Are you looking for someone?" The kid asked.

"A friend of mine was here last night. She didn't come home, so I thought I would check here," Stormy said.

"Oh, is that her car in the parking lot?"

"Yes, it is. Did you see her last night?" Stormy asked.

"Yes, sir. She was drunk, and a friend of hers was helping her get into his van. He said he was taking her home.

Stormy felt his blood go cold. Now he knew Linda was in trouble.

"What can you tell me about the man and his van?" Stormy asked.

"It was a black van...old, maybe late seventies or so. The man was about your height, maybe in his late twenties. I didn't really pay attention to his face. Sorry," the kid replied.

"Do you know which way he drove off to?"

"Yes sir, I was working on my board when they left. He went that way," the kid said, pointing west on Okeechobee Road. "What's wrong? Is he in trouble?"

"We just want to ask him some questions. Thanks for your information, son. If you will give me your name and number, I may need you to look at some pictures for me later. Maybe you will be able to identify him for me. Okay?" Stormy asked.

"Sure thing," the kid said.

Stormy wrote down the name and phone number, and the kid skated off on his board.

On a hunch Stormy quickly dialed Larry's number again, and after getting a voice mail, left a message for him to call as quickly as possible.

Chapter 26

LARRY DROPPED BRENDA OFF at her hotel, with the promise to pick her up in a couple of hours. As he pulled out of the hotel driveway, his phone chirped once, letting him know he had a message. He had turned down the volume while he was with Gerald going through the footage from the street cameras. He turned up the volume and saw he had a voicemail. He pulled over to the curb and played the message. It was from Stormy, and he could sense the urgency in his voice.

Dialing Stormy's cell number, Larry waited as it rang, wondering what Stormy needed. He could tell from the strain in his voice that it was anything but a social call.

"Larry, thanks for calling back so quickly," Stormy said, answering the call.

"No problem, Stormy. What can I do for you?" Larry replied.

"First of all, I need to bring you up to speed on what is happening. You remember Linda Ward, right?"

"Of course, CSI supervisor for your department. Delightful lady," Larry said.

Stormy began with the call that Leo had made to him

in reference to the female bodies discovered in the Miami River. He explained that Leo had reached out to him because one of the bodies was from Hialeah. He finally told Larry about Linda's sister being the last victim.

"Oh my God! I'm so sorry, Stormy. She must be devastated beyond belief," Larry said, in shock.

"She is. But now *she's* missing," Stormy said.

"What? What do you mean she's missing?" Larry responded.

Stormy told him about canvassing the bars along the canal in Hialeah and along the Miami River which it fed into. He told him about the photo from a surveillance camera at one of the bars which showed a person escorting one of the now dead women out into the parking lot. He finished up explaining that he had gone by Linda's house to check on her and how he had found the door open. Then he told him about the strange messages on her answering machine.

"I'm at Triangle Park across from City Hall now. I just talked with a kid on a skateboard who witnessed her with a man last night, around nine o'clock. The kid said the man was helping her into his van...telling the kid that she had too much to drink. I know that's not the case since the message on her machine told her to come to the park last night, that the man meeting her would give her the name of the person who killed her sister," Stormy said.

"Good grief! It sounds like she was abducted by the killer. But for what purpose?" Larry mused.

"I don't know. Dakota and our newest detective, Nickie, are still at her house, waiting for CSI to arrive and determine if there is any other evidence they can obtain. I doubt it. Sounds like Linda only took phone calls from this man, no personal visits. At least they can take the answering machine and clean up the voice...maybe get a clearer sound, maybe isolate any background noises that could help. Right now I'm worried sick about her," Stormy said.

"What can I do to help, Stormy," Larry asked, eager to help.

"I need to run the photo prints I obtained from the bar. There wasn't a clear frontal shot, only a side view, and even that was grainy. We don't have a facial recognition program as high tech as the FBI's. I thought maybe you could pull a little weight and get me to the top of the line...have your people run the photo for me. Time is apparently of the essence now, with Linda missing and possibly abducted," Stormy said.

"Of course, I'll make the call as soon as we hang up. We have a new guy who is really good at his job. When you get downtown, ask for Agent Junior Murray. I'll make sure he takes you right in and runs the photos you have. I would meet you there, but I'm with another Agent from D.C. and can't get away," Larry said.

"Thanks, Larry. I totally understand, and I really appreciate your help," Stormy replied.

"Absolutely no problem. Glad to do it for you, and Linda. Keep me advised, please," Larry said.

"Will do, my friend," Stormy said, ending the call.

Stormy called Dakota and filled her in on his call with Larry. He told her to drop whatever case she and Nickie were working and start driving west from Palm on Okeechobee Road, specifically looking for any black vans. He told her the kid had said it was an older model. If she didn't see one, she and Nickie were to go to CSI and determine if they were able to find anything of value on the answering machine. In the meantime, he told her, he was headed to the FBI office in Miami to have the photo run through their enhanced facial recognition program. He promised her he would call as soon as he learned anything pertinent.

Forty minutes later Stormy entered the FBI building in Miami and was quickly ushered to the office of Agent Murray. Stormy introduced himself. Agent Murray told him he had spoken to Larry and that he would do what he could to help. Stormy opened the manila envelope and withdrew the photos. He handed them to Agent Murray who immediately took them and scanned them into his computer. Then he initiated the facial recognition program.

"Not much quality to go on here," Agent Murray said. "But, I've had results with worse head shots, if that's any comfort."

"At least you're giving it a shot. That's all I ask, Agent Murray," Stormy said.

"Please, Junior will do just fine."

"Junior it is then. I really appreciate you handling this for me," Stormy said.

"Hey, if you have Larry in your corner, you have me there also," Junior said, with a smile. "Now, let's go grab a cup of coffee in the break room while *Annie Mae* does her thing. It could take a while."

"Annie Mae?" Really? You have a name for your program," Stormy said, laughing.

"Well, it's a lot easier than saying *Facial Recognition Program* all the time, isn't it?" Junior said, laughing also.

Chapter 27

CONSUELO GOT HER WISH. Money talked, and she was able to book a suite with an ocean view. She had checked in using yet another phony passport, under the name of Grace Cortez. She had explained to the desk clerk that her luggage would be coming later and to have a bellhop bring it to her room. In reality, she didn't have any luggage. The piece she did have was discarded along with her disguise before reaching the hotel. She planned to go out and shop for the few things she needed, but only after a nice early dinner.

After a bottle of expensive wine was delivered to her room, Consuelo drew a hot bath in the over-sized tub. She stripped down and gently lowered herself into the hot water, the effects immediately relaxing her. She sipped on her glass of wine as she soaked, her mind running through various scenarios involving her upcoming mission, springing *El Scorpion.* After two glasses of wine, a nice bubble bath and a rinsing off in a cold shower, Consuelo dressed in the same clothes she had worn to the hotel. She was desperate to get some new and clean clothes, so she made her way down the elevator to the lobby, where she took a taxi to the nearest upscale shopping mall. As when leaving the hotel, she was careful to keep her face tilted down, out of any camera's view. The only picture the cameras would capture would be the top of her head, hopefully.

After the taxi dropped her off at the shopping center, she headed to the nearest specialty shop for women. She chose some top of the line lingerie, a couple of blouses, and complimenting slacks. She picked out a sunhat with a wide brim for obscuring her face when paired with sunglasses. She then went to a shoe store and purchased a pair of low heels and a pair of tennis shoes. On her way out of the shoe store, she passed a luggage store and stopped in, buying a small suitcase to carry her purchases.

Hailing another taxi, she told him to take her to the Setai Hotel. When she arrived, she kept her head down as she entered the lobby, followed by a bellhop who had taken her suitcase from the taxi.

Once she was in her room, and giving the bellhop a hefty tip, she unpacked the suitcase and began to change clothes. After she was dressed in her new clothes and her makeup refreshed, she made her way down to the Jaya Restaurant in the hotel. It offered Asian-inspired hospitality and she was partial to Asian food. So it was right up her alley.

Consuelo was greeted by a petite Asian girl, probably no more than twenty years of age. She was asked if she wanted to be seated inside or in Setai's serene courtyard, featuring a retractable roof, in case of inclement weather. She chose the courtyard seating, taking away the chance of being trapped inside if someone spotted her and caused problems. At least with the courtyard seating she could make an escape down to the beach if needed. She doubted it would come to that, but she always made sure she placed herself with options.

The hostess allowed her to choose her seat since it wasn't quite the regular dinner time yet. She chose a table near the far northern wall, allowing her to sit with her back protected, also allowing her to see who came and went. The hostess gave her a leather-bound menu and told her the waiter would be over shortly. Consuelo carefully observed her surroundings as the hostess left. Content that she was relatively safe, she began to peruse the menu. She hadn't realized just how hungry she was until she began reading the various offerings. She was amazed at how extensive the selections were.

The selections on the menu ranged from, Vietnamese, Thai, Korean, Indian, Chinese and Japanese. Although she was partial to Thai, she decided to try her next favorite, lamb. When the waiter approached with the customary glass of water, garnished with a slice of lemon, she advised him she was ready to order.

She ordered the lamb cutlets with Tandoor spice rub, curry leaf, turmeric potatoes and lamb Jus. When asked if she wanted anything else to drink, other than the water, she told him to bring her the coldest beer he had. When asked the brand, she asked him if they carried 33 beer, from Vietnam. He smiled and told her they did and that he would make sure it was as cold as she wanted.

Consuelo leaned back, sipping the cold beer that the waiter had brought. With the wide-brimmed hat and her large sunglasses affixed, she let her eyes wander around the courtyard and abutting beach. So far she didn't see anything out of the ordinary, such as someone that didn't belong, or anyone that was caught looking her way and suddenly looking away if she caught their eye. As promised, the beer was ice cold, so much it almost hurt her teeth. But, she loved it! She had acquired a taste for 33 beer when she had carried out a job in Vietnam a few years earlier. Now, whenever she found it in her travels, it was a must.

That particular assassination assignment had been a very close call for her. She had almost been caught when she was spotted leaving her perch from a room in the Imperial Hotel in Saigon. Luckily for her she had been able to swiftly melt into the crowds on Tu Do Street and managed to evade the police.

Soon the meal arrived and her senses were assaulted with the various fragrant aroma's wafting up from the dishes. The waiter left, and she immediately began to eat. God, it was so good!

When Consuelo had finished her meal, she paid the check, leaving a hefty tip. She decided to walk down onto the beach. As her feet touched the sand, and before she had taken two steps, her cell phone began to ring.

Chapter 28

"IT'S ME. PEPE," the voice answered when Consuelo said hello.

"What do you have for me?' Consuelo asked.

"My source says that your target is to be transferred to the Kendall Correctional Facility tomorrow night, around nine o'clock," Pepe responded.

"Will you and your crew be ready? Is everything in place?" asked Consuelo.

"Don't worry. Barring any last-minute changes from the Transport Division, everything will be in place and all you have to do is be at the coordinates I'm sending you. Once you have your package in tow, I expect the balance of the money to be sent to my account."

"It will be. And, thank you. Maybe we'll work together again someday," Consuelo said.

"It will be a pleasure," Pepe said, terminating the call.

As soon as Pepe ended the call he dialed another number. He had a lot of preparations to do before he could implement his plan to spring *El Scorpion* from the transport vehicle.

"Hello." Luis answered.

"Luis, Pepe here. I need you to prepare the van for some night work. I need two six-foot lengths of heavy chain, a portable acetylene torch and tank, the two magnetic signs I had made which are sitting in the office, and some traffic cones. Also, make sure you take three hardhats and the two heavy hooks by the signs to clip onto the ends of the chains. Load all of that into the van, except the magnetic signs. Those you will put on the sides of the van just before you get to the location where you'll be working."

"Sure, boss. Will I be alone or do you want me to take a couple of the guys with me?" Luis asked. Luis was one of Pepe's most dependable men, completely loyal and never questioning any order Pepe gave him. Some of his men liked to play the *gangsta* role and strut around like they were untouchable. In fact, he had fired a couple of his men a while back for failing to follow his orders to a tee. It had seemed to work...so far. The rest of the men had fallen in line and tried to straighten up their act. Luis had never pretended to be anyone other than who he was, a hired gun. Now, Luis was his second-in-command, and he took the role seriously.

"Take Jorge and Mario with you. I'm sending you a text with the location where you need to be at tonight. Make it around eight, and don't to forget to attach the signs to the sides of the van before you get there," Pepe said.

"What will we be doing, boss?" Luis asked.

"Park the van next to the manhole in the middle of the street. Place the cones in the back and front, just like city workers do. Have Jorge help you with whatever you need him to do. Mario is to carry a clip board and answer questions if any residents get curious. He is to tell them that there is a cracked metal rim on the manhole and that you are making repairs. Have him be civil and apologize for any disruption the residents claim are happening. On the clipboard are phony work orders, just in case any *policia* show up and get nosy," Pepe responded.

"Okay, boss. Anything else I need to know?"

"You are to climb down into the manhole and then weld one end of each chain to the inner metal rim. Make sure they are welded solid. I mean solid, they have to withstand the sudden jerking of a vehicle. When you finish, let the two chains drape over the inside ladder, for fast access. It shouldn't take you any more than about an hour, probably less. Once you're finished, put the cover back over the manhole, load the cones and leave. Do you have all that?" Pepe asked.

"*Si,* boss. I'll get right on it as soon as I hang up," Luis replied.

"Make sure you don't get there until eight tonight, and Luis, don't let me down."

"Yes, sir. I understand."

Pepe terminated the call and made another, this one to his cousin, his contact in the Transport Division of the Dade County Court.

"Is everything still on schedule?" Pepe asked, without using names.

"Yes, it's still a go, same time," his cousin answered.

Pepe hung up the phone. The less they talked the less chance of anyone overhearing anything that could jeopardize the operation. His cousin understood, and they would talk later, after he got off work. He was to meet Pepe and bring a package he had requested. It was an orange jumpsuit like the inmates all wore, bearing the DOC J letters emblazoned on the back in white lettering.

Pepe had one more call to make, and this one was really crucial to the success of the operation.

****

Lily Fernandez was a local commercial filmmaker. Her office in Coral Gables had been there for nearly twenty years. She had tried her hand at acting but couldn't break into the big time, so now she specialized in those obnoxious car commercials that permeated the airwaves of the local television stations, night after night. She even had started a school to coach the girls how to stand in front of new cars and jerk their heads left and right, constantly moving their hands to their spiel. Most people laughed at the commercials, but the result was what the dealerships wanted – exposure and for the people to remember their ad.

Years earlier she had borrowed some money from Pepe to start the school. They struck up a friendship, even a romantic fling for a brief period. They both eventually agreed that the romance part would never work, so they continued on as good friends. They still saw each other occasionally, for dinner and sometimes a passionate late night in bed. The sex was good, but they lived in different worlds and the friendship was probably as far as it would ever go.

When Lily's phone rang, and she saw on the caller I.D. that it was Pepe, she assumed he wanted to get together for dinner, and possibly a late-night dessert. She smiled as she answered the call.

"Hello, Pepe. It's been months since I have heard from you."

"Hey, Lily. Sorry I haven't called sooner, but business has been keeping me going like crazy. How about you? Everything going okay?" Pepe replied.

"I'm doing well. Picked up a couple of new accounts, and the coaching school is going great. Life is good," Lily said.

"Would you like to go out tonight for dinner?" Pepe asked.

"I would love to. I need a break," Lily replied.

"Great! I'll pick you up at eight. I have something to talk to you about."

"Okay, I'll be ready, Pepe," Lily said as she hung up the phone.

Chapter 29

LINDA HAD SLEPT FITFULLY during the night. She had used the thin blanket Marc had left for her, but she was still thoroughly pissed that he had taken her clothes off. She was not a prude by any means, but the thought of him seeing her naked made her shudder.

She knew she had to find a way out of this mess, and quickly. There had to be a way, she just had to find it. she had no doubts that when Marc returned, he probably intended to kill her, just as he claimed he had done to her sister and those other girls. What kind of sick mind was she dealing with? He could kill several people just because he had lost his job! He had to be insane and that made him dangerous.

Then it came to her. She remembered her bra. Kicking off the blanket she frantically grappled with her feet to pull the bra close enough to grab it with her hand. Within a minute she had it. Luckily for her Marc had made sure the chains allowed her to reach her mouth so she could eat an energy bar and drink some water.

She held the bra close to her face and began feeling around the cup, bending and pressing with her fingers. Sure enough, there seemed to be a wire stitched around the cup. She quickly put the bra to her mouth and began trying to rip it open. She gnawed at the stitching for several minutes and didn't seem to be making any progress.

Flipping the bra in her hand, she began ripping out the inside of the cup, the material not nearly as stout as the outer layer. Soon she had the thin material covering the layer of foam ripped open and she began biting and pulling the foam from the cup. To her dismay, the stitching on the inside was as tight as the outside. But, now she had one less layer to go through, and she began in earnest, biting and ripping away at the edges.

It took her nearly thirty minutes of gnawing and biting, but her efforts were beginning to pay off. Her mouth was getting sore now, and her teeth ached, but the thread to the inside stitching suddenly started pulling away. She could see the thin wire now and her hopes soared. She redoubled her efforts to pull the wire out, her teeth now really beginning to hurt. But desperation made her work through it and bear the pain. She had to get that wire out. Finally, through torturous effort, she was able to grasp the wire with her teeth. Slowly she pulled and pulled, the wire barely pulling out.

She stopped and lay back, catching her breath, giving her aching teeth and lips a chance to stop hurting. She knew that daylight was soon arriving, and she didn't know how long it would be before Marc showed up. If she didn't get the wire out, she was probably done for. That thought alone spurred her to sit up and renew her attack on the wire. Once she bit down on the thin wire again she pulled with all her might and was rewarded with the wire pulling out about two inches. That wasn't enough, she needed it completely out for what she had planned. With determination she bit on the wire again, now able to get more of it between her teeth. Ever so slowly the wire began pulling out of the stitching. Finally, it jerked free, out of the bra.

She tossed the destroyed bra to the floor and grasping the wire between her fingers. She began to mold it in a certain shape. The final touch was going to hurt since she had to bend the end of the wire into an L shape. But, it wasn't so bad. The wire was so thin she quickly bent it to the desired shape she needed.

Now if it only worked. Several years ago she had attended a class that taught how to open doors with a pick, how to unlock handcuffs, all with a piece of wire. Now she would see if those lessons paid off, or not. If the wire didn't work, she hated to think of what could be in store for her. It just had to work. So she gingerly twisted her fingers with the wire grasped between them and aimed for the keyhole in the cuffs. Her hands were shaking, and she had trouble getting the wire inserted so she stopped and took a deep breath, willing her hands to stop shaking.

Soon, the wire was inserted and she began the process of twisting it in the correct manner. At first nothing happened. Panic began to set in, but she forced her brain to override it. Now was not the time to have a panic attack.

Linda knew that time was of the essence, but she had to stop and relax. Once she felt confident that she could do it. She began twisting the wire, slowly, until she felt a click, and the cuff loosened on her wrist. God, she felt amazing now. Maybe she would get out of here before Marc showed up. With renewed confidence, she inserted the wire into the other cuff and had it open quicker than the first. Pleased with herself, and with great relief, she sat back and rubbed her aching and swollen wrists, gradually feeling the circulation returning.

Linda knew she couldn't afford to waste time, so she stood and cautiously walked to the front of the building, hoping that Marc had really left and wasn't still here and asleep. When she reached the front, she noticed the plywood Marc had placed on the windows she had broken out. Then she saw her clothes, tossed to the floor in a pile. She swiftly raced to the pile and put her clothes back on, *sans* the bra, which was beyond repair now. As she contemplated her next move, she heard a vehicle pulling up to the rear of the store. Panic began to set in again, but with resolve, she shoved it aside and looked around for a weapon. Damn if she was going to allow that maniac to shackle her again. In fact, she was going to make him pay a price for his actions.

Against the plywood she spotted a four-foot piece of a two-by-four, probably discarded after Marc had boarded the windows. Quickly she picked it up and stood behind the door, her grip tight on the wood. She heard the bay door roll up, and the vehicle pull into the bay. Then the van door closed and she heard Marc swearing loudly, as he probably had seen that Linda wasn't where he had left her. Footsteps began to head her way, and she gripped the piece of wood even tighter. As the footsteps reached the doorway she was hiding behind, she swung the piece of wood back in an arc, ready to knock the crap out of Marc when he entered the room.

Then, Marc stepped into the doorway.

Chapter 31

WHILE WAITING IN THE BREAK ROOM, Stormy filled Junior in on the current situation with Linda.

"Do you have any leads on the abduction? Or does this photo we're running have something to do with it?" Junior asked.

Stormy filled Junior in on everything he knew, about the bodies found in the river, one of them being Linda's sister, and the many bars he had visited to see if anyone had seen the murdered girls prior to their untimely deaths. He explained to Junior about getting lucky and pulling a photo of the suspect at one of the bars – getting lucky in the sense that it had been the only bar he checked that had cameras affixed outside the business. Even with those cameras, the shot of his suspect was vague. He explained how Dakota and Nickie were driving around the area in question, looking for any vans that fit the description of the one used in Linda's abduction.

"Have you heard from Dakota yet?"

"No, but I plan to call her once we get back to your office," Stormy replied.

"Well, I don't personally know Linda, but I've heard of

her and nothing but good things. I feel for you and your frustration, so let's get back to my office and see if anything has popped up. We may get lucky...hopefully!" Junior said, as he arose and rinsed out his and Stormy's coffee mugs. After placing them on the counter they both left the break room and headed back to Junior's office.

Back in the office they saw that Annie Mae was still running, the images almost a blur, but no hits as of yet.

"While you make your phone call, and while Annie Mae is still doing her thing, I'll play with the photo and see if I can clean it up some, edit out the surrounding area, enhance the pixels and try to clear it up some," Junior said.

"Okay, I really appreciate it. Time is not really on my side right now. If that creep who murdered those girls, and I'm sure it's him, really has her, God only knows what he's doing with her," Stormy said, as he pulled his cell out and dialed Dakota's number.

"Dakota, anything yet on the van?" Stormy asked when she answered the call.

"God, Stormy, we must have stopped a dozen black, older vans, but nothing so far. Every one of them were either workers or kids. They all have checked out as clean, so far. We have all of their current addresses, which we had dispatch check out, and advised them that we could be wanting to question them again. They all agreed that it would be no problem. Anything on the photo yet?" Dakota asked.

"No, Annie Mae is still running it, but nothing yet."

"*Annie Mae*?" Dakota asked.

"Yeah, Junior gave his program a name," Stormy said with a chuckle.

"Okayyy...well, Nickie and I are heading out west on Okeechobee Road to look for some more vans. I'll let you know if we find anything."

"Alright, Dakota, please do. I'll do the same here," Stormy said, terminating the call.

Stormy placed a call to the Captain and advised him of where he and Dakota stood so far. He assured him he would call as soon as anything in the way of a lead popped up. As he hung up from the call, he heard a ping resonate from the direction of Annie Mae. Junior looked up and said, "Well, well. My girl has got a hit!"

They both rushed over to the computer screen where 'Annie Mae' had been running the scan.

"It's a ninety-two percent probability. That's very good, considering the quality of the photo.

They watched as the screen began loading the actual photo on the hit and the pertinent data concerning the person. When it finished installing the information, Junior heard Stormy swear.

"I know him! I have to get back to the station, ASAP. Could you quickly print out that info and pic for me?" Stormy asked.

"No problem. Who is it?" Junior asked, as he hit a couple of keys and waited as the printer spat out the pages.

"That bastard is one of our own! Or was," Stormy replied, disgust in his voice.

Chapter 32

PEPE DROVE HIS MERCEDES CL to Lily's house in the Gables at a leisurely pace. He was running a little ahead of time and didn't want to arrive too early. He turned up the radio and listened to the seventies channel on his XM station. Most of his men and other older Cubans loved the salsa and Spanish songs, but he was partial to the seventies American music, especially disco. He began singing as "I Love the Night Life" by Alicia Bridges came on; he loved that song.

In the seventies a friend of his had opened a nightclub in Hialeah called *Casanova's*. It was built on the side of a bowling alley owned by his friend, Bill Lamont, who owned Casanova's along with his brother Ron. A strange place to build a club, onto a bowling alley, but, it was hugely popular, especially with the younger crowd which was mostly Latin. Sometimes on the weekend, when there was a guest performer, such as K.C. and the Sunshine Band, the line would stretch for half a block, everyone dressed to the max. He went almost every weekend and had a blast, sitting in the elevated VIP booths. It was no secret that a lot of the clientele were top-tier drug dealers, and they wouldn't tolerate any punk want-a-bees causing trouble. Even though Casanova's hired off-duty policemen for security, *they* took care of things behind the scenes. Those were the days.

Pepe pulled into Lily's driveway exactly on time. He rang the doorbell, and she answered almost immediately.

"I knew you'd be on time," she said. "You somehow always manage to do that."

"I hate people who are late, so I make it a practice to be on time, and never too early. I don't want to be one of those people that are frowned upon for being tagged as an always late arrival," Pepe said, laughing. "I assume you are ready to go."

"Yes, let me grab my clutch, and we'll be on our way. Did you have anywhere special in mind?" she asked, as she exited the door and locked it.

"I don't. Do you?"

"I'm in the mood for Versailles on Southwest Eight, if you don't mind."

"Sounds good to me. I was already thinking of some seafood, so let's go."

They pulled up at Versailles within thirty minutes and Pepe allowed his Mercedes to be valet-parked. They entered the restaurant, and the hostess immediately greeted Pepe. Obviously, he was a frequent customer, the way she went on. Lily wasn't jealous in the least, since Pepe only smiled at the hostess, and lavished his attention on her.

They were seated in a special section, off the books and reserved for special customers. The noise level was greatly diminished in this section and the seating sublime, for a public restaurant. The waiter arrived almost immediately and bore two glasses of water, along with menus for their perusal. Pepe nodded his thanks at the waiter, who smiled as he left them to make their selections.

"Well, you seem to still be a popular customer here, Pepe," Lily said, with a slight smirk.

"I try to make it here at least once every couple of weeks. I'm probably popular because of my generous tips," Pepe said with a hearty laugh.

The waiter returned to the table and asked if they would like beverages, on the house, of course. Lily asked for a glass of rosé and Pepe simply wanted a beer. The waiter left to fetch their drinks and left them alone again.

"I have something to ask of you, Lily. If you can help me, it would be greatly appreciated," Pepe began.

"Let's make our selections first so the waiter won't have to keep coming back, and besides, I *am* hungry," Lily responded. She assumed Pepe had something on his mind, as he wasn't as talkative as he usually was.

They made small talk about her business and how the school was now up and running in the black. Pepe told her he was doing pretty good lately also. The waiter returned, after a nod from Pepe.

"I'll have a small salad and for the entree, the Dolphin Mahi-Mahi medallions in salsa verde," Lily began.

"The same for me, except no salad, I'll have some fried calamari instead," Pepe said, collecting Lily's menu, and along with his passed them to the waiter.

"So, what is this special favor you need from me?" Lily asked, as the waiter left.

"I need the services of one of your actors. Not just whomever you can get, I need certain requirements in their looks," Pepe began, taking a sip of his beer.

"What are the special requirements?" Lily asked.

Instead of giving her a description he simply reached into his jacket pocket and withdrew a photograph. He slid it across the table to her and watched her expression as he took another sip of his beer.

"Is this who I think it is?" she asked, her eyebrows rising slightly.

"Yep...and I need an actor who roughly fits his height and weight. Also, it's important that the facial features resemble the person in the photo as closely as possible," Pepe stated.

Lily looked at the photo for several minutes, taking a couple of sips of wine while she did so. Finally, she looked up from the photo and stared at Pepe.

"Do I even want to know what this is about?" she asked.

"I've known you a long time, and if you really need to know, I'll tell you. But, it's better if you don't know, for your own protection," Pepe said.

"Will my actor be in any sort of danger?"

"No, quite the contrary. He will believe that he is playing a part in a movie. That's all he needs to know. I'll pay you whatever you ask, but I need him tomorrow at the latest," Pepe said.

"Wow...talk about pressure. Actually, I do have someone in mind who resembles El...err...the man in the photo," Lily said, knowing Pepe had not spoken the subjects name out loud, clearly not wanting anyone nearby to overhear the name.

"That would be great. When could I see a photo of

him?"

"I have one on my phone. I keep a photo file here for easy access. Hang on, I'll pull it up," Lily said, as she began scrolling through her phone.

"Ahhh...here it is," she said, handing her phone over to Pepe.

Pepe stared at the actor in the photo and was surprised at how close the resemblance was to *El Scorpion*. The actor was a few years younger, but the facial features fit like a brother.

"What is his height and weight?" Pepe asked.

Before Lily could answer, their appetizers arrived, and Pepe laid the phone face down on the table, to keep the waiter from seeing the image. Once the waiter left, they picked at their food. Pepe turned the phone over and looked at the image again.

"He is about an inch shorter than your man, but the weight seems to be spot on," Lily said.

"I can live with an inch shorter. I must admit, he is closer to the looks than I expected to find," Pepe said.

"How much?" Pepe asked.

"Three thousand," Lily responded.

"Wow, he makes pretty good money."

"Actually, he gets the going rate for an actor with no recognition. Two thousand of it is mine," Lily said with a smile.

"I have no problem with that. After all, you have a business to run."

"So, what's the plan? In other words, what am I to tell the actor?" Lily said.

"Tell him it's a movie about a jailbreak. Also, he is to

think that tomorrow night is a dry run, no actual filming. I'll tell him it will be to determine if he is right for the part," Pepe said.

"And, about the following day or so, when he wants to know if he has the part?"

"We'll tell him that he has the part right afterwards and that he'll have to be ready to go then. He can easily handle the role I need for him to portray. Hell, I could do it, and I'm no actor," Pepe said.

"You've really thought this through, haven't you, Pepe," Lily said.

"In my line of work, you have to know what you're doing. A mistake could be fatal," he said.

"Where do you want me to send him? And what time?" Lily asked.

Pepe slid over a business card with an address of a warehouse in Hialeah. He had already set the scene with cameras and components of the film business, which he had borrowed from a friend.

"Tell him to be at this address at seven tomorrow evening. I'll need to run him through the *script*, so to speak," Pepe said. "And Lily, I can't afford a no-show. He *has* to be there."

"He will be. I'll drive him myself, if I have to," Lily said. "And Pepe? Please be careful. I don't know the full extent of what is going on, but I know the players involved and I don't want you to get hurt...okay?"

"Don't worry, my sweet Lily. I'm bullet-proof," Pepe responded, flashing her a big smile.

Chapter 33

BRENDA TOOK A LONG HOT BATH in the spacious tub in her room. She felt refreshed and had really needed a good soaking after her long flight. She pulled her laptop out and checked for messages. The only one was her SAC reminding her to keep him up to date on any progress. After glancing at her watch, she saw that Larry would be returning soon, so she took off the bath robe the hotel had supplied and picked through the clothes she had hung up upon arrival. Most were wrinkle-free, although some would have to hang a little longer. She selected a smart pair of beige slacks and a low-cut blouse to match. It wasn't that she wanted to show her cleavage, just that it was so hot in South Florida this time of the year. She had barely finished applying her make-up when her cell phone chirped. Glancing at the caller I.D. she saw that it was Larry.

"Hey, Brenda. You ready to go? If not, I can wait in the lobby till you're ready," Larry said when she answered.

"Give me five minutes and I'll be right down," she responded.

Checking herself in the mirror again, she grabbed her handbag and headed for the elevator, feeling almost human again after her bath.

"Hey Larry. Sorry I wasn't ready and waiting for you. I just had to take a good hot bath to unwind," Brenda said, as she stepped from the elevator and met Larry.

"No problem at all. What's on the agenda now?" Larry asked.

"I think we need to do some old-fashioned door-knocking," she replied.

"Door-knocking?"

"Just an old term my dad used all the time. It means we start walking from hotel to hotel showing her picture and hope we don't have to do it all day," Brenda said, smiling at Larry.

"I don't know how far we'll get just showing the picture," Larry said.

"Well, you're right, but it would take forever to go through the camera footage of every hotel we check," Brenda replied. "We'll see how it goes and maybe we'll get lucky."

When they arrived on Miami Beach they parked the car near the biggest cluster of hotels near where they last thought Consuelo was headed.

"God, it's hot down here in Florida. I hope we don't have to walk too much," Brenda said, heading to the nearest hotel from where they had parked.

"It's a dry heat," Larry said, somewhat smugly.

"I bet you tell that to all the girls," Brenda replied, laughing.

"Well, at least there is the ocean breeze here...unlike the interior," Larry said.

"Yep, there is that."

Once they entered the hotel, they walked directly to the front desk and asked for the manager. After showing the photo to him and the desk clerks, they were told they didn't recognize the woman. They left and for the next hour hit hotel after hotel, with no results.

"Well, do we keep going? Or do you have a plan B?" Larry asked.

"Let's do one more. I think she has an affinity for luxury, based on her previous accommodations, so let's check out that one across the street, the Setai."

"That *is* luxury. The Setai is one I surely couldn't afford," Larry said, as they crossed the street.

Once they were inside and introduced to the manager, he told them he had not been there all morning but had been attending a Chamber breakfast. He didn't recognize the woman in the photo and deferred them to the desk clerk. She looked at the picture and studied it for a full minute before saying, "She sure looks familiar. A woman checked in earlier, wearing a wide-brimmed hat and sunglasses. It could have been her."

They went back to the manager and asked if they could see the camera footage since the clerk thought she recognized the woman. He consented and took them to the security office and were introduced to the head of security, Randall Clark. Once they were seated he began to rewind the footage. When he reached the beginning of coverage for early in the morning they watched as he slowly sped it up. Brenda had told him they were looking for any woman wearing a wide-brimmed hat and sunglasses. In about thirty minutes a woman sporting the attire they were watching for appeared, walking to the check-in desk.

"Freeze it right there. Now back it up a little," Brenda asked Randall.

When the woman came back into the frame she had him enlarge it onscreen. She immediately dismissed it as being Consuelo, since the woman was obviously much younger and black. Randall started the footage moving again, and Larry asked, "I'm going to grab a soda, do you want something?"

"No, thank you. How 'bout you, Randall?"

"No, but thank you. I have bottled water in the fridge if you want."

"Sure, I'll take one instead of a soda," Larry said, as he walked over to the fridge in the corner of the room.

Not ten minutes after the first hit, Brenda spotted another woman fitting the description. She had Randall freeze it and back it up, then enlarging the image.

"That's her!" Brenda said. "She was trying to keep her face from the cameras, but this shot caught her before she could hide from it," Brenda took the photo and passed it around to Larry and Randall. They looked back and forth between the screen and the photo and both agreed that it was most likely the same person, Consuelo.

Randall printed out a copy and wrote the time-stamp number on the back. Brenda and Larry thanked him for his assistance and left the security office, returning to the front desk. After being shown the time-stamp, the clerk checked to see who had checked in at that time.

"It shows a woman named Grace Cortez checked in using her passport for identification," the desk clerk said.

"Can you tell me what room number, please," Brenda asked.

"She is in room 1004."

"Would you summon the manager for me, please."

Once the manager arrived he was updated on the identification on the photo, and it was confirmed that the woman checked in. Brenda asked if they would ring the room to see if she was in but to give an excuse of housecleaning or something, so as to not arouse suspicions. The manager called the room and after several rings it was obvious no one was there, or at the least not answering at this time. The clerk hung up without leaving a message. Brenda asked the manager if it was possible to get a key to the room and as expected, denied, citing that a warrant would be needed. He attempted to explain it was the policy of the hotel for the protection of the guests. Brenda had heard it all before and knew from the start it would be a snag – nothing came easy these days. She thanked the manager and told him she would obtain a warrant. She also advised the manager and the clerk, nothing, and she meant nothing, was to be said to the woman known as Grace Cortez that they had been asking about her.

Walking away from the desk Larry asked Brenda what their course of action would be now. Were they going to try to obtain a warrant? Would this Grace person be checked out by the time some judge finally signed it? Brenda walked over to the far side of the expansive lobby and took a seat on a couch, a faux palm tree blocking them from the front desk. She opened her briefcase and pulled out some papers as a ruse. Larry figured it out immediately and took a seat also, pulling out his cell and pretending to talk into it.

The plan was to stakeout the lobby for as long as they

could. They had a photo and maybe they would get lucky. Consuelo, AKA Grace Cortez, could very well walk into the lobby while they were there. Maybe she was just out getting a bite to eat or doing some shopping. All they could do was wait, so they made themselves comfortable.

****

Consuelo re-entered the hotel through the restaurant where she had just eaten. She decided to have a cold beer, so she had walked into the hotel bar, tucked away opposite the front desk. The was lobby visible through tinted windows. The room was dark, and she sat at the far end, away from the window facing the front desk.

As she nursed her beer, her mind processing the coming night and the plan for springing *El Scorpion*, she glanced out the window and saw the woman and man at the desk, talking to the manager, she presumed. Immediately she pegged them for Federal agents, having seen enough of them in the past years. They all seemed to dress the same, walked with the same swagger, exuding authority.

She watched them carefully, aware they couldn't see inside the bar with the tinted windows. She was prepared to bolt through the rear if they decided to approach the bar. She watched as they shook the manager's hand and walked away. She followed them with her eyes as they took a seat on one of the many couches in the lobby, pulling out papers and pretending to be busy studying them. She took notice of them scanning the lobby and front door, trying not to be obvious.

There was nothing in her room other than some clothes,

since she made it a habit to take her passports and anything else of importance with her each time she left. As in the past, she never knew if she would be returning, and this was one time she definitely wouldn't be.

Consuelo beckoned the bartender, who slowly walked her way.

"I have a favor to ask of you," she said.

"Yes, ma'am. What can I do for you?" he asked.

"I just noticed that my ex-husband is in the lobby, and I need to get out of here without him seeing me. Is it possible to leave by the rear door?" Consuelo asked, lightly placing her hand on top of the bartender's.

The bartender looked through the tinted windows and seeing several men in the lobby thought nothing of it. He had seen almost everything imaginable during his ten years here.

"Sure, hon, follow me," he said as he left the back of the bar and led her to the rear door, which opened to the area of the beach she had just left thirty minutes earlier.

"Thanks, I really appreciate it. He can be such a pain and loud mouth, and I don't need his crap today," Consuelo said, giving the bartender a hug and pushing a fifty-dollar bill into his hand.

Out on the beach, she strolled about two blocks south before turning and walking out onto the sidewalk in front of another hotel. Keeping her hat brim pulled down to cover her face from street cameras, she hailed a taxi and soon was headed to downtown Miami, putting some distance between her and the agents she had spotted in the lobby. She didn't give a second thought about leaving her clothes in the room. She could always buy more.

The main thought that ran through her mind was how they were tracking her. She could figure out why – she had done some pretty bad things in her life. She was almost certain it was the Feds, by the way they dressed and carried themselves.

Consuelo decided she would have to be a lot more vigilant, especially now that she knew she was being followed.

Chapter 34

As stormy raced back to Hialeah, he called Captain Carter and apprised him of the new developments. He told the Captain he was headed to the office and would call Dakota to meet him there. They needed to put their heads together and figure out where to start their search for Linda, and it had to be done quickly. There was no telling what Marc had planned for her, but, based on what he had already done, Stormy had an idea of what he was going to do. Dread and concern filled his whole being, and God help Marc if he killed her. They just had to find him, and very quickly, before he could do Linda harm.

"Dakota. I need you and Nickie back at the Bureau, ASAP," Stormy said, when she answered.

"Why? What's going on Stormy?" Dakota asked.

"I have some disturbing news. I got a hit on the photos we obtained from the bar. You'll never guess who it is!" Stormy replied.

"Who? Someone we know?" Dakota said.

"I'll tell you at the office. Captain Carter is waiting for us. Step on it!" Stormy said, hanging up the call.

Captain Carter and Stormy were just getting started

when Dakota and Nickie entered the office. They all moved down the hall to the conference room, at the Captain's request. Once they were inside and the door closed, everyone took a seat at the table.

"I'll let Stormy fill you in on what he's found," Captain Carter said, relinquishing the floor to Stormy.

"As you are aware, I was down at the FBI office in Miami, using their facial recognition program to run the photos we obtained from the bar. Their program is second to none, but I wasn't even sure if there was enough of a frontal shot to get any kind of a match. Well, after running the photo for about thirty minutes, the program came through, and it came up with a match," Stormy began.

"Who is it?" Dakota asked.

"None other than a former employee of ours. *Marc Butler*!" Stormy said.

There was stunned silence in the room for a full minute before anyone spoke.

"Oh my God! You mean the CSI newbie that Linda let go?" Dakota asked.

"The one and only. Sounds like he holds a grudge," Stormy replied.

"To say the least," Captain Carter interjected.

"But he seemed like such a nice guy," Dakota said, not believing what she was hearing.

"Even *Hannibal Lecter* was a nice guy, albeit on the surface," Captain Carter said.

"I know Linda told me once that she thought he lived on a houseboat, somewhere on the river by Okeechobee Road. Nickie, go call HRS and get us his address. If they give you a problem, refer them to the Captain," Stormy said.

"Yes, sir. On it," Nickie replied, swiftly exiting the room.

"I take it you and Nickie didn't have any luck finding the van," Stormy said to Dakota.

"You wouldn't believe how many old black vans there are in this city," Dakota replied.

"Well, putting myself inside his head, I think Marc has already dumped the van, especially since he had contact with a witness when he was putting Linda inside it," Stormy said. "We may have to put the search for the van on the back burner, for now."

"What now, Stormy?" Dakota asked.

"Well, if the Captain agrees, I don't want Marc's name released as a suspect yet. What we know stays among the four of us, five if we count Junior at the FBI. I don't want him totally disappearing if he sees the news. Do you concur, Captain?" Stormy asked.

"I believe you're right. There will be an uproar, especially with the media, once they find out we had a suspect and didn't let them know. We can't sit on it for long, so how much time do you figure you and your team will need?"

"At least twenty-four hours, maybe a little longer," Stormy said.

"Where do we start?" Dakota asked.

"According to my witness, the kid at the park, the van headed west on Okeechobee Road. That's where we have to begin. I don't believe Marc would be stupid enough to take Linda to his houseboat, so where would he go? He was from Georgia, so I doubt he has family down here, although we still have to check it out. Maybe he has a garage or warehouse somewhere that he could have pulled the van into. I believe we should concentrate on looking at small warehouses from Palm Avenue west on Okeechobee Road," Stormy said.

"Sounds as if we need more manpower. That's a lot to cover," Captain Carter said.

"No, the more people who know that it's Marc we're looking for, the more likely it will get out. We'll have to split up and each take a car. I'll pull up a map of the warehouses in the area we need to focus on. Dakota, do you think Nickie is ready for this?" Stormy asked.

"Oh yeah. She's got her head on straight. I think she's going to be a great detective," Dakota said.

"Stormy, I'm going to take a car and help. You can use the extra manpower," Captain Carter said.

"Great, Captain. The help is appreciated."

Nickie returned to the office, a smile on her face. She placed a sheet of paper on the table containing the address of one Marc Butler.

"Did they give you a hard time? I know how HRS can be when it comes to releasing personal information on its employees," Captain Carter asked.

"Yes, at first, Captain. But it wasn't something I couldn't handle, so there's your address," Nickie replied, a glimmer of a smile on her face.

"Good job, Nickie. If there's any fallout, I'll take care of it," Captain Carter replied.

"We need to get with zoning and planning and pull up the locations of all the small warehouses from Palm Avenue west to the outer city limits along Okeechobee Road.

That will have to be our starting point for now, since that's where the kid in the park saw the van heading with Linda inside. Since Nickie has already gotten her feet wet with HRS, she can go to Planning and Zoning and pull the locations," Stormy said.

Nickie rolled her eyes in mock frustration, and patted Dakota on the shoulder as she left the room. Dakota smiled at Stormy and raised her eyebrows.

"What? Someone has to do it," Stormy said, with a laugh.

"Alright, let's lay out a grid for each of us to hit up. Nickie should be back in an hour or so, and we should be done by then. The sooner we get started the better," Captain Carter said.

After several cups of coffee among them, they finally had a grid system planned out. Just as they were about to take a break, Nickie walked in, a manila folder under her arm.

"My God! I didn't realize how many warehouses there are in this city. At least we don't have to go to all of them...do we?" Nickie said, placing the folder on the table.

"Actually, there are over two thousand warehouses and factories in Hialeah. A lot for a city this size," Stormy responded. "I agree with you, let's hope we don't have to cover them all."

"I'll make copies of the grids we completed, and we can overlay them with the locations on a light table and draw out the sections for each of us," Dakota said.

"Great! That will be a lot easier than writing them all down," Stormy said. "When we head out I'm going to check out Marc's address. Maybe I'll get lucky, and he'll be there. If not, I'll begin searching my grid."

Once the maps were placed over the locations on the light table, each one was traced with the grid, a different one for each of them. They finally had a starting point. Everyone took their assigned grid and headed for their cars.

Chapter 35

After leaving Linda cuffed in the abandoned store, Marc had driven back home. He parked the van at a used car lot three blocks from his houseboat. The car lot was closed, so he wasn't too worried about parking there. He was worried about the kid at the park seeing him put Linda inside the van. If the police came and by chance the kid was there, he could possibly go to them and tell what he saw. He decided to dump the van into the canal further outside of Hialeah's city limits. This would be his first priority after checking to see how Linda was faring.

Marc spent a restless night, getting very little sleep. He had expected to hear a knock on his door at any moment. Finally, he got up about seven. After showering and dressing, he left and walked to the van. It was where he had left it, and there was no police presence. Across from the car lot was a Cuban cafe, the smells of fresh Cuban bread baking and wafting through the air. He felt his stomach growl and decided to grab something eat. He walked across the street and ordered two bags of Cuban buttered bread, and two cups of coffee. He began walking back to the van and saw that someone was opening the office of the car lot. He hurried and got in the van quickly. He started the engine and began driving to his destination.

As he drove, he munched on the bread and sipped the steaming hot coffee. When he approached the abandoned strip mall, he drove on past, carefully looking for any police patrol or other cars parked there. Seeing nothing, he turned around as soon as he could and headed back to the strip mall. He pulled in and drove to the back of the buildings, stopping when he reached the one Linda was in. Leaving the motor running, he stepped out and pulled up the overhead door. He got back into the van and slowly drove it inside. Getting out, he quickly pulled the door down and secured it. He reached inside the van and grabbed the bags of bread and the coffee. Turning to take it to Linda, he suddenly let out a curse; then a string of obscenities spewed from his mouth.

He saw that Linda was not chained where he had left her last night. *She was gone!* He dropped the bread and coffee, rushing to the front of the store, thinking she must have pulled down the plywood and gone out the broken window. Like an idiot he had left her clothes in the front, when he should have taken them with him. How did she get out of the handcuffs? She must have had help, there was no other way.

As he approached the doorway he noticed that the plywood was still in place. Where was she? Had she raised the bay door and then closed it upon leaving? Hardly! She would have been in too much of a hurry to escape to take the time to pull the door down.

Marc slowly stepped into the doorway at the front of

the store. As he did, he glimpsed a shadow, and in his peripheral he saw an object coming toward him. He threw his left arm up in an attempt to protect himself. Suddenly he felt the object hit his forearm and heard the bone crack. Immense pain suddenly engulfed him, radiating from his arm. He quickly reached up as he saw the object, a piece of wood, coming at him again, aiming directly at his head. He reached out with his right hand and grabbed the wood but couldn't hold onto it. Once more Linda swung the piece of two-by-four, this time at his leg, making contact on his thigh.

Marc fell to the floor, attempting to cover his head. Looking up, he saw Linda standing over him, the wood raised over her head for a downward strike. He quickly rolled over, and the blow hit the concrete floor. Swinging his leg good leg out, he forcefully kicked her at the ankles, causing her to fall backwards. Swiftly he was on her, striking her in the jaw. He watched as her body went limp, and the wood fell from her hands. Standing up, he leaned down and grabbed her by the arms and began dragging her back into the bay area. He didn't bother taking her clothes off now. He needed to get her secured quickly so he could check out his forearm. He was sure a small bone was broken. The pain was ever-present.

Once he had her secured with the cuffs, he went into the bathroom and took off his pants to check his leg. A large red welt, which was sure to turn into a huge bruise, was the only damage, but he surely would be limping. Checking his arm, he gently felt along the outer bone and sure enough, he could feel the area where it had broken.

Marc was livid! She had almost done him in, and he

was sure she intended to. He looked around and spotted a stack of orange shop towels. Taking one and folding it over twice, he went to her unconscious body and securely tied it around her eyes. He took his knife from the van and cut another towel in half, and with a roll of duct tape, placed a gag in her mouth and taped it shut.

Marc had planned to make her punishment swift, but now he was going to teach her a lesson before he killed her.

He planned to go dump the van into the canal when it got dark, but he would put her body inside it first. It could be years before anyone found the van in the deep canals lining Okeechobee Road, if ever. But, he would also need transportation to get away from here, and it was too far to walk unnoticed, day or night. If he had been thinking straight, he would have thought to bring a bicycle or small motorbike.

He couldn't take the chance of driving the van back into Hialeah. It was possible, maybe a long-shot, but the kid may have given the police a description of him and the van, and even told them about him putting a helpless woman inside.

The situation seemed to be unraveling, but Marc decided to think on it later with a clearer mind. Now, he had no choice but to sleep here tonight. He went over to the van and picked up the bags of bread. He walked over by Linda and took a bottle of water, now that the coffee was spilled all over the bay floor. Sitting at a dusty desk in one corner of the bay, he slowly munched on the bread and sipped a little water, all the while trying to think of a way to leave once he had finished with Linda and dumped the van.

Suddenly he heard a vehicle stop outside the front of

the building. He held his breath, figuring it was the police doing a check. Then, he heard the engine as the car slowly pulled away. He quickly ran to the plywood, peering through one cracked open edge. It wasn't a police car; it was a private security guard. The car was marked in about ten-inch letters on the door, *Atlas Security*, and had a light bar on top with amber lights. It was now driving slowly around the building, presumably to check the backside, and more than likely, the store with the plywood on the window.

The lien-holder of the property, or someone, had obviously hired a security firm to check the property, probably to make sure no transients or vagrants broke in and crashed there.

Then a light bulb went off in his head. Maybe he did have a way out of here after all.

Chapter 36

LARRY AND BRENDA HAD BEEN SITTING on the couch in the lobby of the hotel for three hours now, waiting for Consuelo to return. Each, in turn, had gone to the restroom, purchased water and read the same magazines till their head could take no more.

"I think I'll go into that bar across the lobby and show her picture around. Maybe she's been in there before. At least it's something to do other than just sit here," Larry said.

"Sure, go ahead, Larry. Stretch your legs and leave me sitting here," Brenda said, laughing.

"I'll be right back, and then you can check out the restaurant and stretch your legs," Larry said.

Larry walked across the lobby floor and into the open door of the lounge. He slowed his walk inside so his eyes could adjust to the sudden darkened room. The couch he and Brenda had been perched on for hours was in the brightest part of the lobby. He saw a young, tanned and slightly muscular man tending bar. He noticed the man's eyes never left him. Was it that obvious he was a Fed or did the bartender think he knew him. In any event, Larry walked straight to the bar, pulling the photo from his jacket pocket.

"Hi, could I take a minute of your time?" Larry asked, as he stopped in front of the bartender.

"Sure, what can I do for you?" the bartender asked, his eyes boring into Larry's.

"I wonder if by chance you have seen this woman," Larry asked, as he placed the photo on the counter.

"Are you her ex-husband?"

"Why would you ask that?"

"Look, this is a nice place, and we don't tolerate trouble here. If you have a problem with your wife or ex-wife, take it somewhere else," the bartender stated, placing his hands on the bar top, purposefully flexing his muscles.

"Okay, sport. Number one, she's not my ex or anything else to me. Number two, you obviously recognized her from the photo. Number three, and I want you to listen very carefully, is that I'm not intimidated by you," Larry said, suddenly pulling his credentials out and placing the badge on the counter top. "I'm Special Agent Foresman with the Federal Bureau of Investigation. Do I have your attention now, son?"

"Sorry, sir. It's just that the woman said her ex was in the lobby and was going to cause problems for her. I thought it was you she was referring to," he responded, a nervous tic developing at the corner of his eye.

"When exactly did she tell you this?" Larry asked, his heart racing.

"About an hour ago."

"And where is she now?" Larry asked.

"She didn't want to leave through the front door, afraid

her ex would see her and cause a scene. I agreed to let her leave through the back door. Am I in trouble, sir?" The bartender asked, a bead of sweat forming on his upper lip.

"No, you had no way of knowing she was lying to you. Can you show me the back door she left from?"

The bartender led Larry to the rear of the bar and out into the storage area. Pointing to a door, he said, "She went through there."

"Where does that lead to?" Larry asked.

"Out onto the beach area."

"Show me, please," Larry said.

The bartender opened the door and propped it with a broom. Larry walked outside and saw that it indeed led to the beach, the sand only ten feet away from the door. He scanned the beach in both directions, but in vain. Consuelo was nowhere to be seen, and he hadn't expected to be that lucky. After all, it had been over an hour now, so she could be anywhere. She had enough of a head start to be many miles away by now.

Reluctantly, he walked back inside the bar and headed to Brenda. Before leaving, he gave his card to the bartender, "If you see her again, please call me." He knew Consuelo was long gone and would not be back here, so he didn't expect a call.

"So, evidently she was sitting in the bar watching us watch her," Brenda said, after Larry had relayed what he had found out.

"Yep, she's a cool one alright," Larry said.

"What room number did the clerk say she was registered in?" Brenda suddenly asked.

"Room 1004. Why? We can't go in there without a warrant," Larry responded.

"Let's just go up and have a look anyhow. Maybe she returned to get her things from another direction. We can at least knock on the door," Brenda said, rising and heading for the elevator.

When they reached the tenth floor, they walked down the long hallway. As they approached the room, they saw a maid's cart in front of the door, the maid inside cleaning. Brenda smiled at Larry and told him to wait outside. She stepped into the room, startling the maid.

"Oh, I'm sorry I startled you. I just need to get something from my luggage," Brenda said, heading for the closet as if she belonged there.

"No problem, ma'am," the maid said, walking into the bathroom to clean.

Brenda opened the small closet and noticed that there was only one small piece of luggage. She quickly opened it and ruffled through the sparse collection of women's clothes inside. Finding nothing of interest, she went to the dresser and quickly opened the drawers, still finding nothing. Just as she was heading to the night stands to check those drawers, she heard Larry call out, "Let's go, darling. We'll find it later."

Realizing he would have a darn good reason for calling her darling, and halting her search, she took one last look around the room, still seeing nothing worth looking at. She scurried out of the room and was met at the door by Larry.

"A security guard just got off the elevator. I don't know if the maid knows what Consuelo looks like and put two and two together, realizing you're not her, and called for security," Larry said, as they walked down the hallway.

They passed the guard and smiled and nodded; the guard nodded back. Once they were at the elevator, Larry looked back and saw that the guard had walked past Consuelo's room, knocking on another door. The elevator opened, and they stepped inside and rode down to the lobby in silence.

"Good call, Larry. It could have gone down like you said. Lucky for us it didn't," Brenda said, walking out of the elevator and over to the couch they had graced for several hours earlier.

"Now what?" Larry asked Brenda. "She played us, and we have no idea where she has gone."

"If she pegged us for Feds, and I'm sure she did, she will probably go to ground, maybe even attempt to leave the country. We can't possibly pull the camera footage in every hotel and motel in Dade County. Let's get an early dinner. Maybe putting our heads together, we can come up with another way to find her," Brenda said, heading for the front door of the hotel.

Chapter 37

STORMY DROVE FAST, slightly above the speed limit, heading for Marc's houseboat. He punched the address into the navigation system, not wanting to waste time searching along Okeechobee Road. He wove in and out of traffic, some cars blowing their horns at him, which he ignored. The navigation system took him directly south down LeJuene Road, all the way to Okeechobee, where it directed him to turn west. He took the turn and maintained a fast speed, every minute counting now, Linda's safety of the utmost concern.

When the disembodied voice from the dash announced he was arriving at his destination, he slowed and quickly spotted the houseboat. A car was parked in the graveled driveway. He slowly drove past and about a half-mile down the road, turned around and headed back. He spotted a gas station almost directly across from the houseboat, so he pulled in and parked by the side of the building. Getting out, Stormy walked casually inside, pretending to look at his phone, in case Marc was watching. When he entered the store he went to the self-service soda machine and drew a small coke. Then he took up a position behind the nearest rack of goods next to the front window. He sipped at the coke and pretended to thumb through a magazine, while in all actuality he was looking across the road at the houseboat, watching for any activity.

He stood and watched for about twenty minutes before the clerk walked over and asked, "You going to buy that book or read it here?"

Stormy turned to the clerk, an older man, maybe the proprietor, and flashed his badge.

"I'm waiting for a friend, and they are running late. Hope it's no problem for me to wait in here, it's so hot outside," Stormy said, politely, and with his most disarming smile.

"No, sir. Take your time. Free refill on the coke, if you like," the man said, turning and walking back to the counter.

After an hour passed, Stormy still hadn't seen any activity or movement at the houseboat. He refilled his cup and walked to the cashier.

"I guess my party is going to be really late, so I'll just get out of here. If someone comes in asking about me, Jack Storm, tell them I had to go and will catch up with them later."

"Sure thing, mister. Have a nice day," the cashier replied.

Stormy walked outside and over to his car. Starting the engine, he turned the air conditioning up to max, the interior heat probably at well over a hundred degrees. *And still there were some idiots who would leave their pets, and even their children, in the car in this heat,* Stormy thought to himself.

Stormy drove across the road and into the driveway of the houseboat, parking behind the car. He ran the tag, and it quickly came back to Marc Butler. Still, he hadn't seen any movement, so he exited his car and walked up to the ramp leading onto the houseboat. The loose graveled driveway caused a crunching sound as he walked, but there wasn't much he could do about it. If Marc was inside and heard the noise, he would know soon enough.

Keeping his gun hand poised near his weapon, he cautiously walked up to the door. He knocked, twice, and hearing no movement he hesitated, but only for a minute. He had no intention of leaving to obtain a search warrant, time was too much of a factor. He would take the heat later if he had to, but he was going inside. Once more he knocked, and then called out, "Hello? Anyone home?"

Stormy tried the door handle, finding it locked. He peered in through the front window but didn't see any sign of anyone. He decided to walk around to the back and check it out before trying to enter the houseboat.

At the rear there was nothing but the deck above the river, running across the length of the house. He tried the rear door, and, to his surprise, it was unlocked – either by accident, or maybe a trap. Pulling his weapon, Stormy slowly turned the door handle, standing off to the side of the door. As the door creaked open, he called out once again, "Anyone home?"

Failing to hear anyone answer, he turned sideways and entered the room, his weapon trained in front of him. The interior was dark, all of the lights off, but enough light filtered in through the windows for him to see clearly. He checked each of the rooms before finally holstering his weapon, satisfied that no one was home.

It was apparent that Marc still lived there, at least up until now. There were a few dirty dishes in the kitchen sink and a few clothes in a pile near the washing machine. Other than that, everything appeared normal for occupancy. He wandered back into the small living room and began looking around, trying to find anything that would give a hint as to Marc's whereabouts.

On the coffee table he espied a stack of papers and ruffled through them. Bingo! He saw a receipt for the purchase of a van, only days earlier, and paid for in cash. What he saw next gave him chills. It was a receipt for handcuffs, chains and other essentials that fit the profile of a person with plans – plans to secure someone, against their will, and that someone was probably Linda.

After looking around for a few more minutes, Stormy found nothing else that gave a clue as to where Marc had gone, or if Linda had even been here on the houseboat.

He walked back the way he had entered, through the rear door. Closing it carefully, he walked back to the front, and after getting into his car, called Captain Carter's cell phone. What he was about to relay didn't need to be over the radio, at least for now. The Captain picked up on the first ring after seeing Stormy on the caller I.D.

"What do you have, Stormy?"

"I'm at Marc's houseboat, Captain. There's no one home, but the back door was open. I entered after announcing myself, and you won't guess what I found.

"Tell me!" Captain Carter said.

"There was a receipt for the purchase of a van a few days ago. Paid for in cash. There was also another receipt, for handcuffs, chain, duct tape, and other stuff. I don't like the looks of where this is going, Captain," Stormy said.

"Should we send CSI over to process the place?" Captain Carter asked.

"No, I don't think we should do that, just yet. I suggest we put some surveillance on the place, just in case Marc returns. If he drives by and sees the CSI unit there, we'll have a much harder time finding him. He'll know we're onto him and probably speed up whatever he has planned for Linda, then try to disappear."

"I'll have our Narc unit send out a couple of guys. I'll personally brief them, but with only what they need to know, for now," the Captain said.

"Good! Thanks, Captain. Advise the surveillance team that Marc's car is in the driveway, which means that he is probably driving the van. I'm heading to my grid now to begin checking the warehouses," Stormy said, hanging up.

Stormy's search group – Dakota, Nickie and Captain Carter – had no way of knowing that their grid search was bringing them closer and closer to the abandoned strip mall where Linda was being held.

Chapter 38

MARC QUICKLY RAISED THE BAY DOOR. Risking a peek outside, he saw the security patrol car slowly inching along from the end of the building. He moved back inside the bay and crouched beside the van, out of sight.

Lincoln Combs had been working for Atlas Security for six years now. He took great pride in his job and had once aspired to be a police officer. His wife had been against it, so he deferred to her wishes. They raised two children throughout the years, and now in his late fifties, he was content to do his job and spend free time with his kids and one grandchild. His wife had passed two years earlier, and now all he had to look forward to when he was home was loneliness and an empty house. But the visits from his children were his saving grace – the one thing that kept him sane. He really had no immediate plans to retire. Heck, he couldn't retire even if he wanted to. What else would he do, other than go crazy being alone. He had no hobbies and not a lot of money to travel. Nope, he planned to work until he died, or until something happened that forced him to retire.

Lincoln was just finishing up his night patrol shift, running late because of a couple of incidents earlier. Nothing major, but still causing him to run late. This was his last checkpoint before punching out. He had to make a thorough inspection of this building. He noticed plywood on the front window of one of the stores, plywood that hadn't been there two days ago when he last checked it.

As he pulled closer to the rear of the store, he noticed the bay door standing open. Pulling up slowly to the open door, he left the car running and exited, slowly walking over to the bay.

"Hello! Anyone there?" he called out.

Hearing no answer, he walked closer and peered inside. He noticed a black van parked in the bay. He didn't see anyone. He figured they must be in the front part of the store. He walked into the bay area past the van, on the opposite side of where Marc was knelt down. As he approached the front of the van his eyes were drawn to the corner where Linda was restrained.

Letting out a gasp, he whirled around, his hand on his gun. Seeing no one, he ran over to the woman chained up in the corner. He noticed she was blindfolded, and both wrists were restrained with handcuffs, each one attached to a length of heavy chain.

"Miss, are you okay?" he asked, as he removed her blindfold.

Linda squinted for a second or two as the ambient light blinded her. Then her eyes widened as she looked over the shoulder of the unknown man kneeling before her. Lincoln quickly turned his head in the direction she was looking. Unfortunately he was too late to duck the piece of wood that he saw descending towards him. As the wood struck the side of his head, blackness overtook him immediately, his limp body falling across Linda's outstretched legs.

Marc leaned down and checked the man for a pulse. Finding that he was still alive, he fetched the duct tape and securely bound the man's arms behind him. Blood was beginning to seep down his face from the gash, but not alarmingly so. He dragged the man to the front of the store, where he placed him on his side. He put tape across the man's mouth and taped his ankles together.

Satisfied that the man was securely bound and going nowhere, he went back into the bay. Looking at Linda, he said, "No one is going to stop me from doing what I have planned. No one."

He replaced the blindfold over Linda's eyes, failing to notice tears welling up. She could only pray that the poor man who had tried to help her would be okay. The tears were for him.

Marc went outside and turned off the engine of the security vehicle. He debated switching it out with the van but decided that the van was probably on the Hialeah Police radar, whereas the security car would be okay for a while. He considered that the man was probably at the end of his shift and that when he didn't show up in the next hour or two, an alert would be sent out. They probably, in fact it was a given, that the company had a regularly scheduled route for the man. They would in all likelihood begin to search here, near the end of the man's route. Marc figured he only had an hour or so to wrap things up and then *get out of Dodge*, so to speak. As he turned to reenter the bay, the radio in the security car suddenly crackled to life.

"Lincoln, come in!" The dispatcher called out.

Marc had an epiphany and rushed to the car. Grabbing the mike, he said through his nose, to disguise his voice as much as he could, "Lincoln here."

"What's the matter with your voice, Lincoln. And why aren't you back at the office. Your shift is over," the dispatcher replied.

"This blasted cold came on really fast. Is it possible to take the car home tonight?" Marc asked, feigning a cough. "I feel like my head's gonna explode."

"Lincoln, you know better that that. Besides, the next shift needs it. We're down one car already," Dispatch responded.

"Okay, but I need to stop by my house and grab something to take. I feel like crap."

"Alright. But hurry up."

"Give me about thirty minutes or so, and I'll be there," Marc said.

Marc walked into the bay, closed the overhead door, and approached Linda. Although she couldn't see him through the blindfold, she could sense his presence looming over her.

"Linda, Linda, Linda. Today is your lucky day. The great and painful things I had planned for you will not happen now. Don't worry, it'll all be over soon, and you'll be able see your sweet sister once again," Marc said, chuckling.

Linda was enraged! She tried to scream at Marc, but the gag prevented anything other than muffled noises. She almost had him when she hit him with the wood. Now, she had to think hard about some way to escape. The next time,

Marc wouldn't be so lucky – if there were a next time.

Allowing about thirty minutes for dispatch to finally send someone looking here for the driver, Marc figured he still had almost an hour. He would dump the van with the bodies inside into the canal behind the shop, and then drive the security patrol car back near his houseboat, where he would abandon it.

It was clear that Marc's mental stability was in doubt. He had clearly gone over the edge.

Chapter 39

BRENDA AND LARRY STOPPED in a local restaurant after leaving the hotel. They were bummed out that Consuelo had been watching them and was able to get away. They had no idea where to go from here. Consuelo could be anywhere in several adjoining cities, even headed out of the country.

"I'll have one of our guys head to the airport and show her picture to security. In fact, I'll send one to the Ft. Lauderdale airport also. Just in case she's leaving Florida," Larry said.

"You can try, but I think she's here for a reason and not leaving just yet," Brenda replied.

The waiter arrived and placed glasses of water on the table and put menus in front of Brenda and Larry. He advised them he would be back to take their order in a few minutes. They told him to take his time.

"Well, where do we go from here? Or do you think we'll be spinning our wheels some more?" Larry asked.

"No, I think we're on the right track. At least I know she's in the Miami area. Coming down here, I wasn't totally sure she would still be here. Now that I'm sure. We'll really have to step it up a notch."

"If you believe she's still in the area, we need to do more than send her photo to the airports. Let my office personnel get with all the surrounding cities that have street cameras, send them her photo, and see if we get a hit," Larry said.

"That would be our best move for now. No telling where she ended up. If you'll make the call, I would appreciate it. I really want to nail her," Brenda said, sipping on her water as she perused the menu.

The waiter returned and took their order. Once he had left, Larry dialed his office and relayed the orders for contacting the other cities in Dade County. He told the agent-in-charge to make sure the others coming in on the night shift were aware of what was going on, and to be notify him immediately if they found something.

Once the meal was delivered to their table, they ate mostly in silence, both scouring their brains for anything, no matter how insignificant, that they may have overlooked. Once they had finished their meal, they ordered coffee and agreed to split a piece of cake. Brenda wasn't much on sweets, but she did occasionally like a bite of something to compliment her coffee.

"Do you think she was responsible for Rolando's death in New Orleans?" Larry asked.

"I'm ninety-nine percent convinced she is. I checked and they did take DNA samples from his body. If she was with him, and especially if she slept with him to throw him off guard, then all I need is a DNA sample from her," Brenda replied.

"Well, let me take you to your hotel so you can get a

good night's sleep. I have a feeling we'll have a long day tomorrow," Larry said.

They split the check, left a hefty tip, and walked out to the car.

Larry dropped Brenda off at the Marriott and promised to call her immediately if anything came up. He told her he would pick her up in the morning around nine.

****

The incessant ringing of Brenda's cell phone woke her from a heavy sleep. It had been a long day, and she had been totally exhausted. Rolling over, she answered the phone, still somewhat groggy.

"Hello, this had better be good," she answered.

"Brenda, rise and shine. I have some good news with reference to your target," Larry said.

"Good God, man. Don't you ever sleep?" she said, as she sat up and swung her legs over the edge of the bed. "Give me fifteen minutes, and I'll meet you downstairs. I assume you are downstairs waiting for me, right?"

"I'll grab us a cup of coffee in the restaurant here. How do you like it?" Larry asked, laughing.

"Hot, hot and black," Brenda replied, jumping out of the bed and rushing to the bathroom for a quick shower.

"See you in fifteen," Larry said, ending the call.

Brenda made it to the lobby in sixteen minutes, feeling slightly refreshed after a quick shower and change of clothes. She exited the elevator and spotted Larry sitting in an over-sized easy chair on the far side of the lobby, sipping his coffee and reading the morning newspaper.

"Good morning, Larry," she said, walking up to him. "I assume that's my coffee on the table."

"Yep, black, hot and strong," Larry replied, putting the newspaper down.

Brenda took a seat in the matching easy chair next to him, picked up her coffee, and took a long slow sip. It was hot and slightly burned the tip of her tongue, but it was what she needed.

"Now, what is such good news that you had to wake me at seven in the morning?" she asked, smiling at him, the cup of coffee still cradled in her hands.

"Well, at least you got to sleep until seven. My guys called me at five," Larry began.

"They must have found something important to have awakened you that early," Brenda said, taking another sip of her coffee.

"The night shift guys were running Consuelo's photo in the facial recognition program when they got a hit. She was seen getting into a Uber a day ago, and they tracked the GPS of the car and followed it to an address on the outskirts of downtown," Larry said.

"Is she still there?"

"Nope, according to my guys she left about twenty or thirty minutes later."

"Were they able to track her from there?" Brenda asked, placing her coffee back on the table, trying to maintain her excitement.

"Yeah, she was dropped off at a small local nightclub several miles away," Larry said, his facial expression indicating there was more.

"And let me guess. She disappeared again," Brenda

said, sensing what was coming.

"Yep, she did indeed. No cameras were available in the area of the club. Once she went inside, she never came out. Not that we could see. She probably went straight in and exited the rear door. She is one smart cookie," Larry said.

"Well, crap! Are we going to the club to interview the staff?" Brenda asked.

"They don't open, in fact no one shows up to work until late in the afternoon. Too much time will have passed. She would be really gone for sure, by then," Larry said. "Although, there is more good news."

"My goodness, aren't you the bearer of glad tidings. What else is there?" Brenda asked, giving Larry her undivided attention.

"The house where the Uber driver initially took her? Guess what is there?"

"I have no idea...family members, maybe. We couldn't get that lucky," Brenda replied.

"Nope, even better. The guy that lives there has been on our radar for some time now. He is a forger of passports. Evidently, Consuelo is getting some new passports, probably in order to leave the country," Larry said, finishing his coffee and tossing the empty cup in a small trash can next to the table.

"My, my, Agent Foresman, you sure know how to make a girl's morning," Brenda said. "Let's go have a chat with this master forger."

"My car awaits," Larry said, laughing, and heading for the front door of the hotel, Brenda beside him.

Chapter 40

AFTER LEAVING THROUGH THE BACK DOOR of the nightclub, Consuelo walked the two miles to her hotel, not willing to trust taking a taxi or Uber this time. The streets were slightly crowded, so she blended in enough for her to feel comfortable at not being seen on a camera, although she hadn't seen any around here.

The hotel she registered at wasn't up to the standards she was used to, but, it appeared that the Feds were getting used to finding her at the higher end hotels. To keep under the radar, for now, she had to take a step down in her accommodations. The room was clean and the small hotel fairly nice, but, it wasn't the Ritz.

****

At almost the exact same time Larry and Brenda were leaving her hotel, Consuelo was stirring in bed. She glanced at the clock on the nightstand, and seeing that it was seven thirty, she arose and walked into the bathroom, and turned on the water in the shower. While she waited for it to heat up, she brushed her teeth, returned to the sparse bedroom and retrieved her lingerie. She returned to the bathroom and hopped into the shower, the hot water almost scalding her at first.

After dressing she donned a large pair of sunglasses, her ever-present wide-brimmed hat and left the room. She walked about two blocks to a small Cuban cafe and had a cup of coffee and toast and eggs. Across the street was a small park with an abundance of trees to shade her. She sat down on a bench and pulled out a burner cell phone from her bag. It was going to be her last night here, and she couldn't wait to leave. The Feds were too prevalent, the heat too oppressive and it would feel good to return home.

First, she had to make airline reservations for her and Juan, in the names on the forged passports. Then she needed to find a car for the long drive to Jacksonville, where she planned for the both of them to fly out of the county. After they arrived in Colombia, she would go her way, Juan his, presumably to find his wife and flee to parts unknown. It would be a good payday, but with the close calls with the Feds, the continuous changing of hotels and other setbacks, she felt she had earned it.

Using her tradecraft, and extreme caution, she made several reservations, all with different airlines, all to different destinations. She had no illusions that the Feds wouldn't soon track down the forger she had used. With the technology available today, CCTV's, satellites and facial recognition programs, not to mention that everyone had a cell phone with a camera, she was sure that she was barely keeping one step ahead of her pursuers.

By booking so many varied and spaced out reservations, it would make it almost impossible for the Feds to be present at all of the airports. She had booked flights at Ft. Lauderdale, Tampa, Miami, and even Atlanta, Georgia. She planned to fly out of Jacksonville and that was the main reason she needed a car. She used several of her many untraceable credit cards to book the flights. Now, if Pepe was successful with his end of the plan, and there were no unforeseen hitches, she and Juan would be on their way to Jacksonville tonight. It would be a good six-hour drive, maybe a little more since she would be using I-75. She needed to arrive about two hours early to perform surveillance at the airport, just in case the Feds were staking it out. She would leave the car in long-term parking, after wiping it down for prints.

Thirty minutes later she had made all the reservations. Now, she had to find a car lot where she could buy a used car – cash, no questions asked. She decided to give Pablo another call to see if he could provide her with a car lot to go to. Better yet, she could have him buy the car and bring it to her.

"Hello," Pablo answered when his phone rang.

"Pablo, do you recognize my voice?" Consuelo said, not chancing using her name on the phone.

"Yes, how are you?" Pablo said, astutely aware of the hazards of using her name on an open line.

"I need another favor. Hopefully, you can come through for me, again."

"Name it, and I'll try. I owe you," Pablo said, referring to her assassination of Rolando for him almost six months earlier. Rolando, rogue cop and serial killer, had almost killed him. Consuelo had gone to New Orleans and taken him out for Pablo, at no cost, just a personal favor. Now, she was collecting on that favor, although she didn't say as much.

"I need a car, or SUV, nondescript and used, and with clean plates. I need it today and delivered to me. Can you do that for me? I'll make it worth your while, in addition to the cost of the vehicle," Consuelo said.

"I can do that. I have a friend who will give me the car and let me pay him after I get back. Just tell me where to deliver it," Pablo said.

"I'll call you back in a few hours and give you a location. Thanks, Pablo. And Pablo, make sure the windows are darkly tinted, please," Consuelo said, ending the call.

Pulling up Pepe's number, she dialed it.

"Pepe here."

"Pepe, everything a go on your end?" Consuelo asked.

"I will be ready. You be around the block from the address I'm sending you via text by nine tonight. I'll be in touch," Pepe said, hanging up.

Chapter 41

BRENDA AND LARRY STOPPED and grabbed a breakfast sandwich and another cup of coffee at a Dunkin' Donut shop. They were on their way to the last place Consuelo was dropped off, at the forger's house in South Miami. They had about a thirty-minute drive so plenty of time to formulate a plan for dealing with the forger.

"So, how did the forger end up on your radar, and I assume he has a name," Brenda said.

"We received a tip about a year ago. One of our guys is still building a case on him. It's hard to get anyone to flip on him, and especially to testify. I called the agent working his case on the way to pick you up. I got his permission to approach him in return for giving him any useful information we obtain," Larry responded.

"Well, we need to approach him without giving him the impression he's under investigation," Brenda said. "How do you feel we should approach him?"

"I suggest we identify ourselves and give him an option of helping us. We can assure him we are only interested in Consuelo, and no one else."

"And if he clams up...refuses to talk to us?" Brenda

asked.

"Then we advise him we have info that Consuelo came to see him, even give him the day and time to convince him we already know she was there. If he still won't cooperate, we advise him we will wait by the curb while the FBI task force obtains a search warrant and tosses his house. That should get his attention," Larry said.

"Yeah, I think that would work. But we can't waste time dickering with him. We have to force his hand quickly," Brenda said.

"I agree. And, as for his name. Pablo Escobar!"

"You're kidding me! Tell me you are," Brenda said laughing.

"Nope, that's his name, but no relation to the real one."

"Wonder if he's a celebrity in the neighborhood," Brenda said, once again laughing.

"According to our info he's not married and about sixty years old," Larry said.

"Well, this should be an interesting interview."

"To say the least," Larry responded, slowing down as he turned onto the street where the man lived.

When they pulled in front of the modest but neat house, Brenda remarked about there not being a car in the drive-way.

"According to the info my agent supplied, there is no driver's license on file for him."

They turned and drove up into the driveway and turned off the engine. Exiting the car they both walked up to the front door and rang the bell.

A bespectacled man who appeared to be in his sixties answered the door. He was short, probably no more than five feet one, or two stretching it. He had tufts of snow white frizzy hair on the sides of his head, the top bald. His glasses were perched on the tip of his nose, and he squinted before pushing them up on his nose.

"Yes, may I help you?" he asked.

"Mr. Escobar, FBI, Agents Skipper and Foresman," Larry responded, presenting his badge.

The man frowned and took a closer look at the badge.

"What can I do for you, agents?" The man asked, displaying no accent.

"May we come in. We have a few questions to ask," Brenda replied.

"I'm sure there must be some mistake. What could you possibly want with me?" he asked.

"Mr. Escobar, do you want to stand out here to talk, allowing your neighbors to see us, and I'm sure they would peg us for who we are. Or may we come in and get the questions out of the way. So far, you're not really in trouble with us, but we think you may be able to help us with another investigation," Larry said.

Looking right and then left down his neighborhood, Escobar pushed the door open and motioned for them to come inside.

Surprisingly, the interior was neat, no stacks of papers, no clothes strewn around, just neat, that's all. There was no appearance of a feminine touch in the décor, validating the info that stated he wasn't married. Escobar motioned for them to sit on the couch, covered in plastic that probably had been on it since the sixties. He took a seat opposite them in an easy chair and leaned forward.

"So, ask your questions, and if I can help, I will do so,"

Escobar said, leaning back into his seat.

"Do you know this woman?" Brenda asked, sliding a photo of Consuelo across the coffee table between them.

Pablo leaned forward again and picked up the photo, appearing to scan it closely. Placing it back on the table he said, "No, never seen her before. Should I know her?"

Brenda picked up the photo and walked over to Pablo, holding the photo out closer to his face.

"Are you sure you don't know her, Mr. Escobar?" she asked. She had noticed a tic on his face when he had looked at it before, indicating he did know her and was lying.

"I told you. I don't know her," he said, a bead of sweat forming on his forehead.

Brenda sat back down, placing the photo in her briefcase. After she closed it she looked up at Pablo and said, "I believe you do know her. She was here last night, and we have proof. If you want to deny knowing her, fine. But, rest assured, we do have proof and that's enough to take you in for further questioning. Now, let me tell you what else we know, also with proof. You're not married, you don't drive and you, sir, are a master forger. From our information, dealing from phony driver's licenses to passports."

"That's a lie…," Pablo began to protest, but he stopped when Brenda held up her hand.

"Sir, it's not a lie, and you know it. We are not here to bust you. All we want is to know what she was doing here last night, although we have an idea. She purchased a passport, right?" Brenda said, waiting for Pablo to process what he had just been told.

"How do I know you won't just arrest me once I agree to tell you what you want to know?" Pablo said, after a few seconds deliberation.

"Well, to be honest, you don't. But we really are only interested in her and the new name she will be using. After you provide us with that information, we will leave you in piece and you can continue on doing whatever you have been doing," Larry said, before Brenda could chime in.

"Do I need an attorney, now?" Pablo asked, the beads of sweat more pronounced now.

"No, sir. Provide us with what we ask, and we will be out of your hair as soon as we can walk through the door," Brenda said.

"Okay, she was here last night. I don't know her name, since she was referred to me by someone else, whose name I will not divulge," Pablo began.

"That's fine, sir. We're only interested in the woman," Larry responded, not relinquishing Consuelo's name.

"If I may, I'll go print out what names she used on the passport," Pablo said, as he arose from his seat.

"Names? You made her more than two passports?" Brenda asked, raising her eyebrows.

"Why, yes. She had both made out in the same last name, possibly her husband, maybe," Pablo said, assuming they knew about both passports.

"Go print them out for us, my partner will go with you," Brenda said.

Pablo and Larry walked into a small room just off the living room. The room had a beat up desk, computer on top and a printer off to the side on a small table. Pablo sat down and typed into the computer and then hit the print button. Larry watched as the printed paper slowly pushed out of the machine, and then another. He walked over and took the sheets of paper and motioned for Pablo to return to the living room.

After taking a seat on the couch again, he showed the papers to Brenda.

"Miguel Soto and Felicia Marie Soto," she read out loud.

"Do you know this Miguel Soto, or what he looks like?" She asked.

"No, I only gave her what she asked for, nothing else. I didn't ask who he was," Pablo said.

The undercurrent in his voice gave doubt to Brenda that he was telling the truth. She asked once again, "Are you sure you don't know him?"

"No, agent, I've told you all I know. We had a deal, or are you planning to arrest me now?" Pablo asked nervously.

"No, Mr. Escobar, we are not arresting you. We gave you our word, and you gave us what we wanted. Have a nice day," Larry replied, standing at the same time as Brenda and heading for the door.

****

Pablo Escobar sat slumped in his chair long after Brenda and Larry had left. He was thankful they hadn't pushed harder for a real name for Miguel. He knew who *El Scorpion* was and knew he wasn't a man to cross. He wouldn't have divulged the name even if they had arrested him, the fear of what could happen overriding any threats from the Feds. Now, he had to get rid of any incriminating evidence in his office. Even with the agents assurances, he didn't trust them. He figured that within days they would raid his house, and he didn't plan for them to find anything, including his computer. He knew they could scan the hard drive even if he erased it and find deleted information. He would get rid of the computer tonight and buy another one in the morning.

****

Once in the car and away from Pablo's house, Brenda broke the silence. She had been in deep thought as they drove away and Larry sensed it, so he kept quiet until she was ready to talk.

"I want to know who the hell Miguel Soto is," she finally said. "Evidently Consuelo is taking someone else with her when she leaves. But who? And how do they play into this?"

"How do you want to proceed now, Brenda," Larry asked.

"First, we need to get to your office and man the phones," she replied.

"Ahh...checking to see if she made airline reservations in those names, I assume," Larry said, smiling.

"Yes! If she is planning to leave the country that would explain why she needed new passports. We need to call all the major airlines, especially the ones with overseas flights. If she booked a flight using both names, then someone is going with her. It may be the reason she's here in the first place," Brenda said. "I'm real curious who Miguel is and why he's so important to her being here."

Chapter 42

STORMY AND THE REST OF HIS TEAM worked as fast as possible, checking out the warehouses in their respective grids. Some of the buildings were legitimate and open for business, others were either up for rent, or sale, or closed for whatever reason. They had no time or basis to obtain search warrants for all of the buildings. Time was a factor now, so they pushed on.

"Dakota, anything on your end?" Stormy asked, on the dedicated channel immune to the media. Captain Carter had made the arrangements for unlimited use of the channel and all HPD personnel were told to stay off of it. It wouldn't sto,p the curious officers from listening in, but that couldn't be helped.

"No, Stormy. I Still have a lot to go to, but nothing at all so far. How about you?" Dakota answered.

"No luck here, either. I'll check with the others, but they would have alerted us if something had turned up."

"Nickie, anything on your end?" Stormy asked.

"Nothing here, but I'm almost through with my grid. If it's okay, I'll swing out to the city limits on Okeechobee and see if I can spot the van. Then I'll return and help you guys in your grid, if that's okay with you," Nickie responded.

"That would be okay, but when you get back, help Dakota, she had the largest grid and could use the help," Stormy said.

"I'll keep you advised," Nickie replied.

"Captain, I'm almost finished with my grid as well as Nickie. I assume you aren't having any luck either," Stormy said, keying the radio.

"No luck here either, Stormy. I still have quite a few to go, so when you finish you can swing over and give me a hand," Captain Carter replied.

"Roger that. Nickie is going to make another run out Okeechobee Road when she is done, which should be any minute now. She will be trying to spot the van, but I doubt it's still around. Marc has probably already dumped it somewhere. I told her to help Dakota when she gets back," Stormy said.

Nickie finished her grid and headed out to Okeechobee Road. She was crestfallen as the team didn't seem to be making any ground in their search. She could feel for Linda, but only imagine the horror she was going through. She had only met Linda a few times in the course of her stint on the road, but she had been impressed with her. She seemed to be a strong woman, smart and always had a smile for others. She could only hope that the strength she had seen in Linda would be enough to sustain her until she was found. And, they would find her! They had to, failure was not an option!

As she drove west on Okeechobee Road, Nickie swept her eyes continuously, right and left, looking everywhere, trying to spot the black van. She was nearing the city limits.

Suddenly she saw an apparently abandoned strip mall on her left, bordering the canal. She noticed that one of the front windows had been boarded up with plywood; none of the stores showed any sign of activity. There were no cars in the front. A large sign was situated on the access road where you turned in. *Property for sale* it read.

She drove on past, and reaching the city limits, she made a U-turn and headed back to help Dakota in her grid search. As she approached the abandoned strip mall, she spotted a car parked in the rear. Two seconds later and she would have missed it. It was tucked in close to the rear of the building where the plywood was on the front window. Her curiosity piqued, she suddenly turned onto the access road and entered the front parking lot of the buildings.

Nickie drove slowly along the empty stores, passing the boarded up one on the end. When she reached the end of the row of buildings, she turned and drove around to the rear. As she made the turn bordering the back of the buildings, she saw the car at the other end.

It was then she spotted the amber light bar atop the car and knew immediately it was a security patrol unit. They were simply checking out the property they were contracted to do. She drove up to the rear of the car and decided to get out and ask the security officer if he had seen a black van during his rounds on patrol.

As she exited her car, she saw that the roll-up bay door was open, and her curiosity getting the better of her, began to approach. *Probably the security officer had stumbled onto a burglary and was inside checking it out,* she thought to herself.

****

Marc hadn't failed to hear the other vehicle approaching. He almost panicked but regained his composure. He could feel things beginning to spin out of control. *All of a sudden everyone has decided to pay this place a visit,* he thought to himself. *Well, there's plenty of room inside the van!*

Marc began walking to the open bay door, planning to pretend to be the security officer. As he stepped through the open door he came face to face with Nickie and saw her eyes suddenly take in the van parked in the bay, a spark of recognition suddenly flashing in her eyes. She attempted to draw her weapon, but Marc was too fast. He grabbed her wrist as her hand closed around the butt of her weapon and twisted it, causing her to jerk back off balance. Instantly Marc put her in a headlock, throwing her to the ground. Nickie struggled but was not as strong as the man on top of her. He quickly pried her hand off the weapon and jerked it from the holster. With his knees pressed hard into her back, he struck her in the back of her head with the weapon.

Nickie was suddenly engulfed in a wave of blackness, stars flashing in her eyes, and she fought hard to stay conscious. She realized that she had just come face to face with Marc, the man they were all looking for, the man who had abducted Linda. In a last-ditch effort, she quickly slid her hand down and keyed her radio. She yelled as loud as she could, "*Marc*!"

At first Marc didn't react. Her yelling his name he could understand, since it was obvious he had been recognized. Then he glanced down and saw that her hand was on her radio, and it dawned on him. She had keyed the mike and yelled his name. He ripped the radio off her waistband and threw it as far across the pavement as he could. Now time was definitely not on his side. He didn't know if anyone knew she was coming here or not, but he had to assume so. He couldn't take any chances. He had to wrap up things and do it quickly.

Looking down at Nickie, he rolled her over and felt around her waist until he found her handcuffs. He hurriedly placed them on her wrists in front of her body, not wasting time to flip her back over and cuff her behind her back. At this point he just didn't have the time.

"That was a stupid stunt girl, smart, but stupid," Marc said. "I should do more than knock your lights out for that." He took her weapon and stuffed it down the back of his waistband.

"Go ahead, guess who's on the way now. They're just down the road, so get ready," Nickie said, thankful she was able to stay conscious.

Marc ran into the front of the store and noticed that the security officer was beginning to come around. He grabbed his arms and began dragging him out to the van. The security officer began to struggle, albeit feebly. Sliding the van's side door open, Marc reached down and hefted the security officer up and into the van. He shoved him inside until he was on the far side of the van, leaving plenty of space for the others.

Rushing back inside the bay area, he approached Linda. He was taking no chances with her, he had experienced firsthand what she was capable of, his damaged forearm a testament. He straddled her body and carefully unlocked one of her cuffed wrists from the chain. Then he released the other and cuffed her wrists together in front. It didn't matter now, because in a few minutes, she, along with the other two, would be drowning in the blackness of the canal at the rear of the store. Their bodies would not be discovered for a long time, if ever, if he was lucky.

Reaching down, he lifted Linda into his arms, cradling her tightly so she couldn't struggle. He carried her over to the open van door and deposited her inside, next to the security officer, not noticing her gag had slipped down off her mouth. Then he repeated the same procedure with Nickie. Once he had put her alongside Linda, and almost out of breath, he closed the van door. Reaching around through the passenger's door, he locked it.

Marc's head was spinning. He was trying hard not to panic. Now, all that was left for him to do was drive the van out the door and then push it into the dark, foreboding canal. Once that was done, he would jump into the security officer's vehicle and get as far away from here as he could. He knew he couldn't go back to his houseboat; the police were probably already there, waiting for him to show up. He would dump the security car downtown and then try to disappear until he could find some way to get out of town. He was so close!

Chapter 43

BRENDA AND LARRY HAD ARRIVED at the FBI office in downtown Miami, and were now seated in Larry's office. An extra phone was quickly brought in by a secretary and plugged into the outlet in the wall. At Larry's request, she had downloaded all of the major airlines on his desktop computer. Larry printed out the page, which contained the phone numbers as well.

Making the first call to American Airlines, they immediately ran into a roadblock. The reservation clerk was reluctant to give out the information until Larry informed her that he was with the FBI. He was transferred to a supervisor who listened to Larry explain that they were tracking down a murderer and fugitive and that time was of the essence. Larry explained that he was only interested in whether or not a flight had been booked in the name of Miguel Soto.

The supervisor told him he would be put on hold while he checked. Within a minute the supervisor returned to the phone and advised Larry that a flight had been booked for two people, one being Miguel Soto, the other Felicia Soto. The destination was to Caracas, Venezuela, for the following day. Larry thanked him and hung up the phone. He turned to Brenda and gave a thumbs-up.

"I've got confirmation that a flight was booked for Miguel and Felicia on American," Larry said.

"Well, looks like we have a big problem, Larry," Brenda replied.

"What kind of a problem?"

"I just got off the phone with Delta, and a flight was booked with them for tomorrow also, in the same names."

"Wow! Consuelo is one smart cookie for sure. She is spending a lot of money just to keep us running in circles. It must be pretty important, whatever she is doing. I bet if we check other airlines, we'll find more bookings," Larry said.

"Let's keep calling and see just how many she has booked so far," Brenda replied.

After spending two hours and getting shut down by a couple of the airlines, they finally put their lists together and were shocked at what they saw. Consuelo had booked seats on airlines from Mexico to Canada and even overseas. There were over a dozen bookings, all within three hours of each other for the same day, tomorrow. There was no way they could cover all those airports between now and flight time the next day, even using agents from the larger cities. Now they had a big problem. How could they sift through all those bookings and narrow it down to one or two. It made sense that they would be wanting to leave the country, but Mexico? Canada? They could even use the booking to Hawaii and take another flight from there to God knows where.

They spread out the sheets of the booked flights on the

desktop and began going over them, one by one, eliminating certain ones on various merits. They could be wrong, but they had to try something.

"What about the Air Canada flight?" Larry asked. "What could be there for them. Obviously, they could sail through customs with those passports, and they could arrive there and book another flight to anywhere in the world."

"True. But we have to use our instincts, gut feelings and narrow it down to a reasonable one or two. That many we could cover with no problem," Brenda said. "Could you have someone bring us some coffee? I have a feeling we're going to need it."

Larry called the secretary and asked her to bring some sandwiches and coffee, even some bottled water.

"We have to assume they will be traveling as man and wife, since the passports have the same last name. That means they will be together wherever they go. It will surely help us spot them at whatever airport we get lucky enough to be at," Brenda said, her eyes jumping from one sheet of paper to another, trying to find a clue as to where they would be tomorrow.

The secretary returned after about thirty minutes, bringing an urn of coffee and a tray of assorted sandwiches. They thanked her and decided to take a quick break and refuel, having not eaten hardly anything for hours. Larry poured Brenda a cup of coffee and one for himself. They each took a sandwich and sat down to eat.

Brenda advised Larry that she had to call her SAC in Washington and bring him up to speed on what they had learned so far. Larry nodded to his desk and phone, and she moved into his seat behind the desk. After she had completed the call, bringing her boss up to date, she grabbed another sandwich, suddenly realizing how hungry she was. Once they finished taking a break and eating, they went back to the table and began perusing the flights once again, hoping against hope that they would see something that would give them a clue as to where Consuelo was going.

Finally, after several grueling hours, they had narrowed the list down to two airports, Miami and Jacksonville. Miami because they were still here and wouldn't think that the Feds would believe they would attempt to leave from the most obvious place. Jacksonville, because she would be hoping that the red herrings she was throwing out – Canada and Mexico, even Hawaii – would prompt them to head there. Besides, she would not want to be in the air that long, seeing as how it would give the Feds more time to prepare agents at the other airports.

"I can have a couple of my agents stake out the Miami Airport, if you want to go to Jacksonville. If we're wrong, and they went elsewhere, at least we made a choice. A choice with not much to go on," Larry said.

"I agree. We can take the agency jet I flew down on and head up to Jacksonville tomorrow, early, so we can get the layout of the airport and the terminal they would be departing from. We'll need an inconspicuous surveillance point, because if Consuelo is as smart as she has been so far, she will spot us quickly. She may even be headed there now and scoping out the terminal. Also, I'm sure they'll have disguises," Brenda said, not entirely comfortable with their choices.

"May I make a suggestion, Brenda?" Asked Larry.

"Sure, what is it?"

"Let's leave tonight. We can be there in two hours, get a room, and after dinner find a good surveillance point, or two."

"Great idea. If you'll drive me back to the Marriott, I'll grab a few things and we can head to MIA. I'll call ahead and have the pilots make sure the jet is fueled up and ready to go," Brenda said.

Gathering up all the flight schedules and times, Larry shut off the office lights, and they headed out the door.

Chapter 44

AT TEN MINUTES BEFORE SEVEN that evening, there was a knock on the warehouse door. Pepe was just finishing up a meal delivered from a nearby take-out restaurant. He had eaten better food, but he needed to be here to greet the *actor* when he arrived. His men had all dressed for the part and had the warehouse floor set up with cameras and boom mikes. It was all for show of course, but the actor wouldn't know that. He would think that he was filming a jailbreak scene, which he really was.

"Welcome, I can see you are a prompt man," Pepe said with a big smile, gesturing for the actor to enter the warehouse. "What is your name, if I may ask. For the credits of course. I ask because some actors use a stage name as opposed to their real moniker."

"Thank you, sir, for giving me a chance to show you what I can do. I'm sure you'll be satisfied with my performance. My real name is Tomas Fernandez, but I prefer to use my stage name, for the credits of course."

"Okay, and what is your stage name?" Pepe asked, as if he really cared. He would never see this guy again after tonight, and of course there would be no movie about a jail-break, but Tomas didn't know that.

"I use the name Sean Conner's," Tomas replied, with a flair as if it meant something to Pepe.

"Great stage name, Tomas, great name," Pepe replied, stoking Tomas' ego and thinking to himself, "*yeah, a play on James Bond. Pathetic, but so what, as long as he gets the job done.*"

Tomas, or Sean as he would have it, was led to the *Wardrobe* section of the warehouse. He found a rack with several hanging orange jump suits, various sizes and all emblazoned with MDCJ, Miami Dade County Jail, on the back. He was instructed to try them on until he found one that fit. Pepe, already knowing the man's size from the description Lily had given him, smiled and played along. Once Tomas had settled on a jumpsuit, he approached Pepe and advised him he was ready. Pepe, still playing the part to keep Tomas in the dark, instructed him to go to *Makeup*. If he was breaking out of a jail, he had to have a little dirt on his hands and face. Pepe didn't know if that was true or not, but it seemed like the right thing to say to an actor.

"So, what jail will I be breaking out of and where is my script?" Tomas asked, after returning from the phony Makeup section.

"Actually, we have decided to change the script...it was at a moment's notice, so we couldn't advise you until you arrived," Pepe replied.

"Then why am I going to be wearing a prisoner's jumpsuit?"

"Well, the part is still the same, only you won't be

breaking out of jail. You will be on location while a prisoner transport is *en route.* You will be switching places with another prisoner actor who is being sprung from the transport van. Actually, you will be changing clothes with the other prisoner, to throw off the cop actors when they begin to look for you. I hope you don't have a problem with the change, do you?" Pepe asked, forcing a concerned look on his face.

"Oh, no sir, not at all. After all, I'm playing an important role, right?" Tomas asked.

"Absolutely Sean. Absolutely," Pepe replied. "That's why I made the changes to the script. A man of your talent needs a bigger role. Although you won't be wearing the jumpsuit on location, I need you in it now, to get in character. Now, if you're ready, let's go over your lines."

Somewhat mollified, Sean beamed at Pepe, reveling in his supposedly higher talent.

Two SUV's were driven into the warehouse. One of Pepe's men donned a jumpsuit and got into one of the vehicles. Sean was directed to get into the other. Pepe walked over and pretended to make sure both parties were in place. Then, he walked over to a fake director's chair, a bullhorn sitting beside it. Sean, having been briefed, sat in the SUV, trying to suppress a smile. He felt this was going to be his big break.

"Action!" Pepe spoke through the bullhorn.

"Scene fourteen, take one," one of Pepe's men said, as he clapped up and down on a prop board.

The driver of the SUV containing Pepe's man, revved the engine a couple of times, insinuating a vehicle driving. Suddenly the engine stopped and the door opened, Pepe's man in the jumpsuit climbed out and ran to the other SUV. He opened the door and quickly entered the vehicle. Sean told the man lines Pepe had given him earlier, "Get out of the jumpsuit."

The two men changed clothes and Sean jumped out of the van, wearing the jumpsuit, and ran out of camera range, then stopped.

"Too slow. Let's do it again," Pepe said.

For the next twenty minutes Pepe made Sean and his men repeat the scene, pretending that as a director he wanted it to be perfect. Actually Pepe was satisfied with the first run, but he had to play the part of a perfectionist – a director.

"Okay, it's a wrap! Great job guys," Pepe said.

It was now seven thirty and four of Pepe's men were already at the ambush site. They hadn't been present for the *screen test*. They had been given the location of a nearby park and were to wait for Pepe.

When the order came to go into action, one man would be stationed in his car a mile from the actual scene, ready to radio ahead to the others that the transport van was on its way. Another man would be carrying an AR15 and standing on the sidewalk on the driver's side. The next man would be on the opposite sidewalk with a walker, pretending to be an old man. The last man, the most important one, would be inside the manhole in the middle of the street. It would take twenty minutes for him to get there and get set up with his actor on site.

"Alright, guys. Load up the cameras and head for the shooting site" Pepe said, having told his guys with the cameras to stay at the warehouse. They wouldn't be needed at the site, the other four were all he needed. He realized he had to hurry. He didn't want the transport vehicle to get there before they were set up or all the planning would be in vain, the job a bust.

"Does this mean I have the part?" Sean asked Pepe.

"Oh yeah Sean, you have the part. Great acting kid… now let's get going," Pepe said.

Sean, now wearing gray sweat pants and a gray sweat shirt, was told to get into the back seat of the SUV parked inside the warehouse. Pepe got into the driver's seat and started the engine. He pulled out of the warehouse and began the drive to south Miami.

Chapter 45

"HEY, DID YOU GUYS HEAR THAT?" Dakota asked on the dedicated channel.

"Yeah, it sounded like Nickie yelling Marc's name. Stormy replied. "Hang on while I attempt to raise her."

Stormy keyed the radio and called Nickie several times, with no answer. He told Dakota and Captain Carter to abandon their grids and to meet him at Okeechobee Road and the Palmetto Expressway, ASAP.

While driving to the Palmetto, Stormy became increasingly worried. The yell into the radio was sudden and unexpected. Nickie wouldn't have done that unless she was in trouble. Then, there was her not answering her radio, another indicator that something was not right. He felt a cold feeling in the pit of his stomach – a feeling that they needed to find Nickie and Linda as quickly as possible. Time could very well be running out for both of them.

When he arrived at the Palmetto, he saw that Dakota was already there, parked on the shoulder of the road, on the north side. He quickly pulled in behind her and got out of his car. She exited also and they met at the rear of her car.

"What do you think, Stormy? Is Nickie in trouble?" Dakota asked, the concern written all over her face.

"It definitely was a call targeted for us to hear. It sounded like she was sending us an alarm call. I think she found Marc and is now in trouble," Stormy replied.

"Yeah, I didn't find her to be one that would panic easily. She must have stumbled onto Marc, and by not answering her radio, she has to be in serious trouble. We need to find her, and find her quickly," Dakota said.

"Captain, you getting close?" Stormy asked, keying his radio.

"Got you in sight. Hang on," Captain Carter responded.

"What do you make of that call from Nickie, Stormy?" Captain Carter asked, once he joined them at the rear of Dakota's car.

"I think she stumbled onto Marc. Maybe she spotted the van and after stopping it, was overcome by Marc before she could call for help," Stormy replied.

"Yeah, but she did manage to yell his name into the radio, so she had that one shot. Evidently he was able to stop her before she could say more," Dakota chimed in.

"Do we have any idea where she was heading?" Carter asked.

"She finished her grid before us and said she was going to drive west on Okeechobee to the city limits, to take another shot at finding the van," Stormy replied.

"Then, that's where we need to go, and fast. Don't worry about lights and sirens now, in fact, they may help us if Marc hears them before he can do anything to her," Captain Carter said.

"I have a feeling that we may find Linda there also,"

Dakota said.

"Let's pray you're right, Dakota, and that they both are unharmed," Stormy said.

All three of them jumped into their cars, and with blue lights on, the dash lit up, sirens screaming, the sped off west on Okeechobee Road. They had no idea where they were going, but if Nickie had told them she was headed that way, then they should find her somewhere down the road. That is unless, she turned off onto another road or street. Then all bets were off on finding her quickly.

It was all Dakota could do to hold it together, even as tough as she was. She could feel the tears trying to surface but refused to let that happen. She was close to Linda but only knew Nickie from a few encounters on the road before she joined the Bureau. She couldn't bear the thought of losing either one of them.

"Stormy, I think now is the time to call in reinforcements. I'm going to have three units head our way, just in case," Captain Carter spoke into the radio.

"I think that's a good idea, Captain. More eyes to try to find them, not to mention that it's after seven and darkness will be falling soon. That will make it even harder to spot them," Stormy replied.

"I'm going to pull over and wait for the units. I'll have to give them a rundown on what and who we're looking for. Once they get and know the facts, we'll head you way," Captain Carter said.

"Okay, Dakota and I will keep going. If we find anything, you'll hear from us immediately," Stormy said.

Stormy and Dakota continued speeding west on Okeechobee Road, lights flashing and sirens wailing. Both were scanning both sides of the road frantically as they drove, hoping and praying that they would find Nickie, and hopefully Linda, in time.

Chapter 46

AT SEVEN ON THE DOT, Pablo called and advised Consuelo that he was *en route* with a car for her. She told him where she was staying and to meet her there. He knew the area and told her he would be there in fifteen minutes, as he had been *en route* for the past fifteen already.

Consuelo placed the few things she would need in her over-sized handbag. She made sure the passports were inside. The few clothes and shoes she had, she placed in a small satchel she had picked up earlier. She was traveling light and anxious to make the rendezvous with Pepe in a couple of hours. She was ready to pick up Juan, The Scorpion, and get out of this hot and crowded city, even the state. She only hoped that by booking nearly a dozen airlines that she would be able to throw a kink into the search she knew the Feds were performing now.

She still had no idea how they had found out she was in Florida, but they had, and were intent on nabbing her. She wasn't going to let that happen. She was, and would be, one step ahead of them all the way. She had to be!

It was only about a twenty-minute drive to the area where Pepe wanted her. When Pablo arrived she would treat him to dinner and then pay for an Uber to take him back to Hialeah. She had been puzzled why Pablo had been so quick to refuse helping her with springing Juan. Maybe he was telling the truth...maybe he didn't have a clue how to carry out such a precise plan. Well, too bad. He would be missing out on a big payday. She had checked her account and saw that Juan had transferred the balance of the money, as promised. Now she would have to do the same for Pepe. A deal was a deal, and she intended to follow through with her end. She had decided to wait until Pepe had actually sprung Juan before transferring the balance she owed him. Again, a deal was a deal, and his final balance depended on him being able to spring Juan, *and* deliver him to her.

****

Pablo pulled up in front of the hotel, and noticed Consuelo standing off to the side of the building. He thought it strange that she had on sunglasses when darkness would soon be falling. He didn't give it another thought as he tooted the horn, causing her to look up in recognition. She walked briskly to the car, head tilted slightly down. Pablo leaned over and opened the door for her. Consuelo climbed into the car, a black, two-year-old Chrysler 300.

"I like it. It will do just fine, Pablo," Consuelo said, looking around the interior.

"I figured you would want something black, not too fancy, but comfortable," Pablo said.

"You did good! It will work out perfect. Now, are you ready for some dinner? My treat, and I'll pay for your ride back home," Consuelo said.

"Where would you like to have dinner?" Pablo asked.

"You pick. I'm not too choosy tonight."

"There's a little place about a mile from here. I've eaten there before, and it's really good. It's called Paladin's Steak House," Pablo said.

"Sounds good to me...I could go for a good rib-eye," Consuelo replied.

Once they arrived and parked the car, Consuelo could feel her belly rumbling, causing her to realize she hadn't eaten in hours. They entered the restaurant and were quickly seated by a front window. The hostess left menus on the table and advised them a server would be over shortly. They briefly scanned the menu, and as they settled on what they wanted, the server arrived, glasses of water in hand.

"Are you ready to order or do you want me to come back?" she asked.

"No, we're ready," Consuelo replied.

She and Pablo both ordered the rib-eye steaks with baked potatoes and green beans. The server collected the menus and left to turn in the order. Consuelo turned to Pablo and asked, "So why didn't you take the job?"

"I told you, it's not in my area of expertise," Pablo replied, telling a half-lie. It *wasn't* his forte, but that wasn't the real reason he turned her down.

"Well, too bad. Could have been a big payday for you. Anyway, thanks for putting me in touch with Pepe...he seems to know what he's doing."

"That's why I put you on to him. He knows more about

that kind of stuff than I do," Pablo said, taking a sip of water.

"Anyway, I'm giving you ten K for referring him to me...call it a finder's fee of sorts," Consuelo said, with a sincere laugh.

The server arrived with their steaks, the aroma of the still sizzling meat assaulting their senses. When the server had left, they immediately began eating their meal, all thoughts of talking over for the next few minutes, at least. Once they had finished and ordered coffee, Pablo asked, "Are you really breaking *El Scorpion* out?"

"No, Pablo, Pepe is breaking him out. I'm just collecting him once he does."

"Okay. Just be careful. Not with Pepe, with *El Scorpion*. I owe you and don't want to see you get hurt, okay?" Pablo said.

"Oh, I'll be fine, Pablo. But thanks for your concern," she replied, glancing at her wristwatch.

"I guess you need to get going. How am I getting back to Hialeah?" Pablo asked.

"Use your phone and call an Uber driver. Here's a hundred to cover it, and I'll get the ten K to you before long," Consuelo said, handing over a hundred-dollar bill.

Consuelo left the money for the bill with an ample tip. She and Pablo walked outside the restaurant. She gave him a hug and said, "Call the Uber. I'll be in touch." She turned and walked to the car.

She was probably going to be a little early for her meet with Pepe, but better than being late.

Chapter 47

THE GULFSTREAM GOVERNMENT JET took off about the time Pablo and Consuelo were finishing their dinner. The plane leveled out at eighteen thousand feet, no need to be higher since the flight was of such a short duration. It wouldn't take long before they would be descending as it was only about an hour and a half flight from Miami to Jacksonville, from take-off to landing.

Brenda had called ahead and made reservations at the hotel at the airport for the two of them. It would make it a lot easier to plan their observation points and have dinner, than to have to get rooms away from the airport. By leaving now they had all night to do what they had to, with no time constraints. But, they would have to be prepared for the next morning and hope they had selected the airport that Consuelo and her mystery guest would be leaving from.

It seemed they had barely taken off their seat belts and had a drink before the pilot advised them to buckle up again. They would be landing in fifteen minutes.

"How confident are you that we made the correct choice?" Larry asked, as he buckled his seat belt.

"Based on certain criteria and through some pertinent

eliminations on the other airports, I give us about an eighty percent probability that we chose correctly," Brenda replied.

"That seems like pretty good odds. I guess we'll know one way or another in the morning," Larry said, looking out the window at the lights of Jacksonville.

The plane made such a smooth landing they barely felt the wheels touch down, the reverse thrust of the jet engines their first indication they were on the ground.

Once the Gulfstream had taxied into a designated hangar reserved for certain government agencies, the ramp was lowered and the two agents deplaned. They both had packed lightly, a small carry-on for each of them. At the bottom of the stairs a small tram was waiting for them. They climbed on, their bags in their laps, and were driven to the main terminal.

The first thing they did was check in at the on-site hotel, declining an offer from a redcap to take their bags up for them. Since they both had their weapons inside, they wouldn't take the chance, besides, the bags hardly weighed anything. Brenda had requested and given adjoining rooms. They each went into their respective rooms to freshen up, intending to have a late dinner.

An hour later they rode the elevator down to the main floor and found a restaurant nearby. Once inside they were seated among the rest of the travelers, tourists and even a flight crew. Brenda opted to eat light, a salad and soup. Larry was a little bolder, choosing a double cheeseburger and fries. Not the healthiest, but what he was craving after the flight.

"Where do we want to start looking for the best vantage

point?" Larry asked, taking a sip of his coke to wash down a big bite of burger.

"Well, first of all, you have a splash of mustard on your upper lip," Brenda said, laughing.

"Thanks, that was on purpose," Larry said, laughing also, picking up his napkin and wiping his lip.

"I think the best strategy will be to have one of us on the second level since we could cover more area from there. Also, one of us needs to be on the ground floor in case we're spotted and they take off," Brenda said.

"Sounds good to me. I'll take the lower level, since I can run faster, you know, not being in heels and all," Larry said, grinning.

"Ha ha...for your information, I plan to have on flats," Brenda said. "But, seriously, we need to both go to the second level and determine the best vantage point to see the gate they will be departing from. Then, we can go to the ground level and find the best observation point for you, one that will keep you from being seen by them, but at the same time allowing you to watch the gate for them."

"Once we see them, don't you think it'll be better if we let them board, then delay the flight while we board and take them?" Larry asked.

"I thought of that, but what if they are armed in some way. You know how easy it is to get those 3-D printed guns through the scanners. I can't jeopardize any of the safety of those passengers in a scenario like that."

"Yeah, I didn't really think of that. You're right. It'll be better to approach them before they board. Hopefully, without them seeing us first, of course. Then they'll probably split up and try to get lost in the crowd," Larry said.

"I'll get with security here and give them a heads-up that we're here to pick up a fugitive and have one of them with us to radio a lock-down on the exit doors if they do show, and try to flee," Brenda said, her mind racing to cover all angles.

They finished their meal, paid the check and headed out to the escalators to reach the second level.

"Over there is Gate Fourteen, the one they'll have to go through to get to the boarding area," Brenda said, nodding in the direction of the gate.

"Yeah, pretty clear view from up here. You get to have all the fun," Larry said.

"Okay, let's go and find you a nice spot downstairs."

They took the escalator down and walked all around the area by Gate Fourteen, frustrated at not finding a good spot to watch from. Suddenly Brenda stopped!

"What's the matter, Brenda?" Larry asked, alarmed at her sudden stop.

"You see that guy over there?" Brenda said, pointing in the general direction of the gate.

Larry looked over and saw a dozen or more guys. He knew she had spotted something, so he had to look closer. Then it hit him. The airport janitor!

"Yeah, I see what you mean. Let's get with the janitorial service for the airport and arrange for me a work shirt and pants," Larry said. "But, if Consuelo is as smart as she has been, it may be a little too obvious."

"If you have a better idea, I'm all ears," Brenda said.

"Well, there's no good spots down here, so let's go with it. I'll try to clean my way around with my back to them as much as possible. You can keep me apprised via my ear piece if they show. At least if they do, I can be on them before they can get very far," Larry said.

They went to the security office and spoke with the Lt. In charge. Brenda and Larry produced their FBI identification and explained that they were staking out the possibility of a wanted fugitive leaving from JAX airport. She told him she would like one of their men to be with her the next morning, just in case the fugitive fled and they needed to have the exits locked down. The main question on the Lieutenant's mind was a valid one, were the fugitives dangerous, and was there any danger to the populace of the airport. Brenda didn't lie to him. She told him she didn't think so but couldn't give any guarantees. As far as being armed, it would be very unlikely due to the scanners and the fugitives not wanting to alert TSA. The Lieutenant seemed to be satisfied with the answer and agreed to have one of his men meet her at six in the morning, in his office. There she would explain everything to the man who would be assigned to her.

Next Brenda asked the Lieutenant if he could get in touch with the janitorial services for the airport and arrange for Larry to be fitted with a logo emblazoned work shirt and a pair of pants. The Lieutenant raised his eyebrows but picked up the phone and made a call.

Within ten minutes a supervisor for the janitorial services arrived. He was not told of the ongoing operation by the FBI, rather he was asked to bring up a shirt and pants for Larry. The supervisor didn't ask any questions and left, promising to be back within fifteen minutes. Larry had given the supervisor his sizes, so there was no need for Larry to go with the man. Sure enough, the supervisor was back in fifteen minutes with the clothing. Larry tried on the shirt over his own. It was just loose enough to fit.

"I think you've found your calling, Larry," Brenda said, emitting a big laugh.

"Yeah, I would probably make more money," Larry muttered, then grinning.

With the major details resolved – the vantage points for observing, the janitor's shirt for Larry, and the arrangement for airport security to supply a man – they decided to call it a night. Brenda advised Larry that they should meet back here at the restaurant at five in the morning, in time to have some breakfast before meeting in the airport security office. It was going to be a busy day.

Chapter 48

J**UST AS PEPE ARRIVED** at the rendezvous point where his men were waiting, several blocks away from the street the ambush would occur, his cell rang. He rolled down his window and told his men to give him a minute.

"Pepe, there's going to be about a thirty-minute delay on the transport," his cousin, the contact in the Transportation Division said.

"I don't have a problem with that, but why the delay?" Pepe asked.

"Something to do with the availability of the transport vehicle. Seems there was a mix-up in scheduling, so they're bringing in another vehicle."

"Do me a favor and call once they are on the way. I don't want my men standing around on a residential street at this time of the night. The residents may get suspicious and call it in," Pepe said.

"I'll call just as soon as they leave. It'll take them probably twenty minutes to reach your location…gotta go, someone coming...I'll call."

Pepe heard the dial tone as his cousin hung up. He knew that his cousin was taking a big risk by calling from work, but he was paying him good money for taking that risk. He exited his car and walked over to his men. They had pulled their car into a city park at Pepe's orders and waited for him to arrive. If a Metro Dade deputy happened to drive by and stop, he would explain that one of the cars wouldn't start and they had called to give them a jump.

"Julio, open the hood of your car and take these jumper cables and hang them over the front."

The man did as he was told, without question. He knew that his boss, Pepe, knew what he was doing at all times and they knew not to question him.

"This is just in case an officer drives by and stops. I'll tell him you needed a jump," Pepe told Julio, not really needing to give an explanation, but doing so anyway.

They had to kill about thirty minutes before getting in position. The time passed fairly quickly, his men smoking and telling jokes, keeping their voices down. Even the laughter at the jokes was kept at low volume. His men knew their business and didn't want to attract attention.

One of the men, a new one to the group, happened to notice the actor sitting in the back seat of Pepe's car and asked, "Who's the new dude?"

"He's going to be playing a part in this escapade. That's all you need to know. He'll be with me. Pepe, keeping his voice low to keep the actor in the car from overhearing, told his men the part the actor would play. The men shook their heads in wonder at the audacity of the plan.

"So, he thinks we're going to be filming everything, like in a real movie," one of the men whispered.

"He will actually be a vital part of this job. He'll be running away from the scene in our target's orange jumpsuit, and you guys are to pick him up when you leave the area," Pepe said.

"Once he hears he news of the breakout and realizes there was no filming, how do you know he won't talk?" One of the men asked.

"Because you're going to take him back to the warehouse and once I get there, I'm going to explain to him what will happen to him and any family he has, if he talks. Of course he still gets paid. That should lessen his wounded pride somewhat," Pepe said.

Pepe's phone chirped and he walked over to the front of his car to answer. He saw the caller I.D. and recognized Consuelo's number. She was smart, her name didn't show up on the screen, only the number.

"I'm here, at the street location you sent me. I'm parked in front of a closed cafe," Consuelo said when Pepe answered.

"Sit tight. I'll give you a heads-up once I'm ready to bring you your package," Pepe said, referring to *El Scorpion.*

"Alright, men, let's get into your positions. It shouldn't be long now before the action starts. Manny is already in position and will call when the transport is a mile from here. Be alert and try to be inconspicuous. We don't need a nosy neighbor calling the police," Pepe said.

The men had already rehearsed their positions back in the warehouse and what each would do, so he didn't need to be there. He would be a block away, waiting for one of his men to rush Juan to his car.

Now, within about thirty minutes, everything should come together.

Chapter 49

SEVERAL HIALEAH PATROL UNITS were speeding towards Okeechobee Road, their overheads flashing and sirens screaming. The call from dispatch had chosen three units to proceed, per Captain Carter's orders, to meet him at the Palmetto overpass and Okeechobee Road. The units had no idea, since dispatch hadn't told them, what they were racing to, other than meeting with Captain Carter, Commander of the Detective Bureau. It would take most of them at least ten minutes to reach Okeechobee Road as they all had been in the North end of town, either on patrol or on a traffic stop.

When the call came out, one officer threw the driver's license into the car he had just stopped for speeding, jumped into his unit and sped off. The driver, certainly confused as to what had just happened, didn't complain about the license flying into his window, since he wouldn't be getting a citation on this day.

Stormy and Dakota continued driving westward on Okeechobee Road, in their individual cars, frantically searching for Nickie and desperate to spot her car. Thankfully, traffic was fairly light, and the few cars that were on the road pulled off to the right after seeing the flashing blue strobes in the grills of the cars behind them.

****

Marc ran around and jumped into the driver's seat of the van and started the engine. Putting it into reverse he slowly backed out of the bay, turning the steering wheel to the left. Before he could put it into the drive position, he suddenly sensed something flying over the top of his head. Linda, rising up from the back of the van, leaned forward and swiftly looped her cuffed wrists up and over Marc's head, coming to rest on his neck. Pulling back with all her might, she felt Marc suddenly turn loose of the wheel to try to dislodge her hands on his neck.

With the van still in reverse, Marc floored the gas pedal, the tires spinning, suddenly gripping the pavement and lurching backwards. With the wheels still turned, the van slammed into the security patrol vehicle. The abrupt stop caused Linda to fall to her knees, tightening her grip on Marc's neck. Then the momentum caused her to slide forward, loosening her grip just enough for Marc to get his hands between her wrists and his neck.

After pulling Linda's hands over his head, Marc shoved the vehicle into park. He leaned around and grabbed Linda's head and slammed it into the console. Stunned, Linda fell back to the floor. Nickie attempted to reach up and grab Marc but couldn't make the stretch over Linda's body.

Marc pulled the weapon he had taken from Nickie from his rear waistband. Turning to Nickie and Linda, he said,

"I ought to shoot both of you and make things a lot easier. But, I won't, I want you to slowly drown, knowing there is nothing you can do to escape."

Marc put the van into drive and gave it the gas. But the wheels only spun, the rear bumper caught on the front of the security vehicle. "Damn, I just can't catch a breake" he thought, exiting the van to try to dislodge the two vehicles.

Running to the rear of the two intertwined vehicles, he saw that they were locked together tightly. The only thing he could do was run into the bay and grab the crowbar he had seen days earlier.

After fetching it, he ran back to the van, quickly glancing inside to make sure his victims were still in place, and began the laborious job of dislodging the two bumpers. One was fiberglass, so he was confident that he could just rip it off in pieces. That would still take time, time that he was running out of now. But he couldn't quit; he was so close.

Marc was in a sweat now, literally, and began furiously swinging the crowbar at the fiberglass bumper of the car, striking it over and over. He began to see the cracks splintering along the top of the bumper, and soon it began to break off into pieces. Finally, the bumper snapped off, and the van was free. He tossed the crowbar to the ground and ran to the front of the van. Once in the driver's seat, he put the gear into drive and headed to the far end of the strip mall, where the canal made the curve around the building. He drove the van up to the edge and got out, after putting the gear shift in neutral. Taking a fast look down Okeechobee Road, and seeing no lights or attention directed his way, he walked to the rear of the van and began pushing it, inching it ever closer to the edge of the foreboding canal.

****

As Stormy and Dakota were leaving the main warehouses and businesses behind, empty spaces flashing past them, they worried that they had missed something. Nickie had surely headed this way, unless she had taken a turn to the right into some of the outer warehouses before getting this far. Still, they kept going, their intention to turn around once they reached the city limits and there was no sighting of Nickie or her vehicle. It was still light enough to see, but darkness was not far off. Then, it would make finding Nickie even harder.

Suddenly, Stormy spotted an abandoned strip mall ahead on his left. He couldn't see any vehicles, so they kept driving on past the mall. As they passed it, Stormy happened to glance back. To his amazement, he saw an old black van perched on the edge of a canal, a man behind it pushing. Shouting to Dakota over the radio, he spun his steering wheel, almost losing control of his car and almost hitting an oncoming vehicle. He straightened the car out and floored the gas, heading the quarter-mile back to the mall. Dakota made the same maneuver and was right on his tail.

"Captain, get out here to the edge of the city limits as fast as you can. There's an abandoned strip mall on the left. We spotted the van in the rear, and I believe Marc is here with it," Stormy shouted into his radio.

Chapter 50

PEPE MADE SURE HIS MEN were ready to be in place and that there weren't any neighbors out and about. There was a street light at the end of the block casting a soft glow, but the area where his men were to be placed was just out of the lighted area. He told his men to remain alert until he got word from Manny that the transport vehicle was approaching, then they were to take their assigned places.

Pepe waited in his SUV, parked around the block near an empty lot. Sean, the actor, sat quietly in the back seat. No one talked, each with their own thoughts as to what was going to occur in the next twenty or thirty minutes. Pepe was calm and confident that everything would proceed according to plan. He was never one to consider an operation going south, rather more positive that success would be the outcome. He also was musing about the huge sum of money he was making from this deal; it was a lot more than he had ever made on any one job. Pepe decided that he probably should send Pablo a little token of his appreciation for referring the job to him, maybe ten thousand. Suddenly he was jolted from his thoughts with the chirping of his cell.

"Boss, the vehicle is in sight now. Should be in your area in about two minutes," Manny said when Pepe answered.

"Okay, Manny, head on back to the warehouse. We have it from here on," Pepe replied.

"Alright, men, time for action. Take your places," Pepe said through the ear pieces his men wore.

The transport van turned down the quiet residential street, a shortcut to the rear of the holding facility where they were taking Juan. Being a residential area, they drove at a speed of about twenty miles per hour. They drove under the street light and were soon in the darkened area of the block. As they drove over the manhole cover in the middle of the street, about halfway down the block, an old man with a walker suddenly stepped out in front of them, causing the driver to slam on the brakes.

"Hey, watch where you're going, old man. I almost ran over you," the transport driver yelled, although the windows were up according to protocol, and the old man probably couldn't hear him.

The old man clutched his chest at the close call and slowly began to shuffle across the street, then changing his mind, turned and walked back across in front of the vehicle to the curb he had stepped out from. The driver in the transport van just shook his head, waiting patiently for the old man to make up his mind which way he was going.

While this was playing out, one of Pepe's men was down inside the manhole, the cover pulled almost closed over him. When he heard the transport slam on its brakes, he quickly raised the manhole cover and slid it to one side on the pavement. Grasping the two chains that had been welded earlier to the inside rim, he wrapped both around the rear axle of the transport van and hooked them together securely He then ducked back down inside the manhole.

When the old man finally made it back to the sidewalk, the driver was just about to move on when out of the corner of his eye he spotted a man on the opposite side of the narrow street, stepping out of the shadows. What really caught his eye was the AR-15 the man was cradling. The man began walking towards the van as he leveled the weapon towards the driver. The driver of the van floored the gas, the powerful engine causing the van to suddenly surge forward. When the van was almost past the man with the weapon, the chains affixed to the rear axle suddenly became taut, causing the van to come to a sudden stop, the rear axle separating from the body of the vehicle. The sudden stop caused the airbags to go off, stunning the driver and his partner, also hindering them from drawing their weapons. By the time they could drag down the airbags from their faces and attempt to draw their weapons, the man with the AR-15 was standing outside the driver's window, aiming the weapon at his face. The old man had discarded the walker and also had a weapon aimed at his partner in the passenger's seat. The driver and his partner quickly raised their hands, and glanced back at their prisoner in the rear, who for some reason, was smiling. They realized then that this was an ambush to break out their prisoner.

The man with the AR-15 walked over to the rear door of the van, raised the stock and smashed out the window. After using the butt of the AR-15 to knock the driver out, he reached inside the window and unlocked the doors. He motioned for Juan to exit the van, quickly. During this action, Pepe's other man on the passenger's side, motioned for the man to roll down the window. Once he did, he slammed him in the temple with the butt of his gun, rendering the guard unconscious. He then walked around past the front of the van, his weapon leveled at the windshield, until he was at the driver's door. Pepe had given strict orders that there were to be no shots fired. Opening the drivers door he reached inside and smashed the radio on the dash, then took the two handheld radios from the two men. It would buy them a little time, but it wouldn't be long before one of the residents would look outside to see what all the commotion was.

The man holding the AR-15 grabbed Juan by the arm and told him to follow him. They broke into a run, heading down the block to where Pepe was parked. As the other man grabbed the handheld radios, he ran in the opposite direction to his car around the corner.

Lights began to come on in several houses, and a couple of neighbors ventured outside to see what was going on. By this time, both of Pepe's men and Juan had vanished, and the neighbors assumed that an accident had happened. One of them called 911, while another went out to the van to render aid to the supposedly injured people inside.

When Juan and the man with the AR-15 reached Pepe's SUV, the rear door was already open. Pepe urged Juan inside quickly. The other man jumped into the passenger's seat, stashing the AR-15 behind the seat.

"There's no time to waste, Senor. Change clothes with the man next to you, and do it quickly!" Pepe said to Juan.

Juan looked at the other man in the rear with him and was amazed at how much the resemblance was to him. The other man was already in the process of stripping off his clothes, and Juan swiftly followed suit. Within sixty seconds they had changed clothes. The other man, smiling at Juan, jumped out of the SUV. On cue, he ran down the street, in the direction that Juan had just come from.

Pepe started the SUV and headed in the opposite direction. He drove toward the location where Consuelo was waiting. The whole incident had only taken about three minutes.

As Sean ran, playing the part he was sure was being filmed, he tried to stay in character, but couldn't keep the smile off his face. This was going to be his ticket to many other movies, he just knew it.

As soon as he approached the wrecked van, he saw a few people milling about in the street, some obviously tending to the *supposedly* injured people in the van. He had to admit, it was a heck of a scene. He ran past the people as he had been instructed according to the script. When he turned the corner at the end of the block, and was out of sight of the neighbors in the street, he was picked up by Pepe's man, who was waiting for him.

Everyone in the street had seen the man running away, adorned in the orange jumpsuit that they knew prisoners wore. They all figured that someone had broken out of the holding facility a few blocks away. It had happened before.

When Metro-Dade deputies arrived on the scene, EMS arriving just behind them, the driver and guard had come to their senses and were standing outside the van. They explained what had happened, and the deputies began taking statements from the residents who had ventured outside. All of the residents told the same story. Especially about the prisoner in the orange jumpsuit running away from the scene. After determining that the prisoner the van had been transporting had escaped, Eagle one, the MDP helicopter, was called for, to use their search lights in the area. That search was destined to be in vain as the man in the orange jumpsuit was already several miles away, riding with Pepe's man.

Pepe met up with Consuelo without incident within two minutes. Juan was swiftly ushered out of the SUV and into Consuelo's car. No words were spoken, and both vehicles sped off in different directions.

Chapter 51

MARC HEARD THE SOUND of the sirens off in the distance on Okeechobee Road, heading his way. He was in full-blown panic mode now, but he had to push the van into the canal. He strained and pushed as hard as he could, but something was hindering the van from rolling forward into the canal. He ran around to the front of the vehicle and spotted a cinder block someone had thrown out in front of the passenger's tire. He quickly shoved it out of the way and ran back to the rear of the van, where he began pushing hard. The van began to move forward now that the block had been removed, slowly at first, but picking up speed.

The van rolled over the edge of the canal, but suddenly it stopped as the undercarriage hung up on the berm. Marc realized that he didn't have the time to push it any longer. He had watched as the two unmarked police cars sped past the mall. Hoping they were going to keep heading away, he watched them for a few seconds. Then, to his dismay, he watched as first one, then the other, made a high-speed maneuver and turned around, heading back towards him.

Time was up! He ran to the security patrol car. Although the bumper was off, the car was still drivable. Then he had an epiphany. Looking inside Nickie's unmarked car, he saw that she had left the keys inside and had left the car running. This was even better than he expected. This car was surely faster than the security car, and he could monitor the radio for any pursuit.

Jumping into the driver's seat, he suddenly winched, feeling Nickie's weapon in his back waistband where he had returned it in the van. He reached back and jerked it out, placing it on the passenger's seat. Slamming the car into drive, he burnt rubber and headed out towards Okeechobee Road. Making a quick turn back towards Hialeah, the car fishtailing, he straightened it out and floored the gas. As he drove east on Okeechobee, he realized that he could have used the car on his way out to nudge the van over into the canal. Too late now, he had to get away.

****

As Stormy and Dakota sped the remaining quarter-mile to the strip mall, they saw the black van perched on the edge of the canal. Stormy, sensing that Marc wouldn't have taken the time to try to dump it with all the sirens going off, felt a coldness hit his gut. The girls were inside the van. As they were almost to the site, they saw Nickie's unit suddenly speed out to the road, and after fishtailing, head away from them. Just as he was about to give chase, he watched in horror as the van began sliding over the embankment, ever so slowly dropping into the canal.

"Stormy, that was Nickie's car. Do you want me to go

after it?" Dakota asked over the radio.

"No, turn in here. The van is going into the canal, and I have a feeling both Nickie and Linda may be inside. It will take both of us to get them out if they're unresponsive."

Stormy and Dakota almost lost control of their cars as they made the turn at thirty miles an hour. Sliding up behind the van, they watched as it slipped into the water, only the rear of the van still visible. The air pocket would only keep it afloat for so long, so they had to hurry. Both jumped out of their cars and rushed to the edge of the canal, just as the van settled even lower in the water. Now, only the top foot of the rear of the van was visible. Then, without warning, the van slid into the water, completely submerged now.

Captain Carter had briefed the three HPD marked units and all were now headed westward on Okeechobee Road. The Captain brought up the rear as the marked units had sped off before he could get ahead of them. As they sped westward traffic was beginning to become an issue. Darkness was beginning to approach, which would make the task a little harder.

Suddenly, Nickie's unmarked unit sped past Captain Carter, confusing him for a second. Then he realized that a man was driving the car. He waited for a break in the traffic and made a U-turn.

In full pursuit he called Stormy, "Stormy, Nickie's unit just passed me going back towards town. What's going on?"

"That was Marc, Captain. We're at an abandoned strip mall near the city limits on the left. Send some help. You go get Marc! Dakota and I are about to take a swim,"

Stormy replied.

Captain Carter wasn't sure what to make of that swimming statement, but he had no time to think about it now. He was in full pursuit of Nickie's car, which he now knew was being driven by Marc. No way was he letting him get away.

It was times like this that he missed the thrill of being on the road, and especially the action. Being the Captain in charge of the Detective Bureau kept him desk-bound most of the time, so this was a change of pace he was more than ready for.

Radioing the three marked units still heading away from him, Captain Carter advised them to watch for Stormy and Dakota ahead on their left and also that Stormy had asked for backup.

****

As the van slipped into the canal, Linda tried to crawl to the front. After clambering over the console, she attempted to open the door. With her hands cuffed it was a laborious effort, and the door wouldn't budge. The outside pressure of the water pressing on the doors made it a futile attempt. She sat in the passenger's seat and tried to kick out the windshield with her feet, but once again, the pressure prevented the glass from breaking. She noticed that water was seeping in through the firewall under the dash. She knew if she couldn't get the front doors open, there was no chance of getting the side doors open. Turning in her seat, she looked towards the back of the van and noticed that it was somewhat tipped downward.

"Nickie, try to move the security man all the way to the back of the van. If the water keeps rising, at least we should have an air pocket."

Nickie, thankful that her hands were also cuffed in front, managed to shuffle and pull the man further into the back.

Fearing the worst was yet to come, she searched frantically in the van for something hard to smash the window. Marc must have thought of that beforehand, because there was nothing of use inside. She climbed over the console and helped Nickie move the man all the way to the rear.

They sat together in the back and watched as the water began rising in the front of the van, now almost reaching the lower part of the front seats. This was not how she had seen her death happening. Now, all they could do was huddle in the back and hope the air pocket would last long enough for help to arrive. What was she thinking...there would be no help, no one knew they were in the van...no one knew the van was in the canal. It seemed like a lost cause, and they were going to die in this dirty, filthy canal, trapped in the van. No, that was not the way she was going out...she *had* to figure something out.

Chapter 52

CONSUELO DROVE THE CAR onto the Palmetto Expressway, maintaining a speed no more than three or four miles above the limit. There was no way that after getting this far she was going to allow herself to be stopped for speeding. Juan sat in the passenger's seat. Neither had spoken much since they left South Miami. There would be plenty of time for talking once they were on I-75 and out of Dade County. There was sure to be an all-points bulletin out by now.

Once they passed the 103rd Street exit she knew from the GPS that they were only minutes from I-75. She had originally considered taking I-95 but quickly dismissed that route. That would be the first place Metro-Dade would be concentrating on, as well as the smaller cities heading north once the BOLO was put out. But the authorities had no idea what kind of vehicle she and Juan were in and the heavily tinted windows would help, although now that it was dark it wouldn't make a difference.

Once on I-75, they headed west towards Naples, but the interstate would turn directly north before long. She would drive all the way to I-10 before heading east to Jacksonville. It would be a long drive, but the airport was north of the city and they had plenty of time, especially not having to drive through Jacksonville.

Their flight wasn't scheduled until nine in the morning and her best guess was that they should arrive there between four and five. She wanted to arrive at the Jax airport with enough time to scope out the booking desks before picking up their boarding passes. She hoped that her subterfuge of booking so many flights under the same names would have the Feds running in circles. She knew for sure that they would be all over Miami International, so *not* flying out of there was a no-brainer. Still, she had a funny feeling in her stomach...so she wanted to spend a couple of hours watching for the Feds and police once she arrived there.

"So, how does it feel to be a free man?" she asked Juan, just to start a conversation.

"I won't really feel free until I set foot on Colombian soil," Juan replied. "And thanks, you managed to do a superb job of breaking me out."

"That's what you paid me for. Now let's concentrate on what is going to happen once we arrive at the airport," Consuelo said.

"What do you mean?"

"We'll be arriving several hours before our flight leaves. Once we get there, I'll park the car in long-term parking, and you'll stay with the car until I come back and get you," Consuelo said.

"Leave me there! Where will you be going?" Juan asked.

"I have to do some surveillance for a while. It's my specialty in my line of work...oh, I forgot, you're in the same line of work so you can appreciate what I have to do. I booked a dozen flights for near the same time, all over the United States and Canada, even Mexico. So, it is a roll of the dice choosing this one to leave from. Let's hope the Feds, who are after me also, for some reason, didn't choose this one to stake out."

"You don't know why they're after you?"

"Nope, but I had to jump from hotel to hotel while planning this. I've managed to stay a step ahead of them, so far," Consuelo replied. "By the way, reach in the bag on the back seat and pull out the folder for me, please," Consuelo asked.

Juan unfastened his seat belt and twisted around to see in the back. He spotted the bag and pulled out the folder contained within. He turned and handed it to Consuelo. She opened the folder and pulled out the two passports, handing them to Juan.

"Ahhh...now I'm Miguel Soto. And you're my wife?"

"Yeah, but don't get any ideas, you're married," Consuelo said, emitting a hearty laugh.

"I also have something else for you. In another bag in the back is another change of clothing for you," Consuelo said, nodding towards the rear.

Juan unfastened his seat belt once again and reached into the back and plucked a bag from the seat. When he opened it he pulled out a pair of khaki cargo pants, a navy blue tee-shirt and a ball cap, the front emblazoned with the Jacksonville Jaguars football team logo. There were even a pair of sneakers. He was surprised to find that they were his sizes. Consuelo had done her homework, and he was impressed.

"Cover your eyes, I need to change pants," Juan said.

"Cover my eyes! I'm driving, you sure you want me to do that?" she asked, once again laughing.

Juan laughed and took off the sweat pants he had switched his jumpsuit for earlier. He slid on the khakis and then, taking off his shirt, put on the tee. He would save the hat for when he was at the airport. It wasn't a total makeover disguise, but subtle, touristy.

When they reached the Gainesville exit, Consuelo took the off-ramp and drove down to the various eating establishments lining the street. She needed coffee and something to eat. They pulled through the drive-up of a Wendy's and both ordered two cheeseburgers each. They also ordered a large fry to split, and in addition to coffee, two bottles of water. Once again she got on I-75 and headed toward I-10, which wasn't that far now. They were making good time, and she would need the coffee and food to sustain her over the next few hours. Juan offered to drive, but Consuelo told him she was fine. Besides, now wasn't the time to take a wrong exit and get lost, since neither of them had ever been to Jacksonville.

Feeling better now that she had some food in her, and the caffeine in the black coffee surging through her system, she prepared for the home stretch.

Before long, they got on I-10. After about an hour, they took the I-295 exit. Shortly after that they approached their destination. All her plans would soon come into play, and hopefully, she had chosen right and there wouldn't be any Feds in the airport.

When they reached the airport, she took the turn onto the long-term parking ramp. After collecting the ticket, she placed it on the dash. She parked between two vehicles that were taller than theirs and she switched off the engine. She exited the car and opened the trunk, retrieving another bag. Getting back into the car she opened the bag and pulled out a blonde wig and a makeup bag.

When she finished, she looked like a totally different person. The blonde wig and the small amount of makeup she applied, changed her looks immensely. She didn't want to overdo it. She downplayed her natural beauty and by putting on the wig, made her dark skin look as if she had been on vacation and had gotten a good tan.

"I wouldn't know you if I passed you on the street now. Good job," Juan said.

"Quit flirting, lover boy," Consuelo said, as she fluffed out her hair and grinned at him.

"I'm married, remember?" Juan said, smiling.

"So you keep reminding me. But, today, you're married to *me,*" Consuelo said, opening the door. "Stay here, I'll be back shortly, and I'll bring coffee, if you want some."

"That would be great. I'll recline the seat and take a nap. Leave the keys so I can crack the window a bit, please," Juan said.

Consuelo tossed the keys over to Juan and after running her fingers through the blonde wig once more, began walking to the elevator. When she reached the ground floor, she spotted a newsstand a few steps away and headed to it. When she was just inside she picked up a magazine and opened it, facing the concourse. She scanned the area but there weren't a lot of passengers here yet. Still, she looked up at the second floor, down the concourse and kept looking until she was satisfied there was no one watching, yet.

She ventured out onto the concourse and walked slowly to a coffee shop. She ordered two coffees and a couple of donuts, then strolled back to the elevator, her eyes continuously flitting back and forth, searching the concourse. She decided that she would give it an hour before trying again. There would be no use in her trying to take a quick nap, the coffee would be a detriment to that.

Chapter 53

MARC PASSED THE THREE HPD patrol cars heading towards the strip mall. As he sped past he glanced into his sideview mirror and his heart suddenly began racing. An unmarked vehicle that he hadn't noticed when he passed the patrol cars, suddenly turned around and was heading in his direction, the blue strobes flashing furiously. Marc shoved his foot on the gas and increased his speed. The one advantage he had now was that he could also use the blue lights and avoid getting blocked by slow drivers.

Captain Carter floored the gas, swerving around several vehicles as he gave chase after Nickie's car. He would be damned if he would let that worthless piece of crap get away. He only hoped that Stormy and Dakota would find Linda and Nickie safe.

He could still see the car speeding away from him, identifiable by the glow of the flashing blues he had turned on. All of a sudden a Lowe's delivery truck pulled out from a side street and directly in his path. Slamming on his brakes, he spun the wheel and came to a stop parallel to the truck, within three feet of broadsiding it. The truck driver frantically pulled his vehicle over to the far lane of Okeechobee and probably breathed a sigh of relief as the police vehicle he had almost crashed with sped past him.

Captain Carter had lost sight of Nickie's car, so he pushed his speed up to seventy miles per hour, swerving in and out around other traffic. A quarter-mile ahead of him he saw the car make a left turn onto Southeast 8th Avenue. He picked up his radio mike and told the dispatcher to have units converge to Southeast 8th Avenue and 103rd Street. He also advised that the perp was driving a stolen unmarked police vehicle, running with the blues on, at a high rate of speed.

Marc knew he was in a world of hurt. If only that unmarked car hadn't spotted him when he drove past. Now, he was being chased and felt sure that the unit chasing him had radioed ahead for assistance. After turning onto Southeast 8th Avenue, he figured that the responding units would be coming from the station north of 103rd Street so he made a right onto Hialeah Drive, barely missing several cars. When he reached Southeast 9th, one block away, he turned southbound and picked up speed.

When Captain Carter reached Southeast 8th Avenue, he ran the light and made the turn northbound. He had lost sight of Marc once again. He pounded the dash in frustration but kept speeding northbound, hoping to catch sight of him. At any rate, there should be several units waiting for him at 103rd Street.

He suddenly caught a glimpse of the car making a right turn onto Hialeah Drive. Within ten seconds he was making the turn also. As he straightened his car out and headed east, he saw Marc suddenly make another turn, this time on

Southeast 9th, after only going once block. Making the turn he floored the gas, now gaining fast on Marc.

Quickly he was on his bumper. He moved out to the side and performed a pit maneuver. After tapping the rear of Nickie's car, Marc spun out and lost control of the car. The car jumped the curb and hit a retaining wall airborne. Captain Carter slid to a stop behind the crashed car and jumped out.

Marc was stunned for only a second. He opened the door and slid out under the deployed air-bag. He was bleeding from his nose where the bag had struck, but that was the least of his worries at the moment. He took off down the sidewalk and within seconds reached Southeast Park. He ran through the park, shoving kids and adults out of the way as he fled.

He risked a glance over his shoulder and saw that no one was chasing him. That was strange, he had seen the car stop behind him. Almost out of breath, he slowed to a fast walk and kept going. He had no way of knowing in his state of mind, but he was only three blocks from Triangle Park where he had abducted Linda.

Captain Carter radioed the crash in to dispatch, and unfastened his seat belt. He watched as Marc bailed out of the car and took off running. He couldn't believe it. The guy had nine lives, evidently. Captain Carter was in good shape but now in his early fifties, he knew he wouldn't be able to catch a young Marc in a foot race. He was about ready to advise dispatch of the situation when an idea came to him.

Observing Marc running west through the park, he took a chance and jumped back into his car. He turned off the blues and siren. He drove down the street and turned east.

After one block he parked in a residential driveway beside another vehicle, got out of his car and crouched down low enough to see through the windows up the block, without exposing himself.

Sure enough, Marc came running out of the park and took a left on the sidewalk and headed straight towards Carter's position. Captain Carter stayed down, biding his time. Marc was now down to a fast walk and apparently out of breath. When he walked past the rear of Captain Carter's vehicle parked in the drive, Carter took a running start and dove onto an exhausted Marc. Just that fast the fight was gone out of Marc. Carter rolled him over and cuffed him behind his back, and none too gently.

Grabbing him under his armpits, he lifted him to his feet and said, "Marc Butler, you're under arrest!"

Chapter 54

STORMY DIDN'T HESITATE. He grabbed a Kel-lite from the car and taking his shoes off, took a deep breath and dove into the canal, next to where he had seen the van slip into the water. The canal was about ten to twelve feet deep and very dark. He couldn't see his hand in front of his face, so he flipped the Kel-lite on, the light spotting the van nose down on the bottom. He shoved the flashlight into his waistband and propelled himself deeper into the water. When he reached the bottom, he clung to the door handle and then retrieving the light, shined it into the van. He couldn't see anyone so he edged himself around to the front of the van, then shined the light through the windshield. Then he saw them! In the rear of the van were Nickie, an unknown man, and Linda.

Linda stared through the windshield, the light diffused but still a beacon of hope. Then she saw Stormy press his face to the windshield, and smile, giving a thumbs-up. Linda began laughing, hugging Nickie and slapping the security officer on the shoulder. Everything was going to be alright. Her best friend had found her, as she knew he would.

The water was now approaching their neck area, but the air pocket was still allowing them to breathe. The only problem now was how quickly they could get out, since the water had risen so fast once the van had sunk.

Stormy hadn't failed to notice the water almost up to their chins and knew he had to act fast. He felt his way back around to the front door and tried to open it. It was locked! So he swiftly swam around to the driver's door and found it locked, too. He had been down almost a minute and a half now and his air was quickly running out. Tapping the glass, he held up two fingers, indicating he would be back in two minutes. He only hoped the water wouldn't rise any further before he returned.

Stormy broke through the top of the water and took deep gulps of air. He had almost waited too long to surface. Dakota was waiting on the bank and reached out and grabbed his arm, helping him climb out.

"Are they in the van?" She asked, dread in her voice.

"Yes, they're in there, along with another man. And they're alive, although the water is rising rapidly. I couldn't get the door opened, so we have to find something to break the glass, and fast."

"You won't be able to swing anything hard enough under water to break it. Use your gun!" Dakota said.

Without saying another word, Stormy took several huge gulps of air, oxygenating his lungs, and dove back into the canal once again. Reaching the van, he pulled the Kel-lite out and aimed it at the side window of the passenger's side. He only hoped the weapon wasn't too waterlogged to fire now. Carefully, making sure he didn't drop it, he pulled his weapon from the holster and without wasting time, pulled the trigger. The sound was a dull thump under the water, but the sweetest sound he had ever heard. When he saw the hole in the window, he slowly fired a circle of them, and then fired a larger circle around the first. Using all nineteen rounds he managed to make three overlapping circles.

Not using precious time to re-holster his now empty weapon, he dropped it into the depths of the water. He used his elbow to slam the window, over and over until it finally collapsed in on itself. Reaching inside he unlocked and opened the door.

His breath was now getting low, but he stuck his head inside the door and motioned for Nickie to swim to him. He noticed that the water was up to their chins now. It wouldn't be too long before the air pocket would be gone, replaced by dirty canal water.

Nickie kicked her legs against the edge of the back seat and propelled herself to the front. She had been astute enough to take a deep breath before doing so. When she reached Stormy, he quickly grabbed her by her cuffed hands and pulled her out of the van. Kicking his feet furiously, he rose to the surface, his arm around Nickie.

Dakota reached out and grabbed Nickie by her chained wrists, pulling her up onto the bank, where she lay on her back gasping for much needed air. When Dakota looked back, Stormy had already gone down again.

When Stormy reached the van again, he motioned for Linda to come to him. She shook her head no, instead, grabbing the man by the elbows and propelling him to Stormy. The water was now up to Linda's nose. Stormy wasted no time admiring her bravery and obligation to help the public. He grabbed the man and rushed to the surface as quickly as he could. Dakota was waiting and tried to help Stormy pull the man to the bank. He was heavier than Nickie and it took thirty seconds longer to get him out of the water and on the bank. Without taking several breaths, Stormy took one long deep one and dove down, hoping it would be enough air to get him and Linda out.

When Stormy reached the van for the last time, he stuck his head inside to motion Linda, but instead saw her floating face up in the back, the air pocket gone now. His heart began beating rapidly, a burning hurt in his chest. She had sacrificed herself to save the man, a man she probably didn't even know, but a life saved any way you looked at it. Stormy refused to believe she was gone. He swam in and over the console and reaching out, grabbed Linda by her hands which were floating limply, cuffed together. As quickly as he could, he pulled her through the front door and, grasping her waist, swam as hard as he could to the surface.

When Stormy reached the surface, Linda was ashen, lifeless, and most certainly dead. With Dakota and Nickie's help they got her onto the bank.

Dakota began crying, as did Nickie. Stormy wasted no time at all. He quickly straddled Linda's lifeless body and began to perform CPR. After almost a minute of chest compression's, there was still no change, Linda remained unresponsive.

Chapter 55

AFTER A SECOND FORAY into the airport an hour later, Consuelo still didn't see any signs that there was a surveillance team present. She returned to the car, the time drawing close for them to approach the gate and obtain their boarding passes.

"Juan, this time we go inside together. I want you to walk as inconspicuously as you can about forty yards behind me. If you see me put my hand into my hair and fluff it, turn around and leave. That will mean I've spotted the Feds, and you need to get away. Here are the car keys. Don't be a hero and try to save me. Just get into the car and drive north to Atlanta. You'll be able to figure out how to get out of the country, just don't use the same passport you have now. Make arrangements to get another, somehow," Consuelo said.

"After getting this far, I'm not leaving you. We'll figure it out," Juan said, in response

"No, I mean it. I'll be able to take care of myself. If they don't spot you, I'll lead them on a chase through the airport. Don't worry about me," Consuelo said. "I'll go down the elevator; you take the stairs. That way we're not together, and it should be just enough to space us apart."

"Okay, but I don't like it," Juan said.

"You don't have to like it, and I appreciate your concern, but let's not worry about it, unless we have to."

They exited the car and headed to the elevator and the stairwell adjacent to it. Juan opened the stairwell door and began walking down to the concourse. Consuelo entered the elevator and punched the appropriate button. The elevator doors closed and the car headed down.

When Consuelo exited the elevator, she paused as if she were reading the overhead signs for incoming and departing flights. She wasn't reading them, she was scanning the area for any sign of anyone watching her. At this point she didn't see anything suspicious, so she began walking to the boarding area. Stopping and looking up at the signs again, she caught a glimpse of Juan walking out of the stairwell, his ball cap pulled down covering his eyes. As planned, he was about thirty or forty yards behind her.

Brenda and Larry had been in their assigned spots for nearly thirty minutes, constantly searching the concourse for any sign of Consuelo and her mystery companion. Larry was in the janitor's shirt and pants, slowly emptying trash cans in plastic bags, wiping down the seats, and doing anything else that he figured a janitor would be doing.

He made it a point to not stare at the boarding area, nor appear to be searching for anyone. He would leave that to Brenda on the second floor. He had glanced up a couple of times and couldn't spot her. She was good! Later he would have to ask just where she had been situated.

Brenda was seated between two fake palms, on a bench that allowed her to see through the protective glass at the edge of the railing. The glass was to keep young children from falling through to the concourse below. Brenda was seated far enough back that she could see the boarding area, but not the elevator area below where she sat. So, she didn't see Consuelo exit the elevator. So far, she hadn't seen any sign of Consuelo, although she figured she would be in some kind of disguise. All of a sudden, a blonde woman walked into her view and turned to look at the overhead signs. The woman's face grabbed her attention immediately. Controlling herself, Brenda slowly stood and casually walked over to the railing and looked at her watch, but she actually looked over it at the woman. There was no doubt, it was Consuelo. Praise be! She had selected the correct airport.

But, where was the man who was supposed to be with her? She watched carefully, before making a move. Whispering to Larry through his earpiece, she said. "I see Consuelo. She is about twenty yards north of your position and wearing a blonde wig, or a dye job. Keep doing what you're doing because I haven't seen her companion yet."

Larry moved ever so slowly as he wiped the seats, edging nearer to the boarding area. He didn't attempt to look up to spot Consuelo, as he was sure she would pick up on it at once. Consuelo had proven she was no fool and knew her trade-craft.

Brenda motioned to the security guard who had stayed back against the wall out of sight. By prearranged signs, he radioed the guards at the exits to be alert and to await his instructions.

Consuelo caught a glimpse of a woman upstairs through the glass ringing the railing. She was sitting on a bench and staring out through the same glass. It could have been coincidental, but from experience, Consuelo didn't think so. Then the woman walked to the railing and pretended to look at her watch, but her eyes told another story. She had spotted her. The woman smelled of FBI.

Consuelo began walking to the far exit, on the opposite side from the elevator and away from the elevator. As she walked she took her hand and ran it through her hair, fluffing it out.

Brenda noticed the sudden change in Consuelo, her changing directions and walking towards another exit, and, the telltale signal of someone by running their hands through their hair.

She said to Larry, "She's onto us. Go get her!"

Brenda ran down the stairs, not bothering to wait for an elevator. She wasn't running to help Larry, she was hoping to see someone else fleeing, someone who had been given the sign. When she reached the bottom of the stairs, she quickly looked around, trying to spot anyone that seemed to be trying to leave the area in a hurry. She couldn't see anyone but kept searching.

Juan saw the signal. Consuelo had been right! There had been the chance that the Feds would choose this airport, or had managed to stake out the majority of them. He quickly turned on his heels and opened the stairwell door. He ran up the stairs. No one noticed, especially the guards who had been briefed. The guard that was supposed to have been at the stairwell door had stopped *en route* to use the restroom. By the time he arrived at his post, Juan had reached the top level and was almost to the car.

He hated leaving Consuelo alone, but she had been adamant. He quickly got into the car, started the engine and drove down the exit ramp. He made sure he stopped and paid the parking fee. Consuelo had made sure to leave a fiver on the dash. Once out and away from the airport, he got onto I-95 and headed north, to Atlanta, as Consuelo had suggested. He had no doubt that there were cameras all over the airport and had captured his face and the tag of the car he was driving. He would have to soon steal a car and change tags to avoid capture. He had no idea what he would do once he got to Atlanta, but he would figure it out. For now, he was still free, and wanted to stay that way.

Chapter 56

THE THREE MARKED UNITS Captain Carter had sent towards Stormy's location arrived. Off in the distance the sounds of EMS sirens could be heard wailing, and heading towards them.

"Come on, Linda! Breathe! Breathe, dammit!" Stormy muttered as he kept the chest compression's going. One of the arriving officers offered to take over for him, but Stormy refused to relinquish his task. He was determined to save Linda!

Suddenly, she coughed, and water spewed out of her mouth, splashing on Stormy's chest. Stormy turned her head to one side so the water could come out faster. Her eyes fluttered open and seeing Stormy leaning over her, concern written all over his face, she looked up at him and said, "What took you so long?"

Stormy laughed, exhaling a big sigh of relief and said, "You scared the hell out of me, girl."

One of the officers reached down and unlocked the cuffs on Linda and Nickie.

By the time the EMS vehicles arrived, Linda was sitting up and taking deep even breaths. She was shivering, so

Stormy took his wet shirt off and draped it around her. She asked to get to her feet and between Dakota and Stormy, they helped her. She was a little wobbly at first but stood still until she regained her balance. The EMS personnel raced over to her with a stretcher and attempted to place her on it.

Captain Carter drove up with Marc cuffed and sitting in the rear of the car, subdued and resigned. He got out and ran over to her. As he came close, Linda turned to Captain Carter and asked, "Before I go to the hospital, could you lower Marc's window for me?"

"Are you sure? You need to get to the hospital and get checked out," Captain Carter replied.

"I just need a second to say something to him, then I'll go. Please!" Linda asked.

"Okay, but make it fast. You really need to get checked out."

Captain Carter walked over to his car, reached in, and lowered the rear window. Marc didn't look up, his head hanging down in despair.

"Look at me, you piece of crap," Linda snapped when she approached the open window.

Marc slowly looked up at Linda. She stared at him for a minute, and then she swung her fist into his face as fast and as hard as she could, connecting solidly with his jaw.

"That wasn't for me, Marc. That was for my sister who can't do it now that you killed her. I hope you rot in hell for what you've done, not only to her but to all those other girls." Then Linda turned and sat down on the stretcher. The EMS tech placed a blanket around both her and Nickie.

"I'm riding with her to the hospital," Dakota said.

"Nickie needs to go also to get checked out."

"I'm fine, Dakota," Nickie said.

"Maybe so, but you won't be once the adrenaline wears off, trust me."

"Is this what I have to look forward to, being a detective?" Nickie asked, laughing.

"Only if Stormy's around. He attracts action like a magnet," Dakota said, also laughing.

The security guard had finally come around and was thankful to be alive. He couldn't stop profusely thanking Stormy for saving his life.

Once the CSI team arrived, the whole area was designated a crime scene and taped off. There were so many flashing blue and red lights that traffic on Okeechobee Road had come to a standstill. Arrangements were made for a wrecker to retrieve the van from the bottom of the canal. Captain Carter took the honor of driving Marc, swollen jaw and all, to the Dade County Jail for processing, smiling all the way. Things had worked out, and he hadn't lost any of his people this day.

Stormy advised the other officers that once the wrecker arrived to tell them that his weapon was at the bottom of the canal. They would probably have to use a magnet to lower into the water and hopefully retrieve it for him. Then he put his shoes back on, got into his car and headed to the hospital to be with the girls.

Chapter 57

CONSUELO RAN TO THE NEAREST EXIT across from the boarding area. When she opened the door she was greeted by an airport security guard. He put up his arms to grab her, but she was too fast, ducking down and running past him. The aged and overweight guard gave chase, soon left far behind in Consuelo's wake.

Larry was through the door only seconds behind Consuelo. Running down the hallway, he encountered the guard, huffing and almost out of breath. The guard didn't know that Larry was in disguise and attempted to stop him, causing him even more delay in catching Consuelo. Once he flashed his I.D. to the guard, he was waved by.

Larry lost sight of Consuelo, her having gone down another hallway. By the time he got to the junction of the two halls, he looked both ways but Consuelo was nowhere in sight.

"Larry? Have you got her?" Brenda yelled through Larry's earpiece.

"NO, I'm in the hallways now but she disappeared. I'm still looking, but ask your guy if there's a way she can get out of the airport from here," Larry answered back.

Larry kept jogging down the hallway, glancing into offices along the way, with no sign of Consuelo.

"Larry. The guard said that if you take the hallway to the left, it leads to a door that will take you out on the tarmac where the planes are boarded. Maybe she went that way," Brenda said.

"I'll check it out. I'll get back to you as soon as I'm outside," Larry replied.

Larry had turned right in the hallway and now had to run back the way he had come. Soon he saw a door that was marked, "Airport Personnel Only." He burst through the door, ignoring the alarm that suddenly sounded, and then was outside on the tarmac.

There were several planes pulled up to the terminal and baggage handlers loading luggage into their bellies. He looked all around, and not seeing Consuelo, ran further out on the tarmac, to the rear of the planes. There were two planes taxiing out to their runways, preparing to take off. Larry kept looking and still didn't see Consuelo.

"Brenda, I'm out on the edge of the runway and still no sign of her. Maybe she's still inside," Larry said.

"You stay out there and keep looking, I'll go into the hallways and look for her there," Brenda said.

Larry kept walking between the parked planes and even looking under them. There was no way she could get onto any of the planes since they were parked against the terminal with the accordion loading dock affixed.

Suddenly, he caught a glimpse of someone running across one of the runways. It was a woman with blonde hair. It was her! She had nearly a hundred-yard start on him, but he took off running after her.

"CONSUELO! STOP! FBI!" Larry shouted as he ran, aware that his voice was probably not being heard over the roar of the big jets taking off.

Consuelo kept walking at a fast pace, determined to get across the runways and to the fence in the distance. It was only another two hundred yards, and she would be home free. She didn't hear Larry yelling at her, and even if she had, she wouldn't have stopped. She was too close to getting away. She only hoped that Juan had heeded her orders and managed to get in the car and drive away. The noise from the jet engines was deafening, but it was a minor distraction at this point. She kept walking fast towards the fence, which was drawing closer. There was only one more runway to cross and then she would be at the fence.

Consuelo failed to see the Boeing 747 bearing down on her from the west. It was an arriving flight, and the landing gear was already lowered. At almost one hundred and fifty miles an hour, the plane had almost touched down, the nose at about six feet from hitting the runway.

When the front wheels in the nose gear struck her head, she was decapitated immediately. Her headless body slowly dropped to the pavement. Blood spurted from her open neck in a gush, the wind from the jet fanning the droplets wildly in the air.

Larry watched in horror as the plane's wheel struck Consuelo. He also watched as her headless body slowly crumpled to the pavement, the blood flow pooling on the tarmac.

"Larry, have you spotted her yet?" Brenda suddenly asked in his earpiece.

"Yeah, Brenda, unfortunately I have."

Larry explained what he had just witnessed, the plane striking Consuelo and killing her. Brenda said she would alert airport security so that the runway could be shut down.

"Did you find out who was with her?" Larry asked.

"No, all of the exits were manned by airport security guards and none of them reported anyone leaving. In fact, they wouldn't let anyone leave until we said so," Brenda replied.

"Maybe it was a ploy on her part, booking two people to throw us off," Larry said.

"I don't think so. We just got news on a prisoner escape in Miami. Also we compared the photo Consuelo provided to the man that made her the two passports. It appears that the escaped prisoner is none other than, *El Scorpion*, and his was the photo was on the passport," Brenda said.

"Holy cow! So that was the reason she was in Miami. He has to be in the airport somewhere, don't you think?" Larry remarked.

"I wouldn't count on it now. Somehow he has managed to get away, it appears," Brenda said.

After a thorough search of the airport, Juan wasn't found. The arriving passengers were finally allowed to leave and all airport functions resumed.

Chapter 58

One week later

THE MEMORIAL SERVICE for Linda's sister, Stefanie Taylor, was held in the Hialeah Convention Center. Only non-essential personnel with the Hialeah Police Department and the city did not attend. Other agencies throughout Dade County sent representatives, out of respect for Linda, whom they had all worked with over the years. She was well respected as a top-notch CSI Tech, and as a person. The service was beautiful, but a solemn one. There were over five hundred people in attendance to show their respect. Many were ordinary citizens who had come in contact with Linda over the years. Nickie, Dakota, Stormy and Shaunie sat on the front row, Linda between them. They were her best friends and the support and comfort they provided was most comforting to her.

When the service was over, an honor guard stood at the exit of the center. Linda walked slowly out, her arm locked with Dakota on one side, Stormy on the other. The Honor Guard stood at attention as she passed through their line.

When they reached the parking lot, Linda got into the

car with Stormy and Shaunie. They drove her home and asked if she wanted someone to be with her. She replied no, leaned over and gave Stormy a kiss on the cheek.

"I'll be in to work on Monday. It will be a healing process, but I have to stay busy," Linda said.

"I understand, but if you need me, or anything, please call," Stormy said.

Linda promised she would and exiting the car, walked up the walk to her house, turning and giving a wave to Stormy before she walked into her home.

****

Juan, AKA *El Scorpion*, got off I-95 and hot-wired a car on a used car lot in a small town. He left the car he was driving in its place, after taking the license plate off and placing it on the vehicle he would be driving to Atlanta. When he reached the outskirts of the city, he found a small motel. Luckily for him, Consuelo had left her purse in the car and there was plenty of cash. He would need it. He walked to a nearby electronics store and purchased a burner phone. Recalling from memory, he dialed a number. When the party answered, he said,

"I need your help."

****

Captain Roscoe Carter was awarded a special citation for his capture of Marc Butler. He planned to request to be put back into road patrol; having tasted action again, he wanted more. But, his wife convinced him to stay in the

Detective Bureau because he would be of more benefit there and because his retirement was coming up in a few years. She wanted him to be safe for her and the kids, especially the new grandchild that was due any day now. He finally agreed and let the matter drop.

Stormy had been advised on the escape of *El Scorpion*, and at first was shocked. After some thought he realized that there was nothing he could do, it was out of his jurisdiction and there was no way he could traverse the country looking for him. He put it to the back of his mind and intended to forget about it.

Nickie was also awarded a special citation for her part in the investigation of Marc Butler. She was back on duty and expecting her new partner any day now. She was looking forward to many years of being a homicide detective. She couldn't be any happier with her new position and now was among the few that considered Dakota and Stormy her closest friends. She, along with Linda and the security guard, had come within minutes of dying, and she now had a profound respect for life...it was too short to waste.

****

Consuelo was taken to the Jacksonville morgue and her body unclaimed. If no one claimed it within six months, she would be buried in a county-owned cemetery, never to be visited by anyone.

****

Brenda returned to Washington and was debriefed on

her investigation. She was not only awarded a letter of commendation, she was promoted to Special Agent in the field, a position she had always wanted.

When she had left Miami, she had one last dinner with Larry, who also received a commendation. She promised to return for a visit in the near future. For now, she was heading to Seattle to investigate a serial killer the police had been stumped on. She was probably the happiest she had ever been.

****

Marc Butler sat in solitary, awaiting his court appearance. He had been placed in solitary for his own protection when it was learned that the first girl he had killed, Lilly Sanchez, had a brother in the same jail with him.

Three counts of first-degree murder, four counts of kidnapping, three counts of attempted murder, and one count of assault on a police officer all but guaranteed that he would never get out of prison.

Chapter 59

Two weeks later

"OH MY GOD, THEY'RE SO ADORABLE," Dakota exclaimed.

"They look so much alike," Nickie responded.

"Well, they should, they're twins," Stormy said with a smile so big he just couldn't wipe it off his face.

Shaunie had been rushed to the hospital with labor pains. Stormy had received the call at work, and he and Linda sped at breakneck speed to get there. When he arrived, he was just in time to give her a kiss before they wheeled her into the delivery room.

Originally the doctor had thought there was only one baby. When the delivery was made, it proved him wrong; there were twins, a girl and a boy.

"Have you decided on names for them?" Dakota asked.

"Stormy is naming the girl. I'm naming the boy," Shaunie replied.

"What's the name of the boy, Shaunie? Do you have a name picked out for him?" Dakota asked.

"I have a name picked out, but it'll be a surprise. But,

lean over and you'll be the first to know what the name is," Shaunie replied.

Dakota glanced at Stormy, and he nodded his head that he was okay with that. Dakota leaned down and Shaunie whispered into her ear.

Dakota stood up, clasped her hands together and made a big 'O' shape with her mouth, then turning to Stormy, put on a big smile.

"What's the name of the girl, Stormy?" Linda asked.

"Linda Susan Storm!" He proudly proclaimed.

Author

EARL UNDERWOOD WAS BORN AND RAISED in a small town in North Carolina. In 1961, at the age of 20, he and his family moved to Miami, Florida. He served in the United States Army Corps of Engineers from 1964 to 1966 and did a tour of duty in Viet Nam.

Upon returning home, he married Linda Susan Albert and pursued a career in law enforcement. He retired after serving the public for many years. Most of his police career was that of a homicide detective where he received many awards.

After retirement he relocated to Grand Island in Central Florida with his family. Earl enjoys spending time with his four children, Shaunie, Scott, Michael, and Dejah, and his four grandchildren, Victoria, Erica, Zachary, and Mikaella. Family is the most important thing to Earl and his wife Sue.

Earl came out of retirement and served another fourteen years in law enforcement in Central Florida before finally retiring for good in 2003 with a total of almost 32 years. He now spends his time golfing, painting and pursuing his life-long passion of writing.

Earl may be contacted at Underwood914@yahoo.com.

Other Books by Earl Underwood

***Mizuno's' Revenge* (2017)**

<u>Austin Steele Space Adventures</u>

***Austin Steele's New Life on Xova* (2013)**

***The Scourge of Alpha Centauri* (2015)**

<u>Detective Jack Storm Mysteries</u>

***The Cold Smile* (2014)**

***Sting of the Scorpion* (2016)**

***River of Death* (2018)**

<u>Autobiography</u>

***This Is My Story and I'm Sticking to It* (2012)**

The above books are published by Shoppe Foreman Publishing.
For more information go to www.ShoppeForeman.com/Underwood.
To purchase a book in softcover or e-book go to www.Amazon.com.

Made in the USA
Columbia, SC
01 May 2020

95374031R00190